Sydney tried not to stare, but it was hard.

At three feet away, she should have been able to see this man's imperfections—if not quite a wart, then maybe a chipped tooth. Something. Anything.

But he was impossibly gorgeous. The sheer perfection of a Ken doll come to life.

Navy Ken stood. "I'm sorry. Of course, I should have introduced myself. Lieutenant Luke O'Donlon, of the U.S. Navy SEALs."

Sydney didn't have to be an expert on body language to know the feelings of all the males in the room. The jealousy was practically palpable. Lieutenant Luke O'Donlon gleamed. He shone. He was all white and gold and sunlight and sky-blue eyes.

He was a god. The mighty king of all the Ken dolls.

And he knew it.

Dear Reader,

As Silhouette Books' 20th anniversary continues, Intimate Moments continues to bring you six superb titles every month. And certainly this month—when we begin with Suzanne Brockmann's *Get Lucky*—is no exception. This latest entry in her TALL, DARK & DANGEROUS miniseries features ladies' man Lucky O'Donlon, a man who finally meets the woman who is his match—and more.

Linda Turner's *A Ranching Man* is the latest of THOSE MARRYING McBRIDES!, featuring Joe McBride and the damsel in distress who wins his heart. Monica McLean was a favorite with her very first book, and now she's back with *Just a Wedding Away*, an enthralling marriage-of-convenience story. Lauren Nichols introduces an *Accidental Father* who offers the heroine happiness in THE LOVING ARMS OF THE LAW. *Saving Grace* is the newest from prolific RaeAnne Thayne, who's rapidly making a name for herself with readers. And finally, welcome new author Wendy Rosnau. After you read *The Long Hot Summer,* you'll be eager for her to make a return appearance.

And, of course, we hope to see you next month when, once again, Silhouette Intimate Moments brings you six of the best and most exciting romance novels around.

Enjoy!

Leslie J. Wainger
Executive Senior Editor

Please address questions and book requests to:
Silhouette Reader Service
U.S.: 3010 Walden Ave., P.O. Box 1325, Buffalo, NY 14269
Canadian: P.O. Box 609, Fort Erie, Ont. L2A 5X3

GET LUCKY
SUZANNE BROCKMANN

Silhouette®
INTIMATE™ MOMENTS®
Published by Silhouette Books
America's Publisher of Contemporary Romance

For Patricia McMahon

Acknowledgments:
Special thanks to Frances Stepp, expert on a whole lot more
than diving, who somehow always knows to e-mail or Instant
Message me whenever I have a burning research question, and
Mike Freeman, real-life hero. I'm honored to know you both!
Any mistakes that I've made or liberties that I've taken are
completely my own.

 SILHOUETTE BOOKS

ISBN 0-373-07991-5

GET LUCKY

Copyright © 2000 by Suzanne Brockmann

Visit us at www.romance.net

Printed in U.S.A.

SUZANNE BROCKMANN

lives just west of Boston in a house always filled with her friends—actors and musicians and storytellers and artists and teachers. When not writing award-winning romances about U.S. Navy SEALs, among others, she sings in an a cappella group called SERIOUS FUN, manages the professional acting careers of her two children, volunteers at the Appalachian Benefit Coffeehouse and always answers letters from readers. Send her an SASE along with your letter to P.O. Box 5092, Wayland, MA 01778.

IT'S OUR 20th ANNIVERSARY!
We'll be celebrating all year,
continuing with these fabulous titles,
on sale in March 2000.

Prologue

It was like being hit by a professional linebacker.

The man barreled down the stairs and bulldozed right into Sydney, nearly knocking her onto her rear end.

To add insult to injury, he mistook her for a man.

"Sorry, bud," he tossed back over his shoulder as he kept going down the stairs.

She heard the front door of the apartment building open and then slam shut.

It was the perfect end to the evening. Girls' night out—plural—had turned into girl's night out—singular. Bette had left a message on Syd's answering machine announcing that she couldn't make it to the movies tonight. Something had come up. Something that was no doubt, six-foot-three, broad-shouldered, wearing a cowboy hat and named Scott or Brad or Wayne.

And Syd had received a call from Hilary on her cell phone as she was pulling into the multiplex parking lot. *Her* excuse for cancelling was a kid with a fever of one hundred and two.

Turning around and going home would have been too depressing. So Syd had gone to the movie alone. And ended up even *more* depressed.

The show had been interminably long and pointless, with buff young actors flexing their way across the screen. She'd alternately been bored by the story and embarrassed, both for the actors and for herself, for being fascinated by the sheer breathtaking perfection of their bodies.

Men like that—or like the football player who'd nearly knocked her over—didn't date women like Sydney Jameson.

It wasn't that she wasn't physically attractive, because she was. Or at least she could be when she bothered to do more than run a quick comb through her hair. Or when she bothered to dress in something other than the baggy shirts and loose-fitting, comfortable jeans that were her standard apparel—and that allowed the average Neanderthal rushing past her down the stairs to mistake her for a man. Of course, she comforted herself, the dimness of the 25-watt bulbs that the landlord, Mr. El Cheap-o Thompkins, had installed in the hallway light fixtures hadn't helped.

Syd trudged up the stairs to the third floor. This old house had been converted to apartments in the late 1950s. The top floor—formerly the attic—had been made into two units, both of which were far more spacious than anyone would have thought from looking at the outside of the building.

She stopped on the landing.

The door to her neighbor's apartment was ajar.

Gina Sokoloski. Syd didn't know her next-door neighbor that well. They'd passed on the stairs now and then, signed for packages when the other wasn't home, had brief conversations about such thrilling topics as the best time of year for cantaloupe.

Gina was young and shy—not yet twenty years old—and a student at the junior college. She was plain and quiet and rarely had visitors, which suited Syd just fine after living for eight months next door to the frat boys from hell.

Gina's mother had come by once or twice—one of those tidy, quietly rich women who wore a giant diamond ring and drove a car that cost more than Syd could make in three very good years as a freelance journalist.

The he-man who'd barrelled down the stairs wasn't what Syd would have expected a boyfriend of Gina's to look like. He was older than Gina by about ten years, too, but this could well be more proof that opposites did, indeed, attract.

This old building made so many weird noises during the night. Still, she could've sworn she'd heard a distinctly human sound coming from Gina's apartment. Syd stepped closer to the open door and peeked in, but the apartment was completely dark. "Gina?"

She listened harder. There it was again. A definite sob. No doubt the son of a bitch who'd nearly knocked her over had just broken up with Gina. Leave it to a man to be in such a hurry to be gone that he'd leave the door wide open.

"Gina, your door's unlatched. Is everything okay in here?" Syd knocked more loudly as she pushed the door open even farther.

The dim light from the hallway shone into the living room and...

The place was trashed. Furniture knocked over, lamps broken, a bookshelf overturned. Dear God, the man hurrying down the stairs hadn't been Gina's boyfriend. He'd been a burglar.

Or worse...

Hair rising on the back of her neck, Syd dug through her purse for her cell phone. Please God, don't let Gina have been home. Please God, let that funny little sound be the ancient swamp cooler or the pipes or the wind wheezing through the vent in the crawl space between the ceiling and the eaves....

But then she heard it again. It was definitely a muffled whimper.

Syd's fingers closed around her phone as she reached with her other hand for the light switch on the wall by the door. She flipped it on.

And there, huddled in the corner of her living room, her face bruised and bleeding, her clothing torn and bloody, was Gina.

Syd locked the door behind her and dialed 911.

Chapter 1

All early-morning conversation in Captain Joe Catalanotto's outer office stopped dead as everyone turned to look at Lucky.

It was a festival of raised eyebrows and opened mouths. The astonishment level wouldn't have been any higher if Lieutenant Luke "Lucky" O'Donlon of SEAL Team Ten's Alpha Squad had announced he was quitting the units to become a monk.

All the guys were staring at him—Jones and Blue and Skelly. A flash of surprise had even crossed Crash Hawken's imperturbable face. Frisco was there, too, having come out of a meeting with Joe and Harvard, the team's senior chief. Lucky had caught them all off guard. It would've been funny—except he wasn't feeling much like laughing.

"Look, it's no big deal," Lucky said with a shrug, wishing that simply saying the words would make it so, wishing he could feel as nonchalant as he sounded.

No one said a word. Even recently promoted Chief Wes

Skelly was uncharacteristically silent. But Lucky didn't need to be telepathic to know what his teammates were thinking.

He'd lobbied loud and long for a chance to be included in Alpha Squad's current mission—a covert assignment for which Joe Cat himself didn't even know the details. He'd only been told to ready a five-man team to insert somewhere in Eastern Europe; to prepare to depart at a moment's notice, prepare to be gone for an undetermined amount of time.

It was the kind of assignment guaranteed to get the heart pumping and adrenaline running, the kind of assignment Lucky lived for.

And Lucky had been one of the chosen few. Just yesterday morning he'd done a victory dance when Joe Cat had told him to get his gear ready to go. Yet here he was, barely twenty-four hours later, requesting reassignment, asking the captain to count him out—*and* to call in some old favors to get him temporarily assigned to a not-so-spine-tingling post at the SEAL training base here in Coronado, effective ASAP.

Lucky forced a smile. "It's not like you'll have trouble replacing me, Captain." He glanced at Jones and Skelly who were both practically salivating at the thought of doing just that.

The captain gestured with his head toward his office, completely unfooled by Lucky's pretense at indifference. "You want to step inside and tell me what this is all about?"

Lucky didn't need the privacy. "It's no big secret, Cat. My sister's getting married in a few weeks. If I leave on this assignment, there's a solid chance I won't be back in time."

Wes Skelly couldn't keep his mouth shut a second longer. "I thought you were heading down to San Diego last night to read her the riot act."

Lucky had intended to. He'd gone to visit Ellen and her alleged fiancé, one geeky college professor by the name of Gregory Price, intending to lay down the law; intending to demand that his twenty-two-year-old baby sister wait at least another year before she take such a major step as marriage. He'd gone fully intending to be persuasive. She was impossibly young. How could she be ready to commit to one man—one who wore sweaters to work, at that— when she hadn't had a chance yet to truly live?

But Ellen was Ellen, and Ellen had made up her mind. She was so certain, so unafraid. And as Lucky had watched her smile at the man she was determined to spend the rest of her life with, he'd marveled at the fact that they'd had the same mother. Of course, maybe it was the fact they had different fathers that made them such opposites when it came to commitment. Because, although Ellen was ready to get married at twenty-two, Lucky could imagine feeling too young to be tied down at age eighty-two.

Still, he'd been the one to give in.

It was Greg who had convinced him. It was the way he looked at Ellen, the way the man's love for Lucky's little sister shone in his eyes that had the SEAL giving them both his blessing—and his promise that he'd be at the wedding to give the bride away.

Never mind the fact that he'd have to turn down what was shaping up to be the most exciting assignment of the year.

"I'm the only family she's got," Lucky said quietly. "I've got to be there for her wedding, if I can. At least I've got to *try.*"

The Captain nodded. "Okay," he said. That was explanation enough for him. "Jones, ready your gear."

Wes Skelly made a squawk of disappointment that was cut off by one sharp look from the senior chief. He turned away abruptly.

Captain Catalanotto glanced at Frisco, who worked as a

classroom instructor when he wasn't busy helping run the SEAL BUD/S training facility. "What do you think about using O'Donlon for your little project?"

Alan "Frisco" Francisco had been Lucky's swim buddy. Years ago, they'd made it through BUD/S training together and had worked side by side on countless assignments— until Desert Storm. Lucky had been ready to ship out to the Middle East with the rest of Alpha Squad when he'd received word that his mother had died. He'd stayed behind and Frisco had gone—and gotten his leg nearly blown off during a rescue mission. Even though Frisco no longer came out into the field, the two men had stayed tight.

In fact, Lucky was going to be the godfather later this year when Frisco and his wife Mia had their first baby.

Frisco now nodded at the Captain. "Yeah," he said. "Definitely. O'Donlon's perfect for the assignment."

"What assignment?" Lucky asked. "If it's training an all-woman SEAL team, then, yes, thank you very much, I'm your man."

There, see? He'd managed to make a joke. He was already starting to feel better. Maybe he wasn't going out into the real world with Alpha Squad, but he was going to get a chance to work with his best friend again. And—his natural optimism returning—he just *knew* there was a Victoria's Secret model in his immediate future. This *was* California, after all. And he wasn't nicknamed Lucky for nothing.

But Frisco didn't laugh. In fact, he looked seriously grim as he tucked a copy of the morning paper beneath his arm. "Not even close. You're going to hate this."

Lucky looked into the eyes of the man he knew better than a brother. And he didn't have to say a word. Frisco knew it didn't really matter what his buddy did over the next few weeks. Everything would pale beside the lost opportunity of the assignment he'd passed up.

Frisco gestured for him to come outside.

Lucky took one last look around Alpha Squad's office. Harvard was already handling the paperwork that would put him temporarily under Frisco's command. Joe Cat was deep in discussion with Wes Skelly, who still looked unhappy that he'd been passed over yet again. Blue McCoy, Alpha Squad's executive officer, was on the phone, his voice lowered—probably talking to Lucy. He had on that telltale frown of concern he wore so often these days when he spoke to his wife. She was a San Felipe police detective, involved with some big secret case that had the usually unflappable Blue on edge.

Crash sat communing with his computer. Jones had left in a rush, but now he returned, his gear already organized. No doubt the dweeb had already packed last night, just in case, like a good little Boy Scout. Ever since the man had gotten married, he hurried home whenever he had the chance, instead of partying hard with Lucky and Bob and Wes. Jones's nickname was Cowboy, but his wild and woolly days of drinking and chasing women were long gone. Lucky had always considered the smooth-talking, good-looking Jones to be something of a rival both in love and war, but he was completely agreeable these days, walking around with a permanent smile on his face, as if he knew something Lucky didn't.

Even when Lucky had won the spot on the current team—the spot he'd just given up—Jones had smiled and shaken his hand.

The truth was, Lucky resented Cowboy Jones. By all rights, he should be miserable—a man like that—roped into marriage, tied down with a drooling kid in diapers.

Yeah, he resented Cowboy, no doubt about it.

Resented, and envied him his complete happiness.

Frisco was waiting impatiently by the door, but Lucky took his time. ''Stay cool, guys.''

He knew when Joe Cat got the order to go, the team

would simply vanish. There would be no time spent on farewells.

"God, I hate it when they leave without me," he said to Frisco as he followed his friend into the bright sunshine. "So, what's this about?"

"You haven't seen today's paper, have you?" Frisco asked.

Lucky shook his head. "No, why?"

Frisco silently handed him the newspaper he'd been holding.

The headline said it all—Serial Rapist Linked to Coronado SEALs?

Lucky swore pungently. "Serial *rapist?* This is the first I've heard of this."

"It's the first any of us have heard of this," Frisco said grimly. "But apparently there's been a series of rapes in Coronado and San Felipe over the past few weeks. And with the latest—it happened two nights ago—the police now believe there's some kind of connection linking the attacks. Or so they say."

Lucky quickly skimmed the article. There were very few facts about the attacks—seven—or about the victims. The only mention of the women who'd been attacked was of the latest—an unnamed 19-year-old college student. In all cases, the rapist wore a feature-distorting pair of panty hose on his head, but he was described as a Caucasian man with a crew cut, with either brown or dark blond hair, approximately six feet tall, muscularly built and about thirty years of age.

The article focused on ways in which women in both towns could ensure their safety. One of the tips recommended was to stay away—far away—from the U.S. Navy base.

The article ended with the nebulous statement, "When asked about the rumored connection of the serial rapist to the Coronado naval base, and in particular to the teams of

SEALs stationed there, the police spokesman replied, 'Our investigation will be thorough, and the military base is a good place to start.'

"Known for their unconventional fighting techniques as well as their lack of discipline, the SEALs have had their presence felt in the towns of Coronado and San Felipe many times in the past, with late-night and early-morning explosions often startling the guests at the famed Hotel del Coronado. Lieutenant Commander Alan Francisco of the SEALs could not be reached for comment."

Lucky swore again. "Way to make us look like the spawn of Satan. And let me guess just how hard—" he looked at the top of the article for the reporter's name "—this S. Jameson guy tried to reach you for comment."

"Oh, the reporter tried," Frisco countered as he began moving toward the jeep that would take him across the base to his office. Lucky could tell from the way he leaned on his cane that his knee was hurting today. "But I stayed hidden. I didn't want to say anything to alienate the police until I had the chance to talk to Admiral Forrest. And he agreed with my plan."

"Which is…?"

"There's a task force being formed to catch this son of a bitch," Frisco told him. "Both the Coronado and San Felipe police are part of it—as well as the state police, and a special unit from FInCOM. The admiral pulled some strings, and got us included. That's why I went to see Cat and Harvard. I need an officer I can count on to be part of this task force. Someone I can trust."

Someone exactly like Lucky. He nodded. "When do I start?"

"There's a meeting in the San Felipe police station at 0900 hours. Meet me in my office—we'll go down there together. Wear your whites and every ribbon you've got." Frisco climbed behind the wheel of the jeep, tossing his cane into the back. "There's more, too. I want you to hand-pick a team, and I want you to catch this bastard. As quickly as possible. If the perp *is* a spec-warrior, we're going to need more than a task force to nail him."

Lucky held on to the side of the jeep. "Do you really think this guy could be one of us?"

Frisco shook his head. "I don't know. I hope to hell he's not."

The rapist had attacked seven women—one of them a girl just a little bit younger than his sister. And Lucky knew that it didn't matter who this bastard was. It only mattered that they stop him before he struck again.

"Whoever he is," he promised his best friend and commanding officer, "I'll find him. And after I do, he's going to be sorry he was born."

Sydney was relieved to find she wasn't the only woman in the room. She was glad to see that Police Detective Lucy McCoy was part of the task force being set up this morning, its single goal: to catch the San Felipe Rapist.

Out of the seven attacks, five had taken place in the lower-rent town of San Felipe. And although the two towns were high-school sports-team rivals, this was one case in which Coronado was more than happy to let San Felipe take the title.

They'd gathered here at the San Felipe police station ready to work together to apprehend the rapist.

Syd had first met Detective Lucy McCoy last Saturday night. The detective had arrived on the scene at Gina Sokoloski's apartment clearly pulled out of bed, her face clean of makeup, her shirt buttoned wrong—and spitting mad that she hadn't been called sooner.

Syd had been fiercely guarding Gina, who was frighteningly glassy-eyed and silent after the trauma of her attack.

The male detectives had tried to be gentle, but even gentle couldn't cut it at a time like this. *Can you tell us what happened, miss?*

Sheesh. As if Gina would be able to look up at these men and tell them how she'd turned to find a man in her living room, how he'd grabbed her before she could run, slapped his hand across her mouth before she could scream, and then...

And then that Neanderthal who had nearly run Syd down on the stairs had raped this girl. Brutally. Violently. Syd would've bet good money that she had been a virgin, poor shy little thing. What an awful way to be introduced to sex.

Syd had wrapped her arms tightly around the girl, and told the detectives in no uncertain terms that they had better get a woman down here, pronto. After what Gina had been through, she didn't need to suffer the embarrassment of having to talk about it with a man.

But Gina had told Detective Lucy McCoy all of it, in a voice that was completely devoid of emotion—as if she were reporting facts that had happened to someone else, not herself.

She'd tried to hide. She'd cowered in the corner, and he hit her. And hit her. And then he was on top of her, tearing her clothing and forcing himself between her legs. With his hands around her throat, she'd struggled even just to breathe, and he'd...

Lucy had quietly explained about the rape kit, explained about the doctor's examination that Gina still had to endure, explained that as much as Gina wanted to, she couldn't take a shower. Not yet.

Lucy had explained that the more Gina could tell her about the man who'd attacked her, the better their chances were of catching him. If there was anything more she could report about the words he'd spoken, any little detail she may have left out....

Syd had described the man who nearly knocked her over on the stairs. The lighting was bad. She hadn't gotten a

good look at him. In fact, she couldn't even be sure that
he wasn't still wearing the nylon stocking over his face that
Gina had described. But she could guess at his height—
taller than she was, and his build—powerful—and she
could say for a fact that he was a white male, somewhere
between twenty-five and thirty-five years of age, with very
short, crew-cut hair.

And he spoke in a low-pitched, accentless voice. *Sorry,
bud.*

It was weird and creepy to think that a man who'd brutalized Gina would have taken the time to apologize for
bumping into Syd. It was also weird and creepy to think
that if Syd had been home, she might have heard the noise
of the struggle, heard Gina's muffled cries and might've
been able to help.

Or, perhaps Syd might've been the victim herself.

Before they'd headed over to the hospital, Gina had loos-
ened her grip on the torn front of her shirt and showed
Lucy and Syd a burn. The son of a bitch had branded the
girl on her breast, in what looked like the shape of a bird.

Lucy had stiffened, clearly recognizing the marking.
She'd excused herself, and found the other detectives. And
although she'd spoken in a lowered voice, Syd had moved
to the door so she could hear.

"It's our guy again," Lucy McCoy had grimly told the
other detectives. "Gina's been burned with a Budweiser,
too."

Our guy *again*. When Syd asked if there had been other
similar attacks, Lucy had bluntly told her that she wasn't
at liberty to discuss that.

Syd had gone to the hospital with the girl, staying with
her until her mother arrived.

But then, despite the fact that it was three o'clock in the
morning, there were too many unanswered questions for
Syd to go home and go to sleep. As a former investigative
reporter, she knew a thing or two about finding answers to

unanswered questions. A few well-placed phone calls connected her to Silva Fontaine, a woman on the late-night shift at the hospital's Rape Counseling Center. Silva had informed Syd that six women had come in in half as many weeks. Six women who hadn't been attacked by husbands or boyfriends or relatives or co-workers. Six women who had been attacked in their own homes by an unknown assailant. Same as Gina.

A little research on the Internet had turned up the fact that a *budweiser* wasn't just a bottle of beer. U.S. Navy personnel who went through the rigorous Basic Underwater Demolition Training over at the SEAL facility in nearby Coronado were given a pin in the shape of a flying eagle carrying a trident and a stylized gun, upon their entrance into the SEAL units.

This pin was nicknamed a budweiser.

Every U.S. Navy SEAL had one. It represented the SEAL acronym of sea, air and land, the three environments in which the commando-like men expertly operated. In other words, they jumped out of planes, soaring through the air with specially designed parachutes as easily as they crawled through jungle, desert or city, as easily as they swam through the deep waters of the sea.

They had a near-endless list of warrior qualifications— everything from hand-to-hand combat to high-tech computer warfare, underwater demolition to sniper-quality marksmanship. They could pilot planes or boats, operate tanks and land vehicles.

Although it wasn't listed, they could also, no doubt, leap tall buildings with a single bound.

Yeah, the list was impressive. It was kind of like looking at Superman's resume.

But it was also alarming.

Because *this* superhero had turned bad. For weeks, some psycho Navy SEAL had been stalking the women of San Felipe. Seven women had been brutally attacked, yet there had been no warnings issued, no news reports telling women to take caution.

Syd had been furious.

She'd spent the rest of the night writing.

And in the morning, she'd gone to the police station, the freelance article she'd written for the *San Felipe Journal* in hand.

She'd been shown into Chief Zale's office and negotiations had started. The San Felipe police didn't want any information about the attacks to be publicized. When Zale found out Syd was a freelance reporter, and that she'd been there at the crime scene for hours last night, he'd nearly had an aneurism. He was convinced that if this story broke, the rapist would go into deep hiding and they'd never apprehend him. The chief told Syd flatly that the police didn't know for certain if all seven of the attacks had been made by the same man—the branding of the victim with the budweiser pin had only been done to Gina and one other woman.

Zale had demanded Syd hold all the detailed information about the recent attacks. Syd had countered with a request to write the exclusive story after the rapist was caught, to sit in with the task force being formed to apprehend the rapist—provided she could write a series of police-approved articles for the local papers, now warning women of the threat.

Zale had had a cow.

Syd had stood firm despite being blustered at for several hours, and eventually Zale had conceded. But, wow, had he been ticked off.

Still, here she was. Sitting in with the task force.

She recognized the police chief and several detectives from Coronado, as well as several representatives from the California State Police. And although no one introduced her, she caught the names of a trio of FInCOM Agents, as well. Huang, Sudenberg and Novak—she jotted their names in her notebook.

It was funny to watch them interact. Coronado didn't think much of San Felipe, and vice versa. However, both groups preferred each other over the state troopers. The Finks simply remained aloof. Yet solidarity was formed— at least in part—when the U.S. Navy made the scene.

"Sorry, I'm late." The man in the doorway was blindingly handsome—the blinding due in part to the bright white of his naval uniform and the dazzling rows of colorful ribbons on his chest. But only in part. His face was that of a movie star, with an elegantly thin nose that hinted of aristocracy, and eyes that redefined the word *blue.* His hair was sunstreaked and stylishly long in front. Right now it was combed neatly back, but with one puff of wind, or even a brief blast of humidity, it would be dancing around his face, waving tendrils of spun gold. His skin was perfectly tanned—the better to show off the white flash of his teeth as he smiled.

He was, without a doubt, the sheer perfection of a Ken doll come to life.

Syd wasn't sure, but she thought the braids on his sleeves meant he was some sort of officer.

The living Ken—with all of his U.S. Navy accessories— somehow managed to squeeze his extremely broad shoulders through the door. He stepped into the room. "Lieutenant Commander Francisco asked me to convey his regrets." His voice was a melodic baritone, slightly husky with just a trace of Southern California, dude. "There's been a serious training accident on the base, and he was unable to leave."

San Felipe Detective Lucy McCoy leaned forward. "Is everyone all right?"

"Hey, Lucy." He bestowed a brief but special smile upon the female detective. It didn't surprise Syd one bit that he should know the pretty brunette by name. "We got a SEAL candidate in a DDC—a deck decompression chamber. Frisco—Lieutenant Commander Francisco—had to fly out to the site with some of the doctors from the naval hospital. It was a routine dive, everything was done completely by the book—until one of the candidates started showing symptoms of the bends—*while* he was in the water. They still don't know what the hell went wrong. Bobby got him out and back on board, and popped him in the DDC, but from his description, it sounds like this guy's already had a CNS hit—a central nervous system hit,'' he translated. ''You know, when a nitrogen bubble expands in the brain.'' He shook his head, his blue eyes somber, his pretty mouth grim. ''Even if this man survives, he could be seriously brain damaged.''

U.S. Navy Ken sat down in the only unoccupied chair at the table, directly across from Sydney, as he glanced around the room. ''I'm sure you all understand Lieutenant Commander Francisco's need to look into this situation immediately.''

Syd tried not to stare, but it was hard. At three feet away, she should have been able to see this man's imperfections—if not quite a wart, then maybe a chipped tooth. Some nose hair at least.

But at three feet away, he was even more gorgeous. *And* he smelled good, too.

Chief Zale gave him a baleful look. ''And you are…?''

Navy Ken half stood up again. ''I'm sorry. Of course, I should have introduced myself.'' His smile was sheepish. Gosh darn it, it said, I plumb forgot that not everybody here knows who I am, wonderful though I may be. ''Lieutenant Luke O'Donlon, of the U.S. Navy SEALs.''

Syd didn't have to be an expert at reading body language to know that everyone in the room—at least everyone male—hated the Navy. And if they hadn't before, they sure did now. The jealousy in the room was practically palpable.

Lieutenant Luke O'Donlon gleamed. He shone. He was all white and gold and sunlight and sky-blue eyes.

He was a god. The mighty king of all Ken dolls.

And he knew it.

His glance touched Syd only briefly as he looked around the room, taking inventory of the police and FInCOM personnel. But as Zale's assistant passed out manila files, Navy Ken's gaze settled back on Syd. He smiled, and it was such a perfect, slightly puzzled smile, Syd nearly laughed aloud. Any second now and he was going to ask her who she was.

"Are you FInCOM?" he mouthed to her, taking the file that was passed to him and warmly nodding his thanks to the Coronado detective who was sitting beside him.

Syd shook her head, no.

"From the Coronado PD?" he asked silently.

Zale had begun to speak, and Syd shook her head again, then pointedly turned her attention to the head of the table.

The San Felipe police chief spoke at length about stepping up patrol cars in the areas where the rapes had taken place. He spoke of a team that would be working around the clock, attempting to find a pattern in the locations of the attacks, or among the seven victims. He talked about semen samples and DNA. He glared at Syd as he spoke of the need to keep the details of the crimes, of the rapist's MO—method of operation—from leaking to the public. He brought up the nasty little matter of the SEAL pin, heated by the flame from a cigarette lighter and used to burn a mark onto the bodies of the last two victims.

Navy Ken cleared his throat and interrupted. "I'm sure it's occurred to you that if this guy *were* a SEAL, he'd have to be pretty stupid to advertise it this way. Isn't it much more likely that he's trying to make you believe he's a SEAL?"

"Absolutely," Zale responded. "Which is why we implied that we thought he was a SEAL in the article that came out in this morning's paper. We want him to think he's winning, to become careless.''

"So you *don't* think he's a SEAL," the SEAL tried to clarify.

"Maybe," Syd volunteered, "he's a SEAL who wants to be caught.''

Navy Ken's eyes narrowed slightly as he gazed at her, clearly thinking hard. "I'm sorry," he said. "I know just about everyone else here, but we haven't been introduced. Are you a police psychologist?"

Zale didn't let Syd reply. "Ms. Jameson is going to be working very closely with you, Lieutenant."

Ms. not Doctor. Syd saw that information register in the SEAL's eyes.

But then she realized what Zale had said and sat back in her chair. "I am?"

O'Donlon leaned forward. "Excuse me?"

Zale looked a little too pleased with himself. "Lieutenant Commander Francisco put in an official request to have a SEAL team be part of this task force. Detective McCoy convinced me that it might be a good idea. If our man is or was a SEAL, you may have better luck finding him."

"I assure you, luck won't be part of it, sir."

Syd couldn't believe O'Donlon's audacity. The amazing part was that he spoke with such conviction. He actually believed himself.

"That remains to be seen," Zale countered. "I've decided to give you permission to form this team, provided you keep Detective McCoy informed of your whereabouts and progress."

"I can manage that." O'Donlon flashed another of his smiles at Lucy McCoy. "In fact, it'll be a pleasure."

"Oh, ack." Syd didn't realize she'd spoken aloud until Navy Ken glanced at her in surprise.

"And provided," Zale continued, "you agree to include Ms. Jameson in your team."

The SEAL laughed. Yes, his teeth *were* perfect. "No," he said, "Chief. You don't understand. A SEAL team is a team of *SEALs*. Only SEALs. Ms. Jameson will—no offense, ma'am—only get in the way."

"That's something you're just going to have to deal with," Zale told him a little too happily. He didn't like the Navy, and he didn't like Syd. This was his way of getting back at them both. "I'm in charge of this task force. You do it my way, or your men don't leave the naval base. There are other details to deal with, but Detective McCoy will review them with you."

Syd's brain was moving at warp speed. Zale thought he was getting away with something here—by casting her off on to the SEALs. But *this* was the real story—the one that would be unfolding *within* the confines of the naval base as well as without. She'd done enough research on the SEAL units over the past forty-odd hours to know that these unconventional spec-warriors would be eager to stop the bad press and find the San Felipe Rapist on their own. She was curious to find out what would happen if the rapist *did* turn out to be one of them. Would they try to hide it? Would they try to deal with punishment on their own terms?

The story she was going to write could be an in-depth look at one of America's elite military organizations. And it could well be exactly what she needed to get herself noticed, to get that magazine editor position, back in New York City, that she wanted so desperately.

"I'm sorry." O'Donlon started an awful lot of his sentences with an apology. "But there's just no way a police social worker could keep up with—"

"I'm not a social worker," Syd interrupted.

"Ms. Jameson is one of our chief eyewitnesses," Zale said. "She's been face to face with our man."

O'Donlon faltered. His face actually got pale, and he

dropped all friendly, easygoing pretense. And as Syd gazed into his eyes, she got a glimpse of his horror and shock.

"My God," he whispered. "I didn't…I'm sorry—I had no idea…."

He was ashamed. And embarrassed. Honestly shaken. "I feel like I should apologize for all men, everywhere."

Amazing. Navy Ken wasn't all plastic. He was at least part human. Go figure.

Obviously, he thought she had been one of the rapist's victims.

"No," she said quickly. "I mean, thanks, but I'm an eyewitness because my neighbor was attacked. I was coming up the stairs as the man who raped her was coming down. And I'm afraid I didn't even get that good a look at him."

"God," O'Donlon said. "*Thank* God. When Chief Zale said…I thought…." He drew in a deep breath and let it out forcefully. "I'm sorry. I just can't imagine…." He recovered quickly, then leaned forward slightly, his face speculative. "So…you've actually *seen* this guy."

Syd nodded. "Like I said, I didn't—"

O'Donlon turned to Zale. "And you're giving her to *me?*"

Syd laughed in disbelief. "Excuse me, I would appreciate it if you could rephrase that…."

Zale stood up. Meeting over. "Yeah. She's all yours."

Chapter 2

"Have you ever been hypnotized?" Lucky glanced over at the woman sitting beside him as he pulled his pickup truck onto the main drag that led to the naval base.

She turned to give him a disbelieving look.

She was good at that look. He wondered if it came naturally or if she'd worked to perfect it, practicing for hours in front of her bathroom mirror. The thought made him smile, which only made her glower even harder.

She was pretty enough—if you went for women who hid every one of their curves beneath androgynous clothes, women who never let themselves smile.

No, he mused, looking at her more closely as he stopped at a red light. He'd once dated a woman who'd never smiled. Jacqui Fontaine. She'd been a beautiful young woman who was so terrified of getting wrinkles she kept her face carefully devoid of all expression. In fact, she'd gotten angry with him for making her laugh. At first he'd thought she was joking, but she'd been serious. She'd asked him back to her apartment after they'd seen a movie, but he'd declined. Sex would have been positively bizarre. It would have been like making love to a mannequin. The thought still made him shudder.

This woman, however, had laugh lines around her eyes. Proof that she did smile. Probably frequently, in fact.

She just had no intention of smiling at *him*.

Her hair was thick and dark, curling around her face, unstyled and casual—cut short enough so that she probably could get away with little more than raking her fingers through it after climbing out of bed.

Her eyes were dark brown and impossibly large in a face that could only be called pixielike.

Provided, of course, that pixies had a solid dose of unresolved resentment. She didn't like him. She hadn't liked him from the moment he'd walked into the San Felipe police-station conference room.

"Cindy, wasn't it?" He knew damn well that her name was Sydney. But what kind of woman was named *Sydney?* If he was going to have to baby-sit the woman who could potentially ID the San Felipe Rapist, why couldn't she be named Crystal or Mellisande—and dress accordingly?

"No," she said tightly, in a voice that was deceptively low and husky, unfairly sexy considering she clearly didn't want anyone looking at her to think even remotely about sex, "it wasn't. And no, I've never been hypnotized."

"Great," he said, trying to sound as enthusiastic as possible as he parked in the lot near Frisco's office. *His* office now, too, at least temporarily. "Then we're going to have some fun. A real adventure. Uncharted territory. Boldly going, etcetera."

Now Sydney was looking at him with something akin to horror in her eyes. "You can't be serious."

Lucky took the keys out of the ignition and opened the truck's door. "Of course not. Not completely. Who'd ever want to be completely serious about anything?" He climbed out and looked back inside at her. "But the part

I'm not completely serious about is whether it's going to be fun. In fact, I suspect it's going to be pretty low key. Probably dull. Unless while you're under, I can convince the hypnotist to make you quack like a duck.''

If she *were* a Crystal or a Mellisande, Lucky would've winked at her, but he knew, without a doubt, that winking at Sydney would result in her trying to melt him into unidentifiable goo with her death-ray glare.

Most women liked to be winked at. Most women could be softened up with an appreciative look and a compliment. Most women responded to his "hey, baby" body language and subtle flirting with a little "hey, baby" body language and subtle flirting in return. With most women, he didn't have to wait long for an invitation to move from subtle flirting to flat-out seduction.

Sydney, however, was not most women.

"Thanks, but I don't want to be hypnotized," she told him as she climbed awkwardly down from the cab of his truck. "I've read that some people are less susceptible to hypnotism—that they just can't be hypnotized. I'm pretty sure I'm one of them."

"How do you know," Lucky reasoned, "if you've never tried?"

His best smile bounced right off her. "It's a waste of time," she said sternly.

"Well, I'm afraid I don't think so." Lucky tried his apologetic smile as he led the way into the building, but that one didn't work either. "I guess you'll have an opportunity to prove me wrong."

Sydney stood still. "Do you *ever* not get your way?"

Lucky pretended to think about that for a moment. "No," he finally said. He smiled. "I always get my way, and I'm never completely serious. You keep that in mind, and we'll get along just fine."

Sydney stood in the building's lobby watching as Lieutenant Luke O'Donlon greeted a lovely, dark-haired, very pregnant woman with a stunner from his vast repertoire of smiles.

"Hey, gorgeous—what are you doing here?" He wrapped his arms around her and planted a kiss full on her lips.

His wife. Had to be.

It was funny, Syd wouldn't have believed this man capable of marriage. And it still didn't make sense. He didn't walk like a married man. He certainly didn't talk like a married man. Everything about him, from the way he sat as he drove his truck to the way he smiled at anything and everything even remotely female, screamed bachelor. *Terminal* bachelor.

Yet as Syd watched, he crouched down and pressed his face against the woman's burgeoning belly. "Hello in there!"

Whoever she was, she *was* gorgeous. Long, straight, dark hair cascaded down her back. Her delicately featured face held a hint of the Far East. She rolled her beautiful, exotic eyes as she laughed.

"This is why I don't come out here that often," she said to Syd over the top of O'Donlon's head as he pressed his ear to her stomach, listening now. "I'm Mia Francisco, by the way."

Francisco. The Lieutenant Commander's wife.

"He's singing that Shania Twain song," O'Donlon reported, looking past Syd and grinning. "The one Frisco says never leaves your CD player?"

Syd turned to see a teenaged girl standing behind her— all long legs and skinny arms, surrounded by an amazing cloud of curly red hair.

The girl smiled, but it was decidedly half-hearted. "Ha, ha, Lucky," she said. "Very funny."

"We heard about the diving accident," Mia explained as O'Donlon straightened up. "They weren't releasing any names, and we couldn't reach Alan, so Tasha talked me into driving out to make sure Thomas was okay.''

"Thomas?"

"King," Mia said. "Former student of mine? You remember him, don't you? He's going through BUD/S training with this class.''

"Yeah." O'Donlon snapped his fingers. "Right. Black kid, serious attitude.''

"It wasn't Thomas," the red-haired girl—Tasha—informed him. "It was someone else who got hurt.''

"An ensign named Marc Riley. They've got him stabilized. He's in a lot of pain, but it's not as bad as they first thought." Mia smiled at Syd again, friendly but curious, taking in her shapeless linen jacket, her baggy khaki pants, her cloddish boots and the mannish blouse she wore buttoned all the way to her neck.

Syd had no doubt that she looked extremely different from the usual sort of women who followed Lieutenant O'Donlon around.

"I'm sorry," Mia continued. "We didn't mean to shanghai Lucky this way.''

Lucky. The girl had referred to O'Donlon by that name, too. It was too perfect. Syd tried her best not to smirk.

"It's not a problem," she said. "I'm Syd Jameson.''

"We're working together on a special project," the man who was actually nicknamed *Lucky* interjected, as if he were afraid Mia might assume they were together socially. Yeah, as if.

"Is that the same project Lucy McCoy kicked us out of Alan's office to talk to him about?" Mia asked.

Lucky started to speak, then put his hands over Tasha's ears and swore. The girl giggled, and he winked at her before looking at Mia. "Lucy's already here?''

"Tell Alan it's my fault you're late.''

"Yeah, great." Lucky laughed as he waved good-bye, leading Syd down one of the corridors. "I'll tell him I'm delayed because I stopped to flirt with his wife. *That'll* go over just swell.''

Syd had to run to keep up. She had no doubt that whatever excuse O'Donlon gave for being late, he would be instantly forgiven. Grown men didn't keep nicknames like Lucky well past adolescence for no reason.

Lucky.

Sheesh.

Back in seventh grade, Syd had had a nickname.

Stinky.

She'd forgotten to wear deodorant one day. Just one *day,* and she was Stinky until the end of the school year.

Speaking of stinky, she'd have dressed differently if she'd known she was going to be running a marathon today. Lieutenant Lucky O'Donlon was well out in front of her and showed no sign of slowing down. How big was this place, anyway?

Not content to wait for an elevator, he led the way into a stairwell and headed up.

Syd was already out of breath, but she pushed herself to keep up, afraid if she let him out of her sight, she'd lose him. She tried to keep her eyes glued to his broad back, but it was hard, particularly since his perfect rear end was directly in her line of sight.

Of course he had a perfect rear end—trim and tiny, about one one-hundredth the size of hers, and a perfect match for his narrow hips. She shouldn't have expected anything less from a man named Lucky.

She followed his microbutt back out into the hallway and into an empty outer office and...

Syd caught her breath as he knocked on a closed door. The SEAL wasn't even slightly winded, damn him, and here she was, all but bent over, hands on her knees, puffing and wheezing.

''Smoker?'' he asked, almost apologetically. Almost, but not quite. He was just a little too amused to be truly sorry.

"No," she said. She was more out of shape than she'd realized. She'd always enjoyed running, but this spring and summer she hadn't quite managed to get started again.

The door opened, and standing in the inner office was a man who could have been a mirror reflection of Lucky. His hair was a slightly different color, and his face was more craggy than pretty, but the widths of the two men's shoulders were close to exact.

"I have a meeting with Admirals Forrest and Stonegate," the man said in a way of greeting. "Lucy's already here. Hear her out, and do whatever you've got to do to catch this guy. Preferably before the end of this week."

He looked from Lucky to Syd. His eyes were different from Lucky's and not just in color. He seemed capable of looking past the unruly hair that was falling into her own eyes, past the high neck of her shirt, past her near-permanent expression of slightly bored, slightly raised-eyebrow disbelief that she'd adopted after too many years of being given nicknames like Stinky.

Whatever he saw when he looked at her made him smile.

And it wasn't a condescending smile, or a "wow, you are such a freak" smile, either.

It was warm and welcoming. He held out his hand. "I'm Alan Francisco." His grip was as pleasantly solid as his smile. "Welcome to Coronado. If there's anything you need while you're here, I'm sure Lieutenant O'Donlon will be more than happy to provide it for you."

And just like that, he was gone. It wasn't until he was out the far door that Syd realized he'd moved stiffly, leaning heavily on a cane.

With a jolt, she realized she was standing there gazing after Alan Francisco. Lucky had already gone into the lieutenant commander's office, and she followed, shutting the door behind her.

Surprise, surprise—Lucky had his arms wrapped around

Detective McCoy. As Syd watched, he gave her a hello kiss.

"I didn't get to say hello properly before," he murmured. "You are looking too good for words, babe." Keeping his arm looped around her shoulders, he turned to Syd. "Lucy's husband, Blue, is XO of SEAL Team Ten's Alpha Squad."

Lucy's husband. Syd blinked. Lucy had a husband, who was also a SEAL. And presumably the two men were acquaintances, if not friends. This guy was too much.

"XO means executive officer," Lucy explained, giving Lucky a quick hug before slipping free from his grasp, reaching up to adjust the long brown hair that had slipped free from her ponytail holder. She really did have remarkably pretty eyes. "Blue's second in command of Alpha Squad."

"Blue," Syd repeated. "His name's really *Blue?*"

"It's a nickname," Lucy told her with a smile. "SEALs tend to get nicknames when they first go through BUD/S training. Let's see, we've got Cat, Cowboy, Frisco—" she ticked the names off on her fingers "—Blue, Lucky, Harvard, Crow, Fingers, Snakefoot, Wizard, Elmer, the Priest, Doc, Spaceman, Crash…"

"So your husband works here on the Navy base," Syd clarified.

"Some of the time," Lucy said. She glanced at Lucky and what that look meant, Syd couldn't begin to guess. "Alpha Squad went wheels up while we were downtown."

Syd couldn't guess the meaning of Lucy's words, either. "Wheels up?" She was starting to sound like a parrot.

"They've shipped out," Lucky explained. He leaned back casually, half sitting on Lieutenant Commander Francisco's desk. "The expression refers to a plane's wheels leaving the ground. Alpha Squad is outta town."

Again, Lucy and Lucky seemed to be communicating with no words—only a long, meaningful look. Was it pos-

sible that this blue-eyed blond god was having an
with the wife of a superior officer? Anything was possible,
but that seemed a little too sordid.

"What you've done," Lucy said quietly, breaking the
silence, "is going to mean everything to Ellen. Looking
back, you *know* it's going to be worth it."

"I could still be shipped out myself," he countered. "If
something big came up, and I was needed, I wouldn't even
be able to attend my *own* wedding."

Syd cleared her throat. She didn't know what they were
talking about, didn't *want* to know. She wasn't interested
in Ellen—whoever she was—or what Lucky and Lucy Mc-
Coy did behind her husband's back. She just wanted to help
catch the rapist, get her story and be off to New York.

"I'm okay, you know," Lucky told the detective. "And
I'll be even more okay if you'll meet me for dinner one of
these nights."

Lucy gave him a quick smile, glancing at Syd, obviously
aware that the two of them weren't alone. "You've got my
number," she said. She sat down at the conference table
that was over by the window. "Right now, we need to go
over some task-force rules, talk about your team."

Lucky sat at the head of the table. "Great. Let's start
with *my* rules. You let me form a team of SEALs, you don't
hammer me with a lot of useless rules and hamper me with
unqualified people who will only slow us down—" he shot
Syd an apologetic version of his smile "—no offense—and
then we'll catch your guy."

Lucy didn't blink. "The members of your team have to
meet Chief Zale's approval."

"Oh, no way!"

"He—and *I*—believe that since we don't know who
we're dealing with, and since you have plenty of alterna-
tives for personnel, you should construct your team from
SEALs or SEAL candidates who *absolutely*—no question—do not fit the rapist's description."

Syd sat down across from Lucky. "So in other words, no one white, powerfully built, with a crew cut."

Lucky sputtered. "That eliminates the majority of the men stationed in Coronado."

Lucy nodded serenely. "That's right. And the majority of the men are all potential suspects."

"You honestly think a real SEAL could have raped those women?"

"I think until we know more, we need to be conservative as to whom we allow into our information loop," she told him. "You'd be a suspect yourself, Luke, but your hair's too long."

"Gee, thanks for the vote of confidence."

"The second rule is about weapons," Lucy continued. "We don't want you running around town armed to the teeth. And that means knives as well as sidearms."

"Sure," he said. "Great. And when we apprehend this guy, we'll throw spoons at him."

"You won't apprehend him," she countered. "The task force will. Your team's job is to help locate him. Track him down. Try to think like this son of a bitch and anticipate his next move, so we—the police and FInCOM—can be there, waiting for him."

"Okay," Lucky said. He pointed across the table at Sydney. "I'll follow your rules—if you take her off my hands. After we do the hypnotist thing tomorrow afternoon, all she's going to do is get in the way." He looked at Syd. "No offense."

"Too bad," she said, "because I *am* offended."

Lucky looked at her again. "I don't know what Zale has against you, but it's obvious he doesn't like *me*. He's trying to make it close to impossible for my team to operate by assigning me…"

"I'm a reporter," Syd told him.

"…what amounts to little more than baby-sitting duty and…" His impossibly blue eyes widened. "A reporter."

Now he was the parrot. His eyes narrowed. "Sydney Jameson. S. Jameson. Ah, jeez, you're not just a reporter, you're *that* reporter." He glared at her. "Where the hell do you get off making us all sound like psychotic killers?"

He was serious. He'd taken offense to the one part of her story the police had actually requested she include. "Cool your jets, Ken," she told him. "The police wanted me to make it sound as if they actually believed the rapist was a SEAL."

"It's entirely likely our man is a SEAL wannabe," Lucy interjected. "We were hoping the news story would feed his ego, maybe make him careless."

"Ken?" Lucky asked Syd. "My name's Luke."

Oops, had she actually called him that? "Right. Sorry." Syd gave him the least sorry smile she could manage.

Lucky looked at her hard before he turned to Lucy. "How the hell did a reporter get involved?"

"Her neighbor was attacked. Sydney stayed with the girl—and this *was* just a girl. She wasn't more than nineteen years old, Luke. Sydney was there when I arrived, and oddly enough, I didn't think to inquire as to whether she was with UPI or Associated Press."

"So what did you do?" Lucky turned back to Syd. "Blackmail your way onto the task force?"

"Damn straight." Syd lifted her chin. "Seven rapes and not a single word of warning in any of the papers. It was a story that needed to be written—desperately. I figured I'd write it—*and* I'll write the exclusive behind-the-scenes story about tracking and catching the rapist, too."

He shook his head, obviously in disgust, and Syd's temper flared. "You know, if I were a man," she snapped, "you'd be impressed by my assertive behavior."

"So did you actually see this guy, or did you just make that part up?" he asked.

Syd refused to let him see how completely annoyed he made her feel. She forced her voice to sound even, controlled. "He nearly knocked me over coming down the stairs. But like I told the police, the light's bad in the hallways. I didn't get a real clear look at him."

"Is there a chance it was good enough for you to look at a lineup of my men and eliminate them as potential suspects?" he demanded.

Lucy sighed. "Lucky, I don't—"

"I want Bobby Taylor and Wes Skelly on my team."

"Bobby's fine. He's Native American," she told Syd. "Long dark hair, about eight feet tall and seven feet wide—definitely not our man. But Wes..."

"Wes shouldn't be a suspect," Lucky argued.

"Police investigations don't work that way," Lucy argued in response. "Yes, he *shouldn't* be a suspect. But Chief Zale wants every individual on your team to be completely, obviously not the man we're looking for."

"This is a man who's put his life on the line for me—for your husband—more times than you want to know. If Sydney could look at Skelly and—"

"I really don't remember much about the man's face," Syd interrupted. "He came flying down the stairs, nearly wiped me out, stopped a few steps down. I'm not even sure he turned all the way around. He apologized, and was gone."

Lucky leaned forward. "He *spoke* to you?"

God, he was good-looking. Syd forced away the little flutter she felt in her stomach every time he gazed at her. She really was pathetic. She didn't like this man. In fact, she was well on her way to disliking him intensely, and yet simply looking into his eyes was enough to make her knees grow weak.

Obviously, it had been way too long since she'd last had sex. Not that her situation was likely to change any time in the near future.

"What did he say?" Lucky asked. "His exact words?"

Syd shrugged, hating to tell him what the man had said, but knowing he wouldn't let up until she did.

Just do it. She took a deep breath. "He said, 'Sorry, bud.'"

"Sorry...*bud?*"

Syd felt her face flush. "Like I said. The light was bad in there. He must've thought I was, you know, a man."

Lucky O'Donlon didn't say anything aloud, but as he sat back in his seat, the expression on his face spoke volumes. His gaze traveled over her, taking in her unfeminine clothes, her lack of makeup. An understandable mistake for any man to make, he telegraphed with his eyes.

He finally looked over at Lucy. "The fact remains that I can't possibly work with a reporter following me around."

"Neither can I," she countered.

"I've worked for years as an investigative reporter," Syd told them both. "Hasn't it occurred to either one of you that I might actually be able to help?"

Chapter 3

This shouldn't be too hard.

Lucky was a people person—charming, charismatic, likeable. He knew that about himself. It was one of his strengths.

He could go damn near anywhere and be best friends with damn near anyone within a matter of hours.

And that was what he had to do right here, right now with Sydney Jameson. He had to become her best friend and thus win the power to manipulate her neatly to the sidelines. Come on, Syd, help out your old pal Lucky by staying out of the way.

His soon-to-be-old-pal Syd sat in stony silence beside him in his pickup truck, arms folded tightly across her chest, as he drove her back to her car which was parked in the police-station lot.

Step one. Get a friendly conversation going. Find some common ground. Family. Most people could relate to family.

"So my kid sister's getting married in a few weeks."

Lucky shot Syd a friendly smile as well, but he would've gotten a bigger change of expression from the Lincoln head at Mount Rushmore. "It's kind of hard to believe. You know, it feels like she just turned twelve. But she's twenty-two, and in most states that's old enough for her to do what she wants."

"In *every* state it's old enough," Syd said. What do you know? She was actually listening. At least partly.

"Yeah," Lucky said. "I know. That was a joke."

"Oh," she said and looked back out the window.

O-kay.

Lucky kept on talking, filling the cab of the truck with friendly noise. "I went into San Diego to see her, intending to tell her no way. I was planning at least to talk her into waiting a year, and you know what she tells me? I bet you can't guess in a million years."

"Oh, I bet I can't either," Syd said. Her words had a faintly hostile ring, but at least she was talking to him.

"She said, we can't wait a year." Lucky laughed. "And I'm thinking murder, right? I'm thinking where's my gun, I'm going to at the very least scare the hell out of this guy for getting my kid sister pregnant, and then Ellen tells me that if they wait a year, this guy Greg's sperm will expire."

He had Syd's full attention now.

"Apparently, Greg had leukemia as a teenager, years and years ago. And before he started the treatment that would save him but pretty much sterilize him, he made a few deposits in a sperm bank. The technology's much better now and frozen sperm has a longer, um, shelf life, so to speak, but Ellen's chances of having a baby with the sperm that Greg banked back when he was fifteen is already dropping."

Lucy glanced at Syd, and she looked away. Come on, he silently implored her. Play nice. Be friends. I'm a nice guy.

"Ellen really loves this guy," he continued, "and you should see the way he looks at her. He's too old for her by about seventeen years, but it's so damn obvious that he loves her. So how could I do anything but wish them luck and happiness?''

Syd actually graced him with a glance. ''How are your parents taking this?''

Lucky shook his head, glad at the perfect opportunity to segue into poor-little-orphaned-me. This *always* won him sympathy points when talking to a woman. ''No parents. Just me and Ellen. Mom had a heart attack years ago. You know, you really don't hear much about it, but women are at just as much risk for heart disease as men and—'' He cut himself off. ''Sorry—I've kind of turned into a walking public service announcement about the topic. I mean, she was so young, and then she was so gone.''

''I'm sorry,'' Syd murmured.

''Thanks. It was roughest on Ellen, though,'' he continued. ''She was still just a kid. Her dad died when she was really young. We had different fathers and I'm not really sure what happened to mine. I think he might've become a Tibetan monk and taken a vow of silence to protest Jefferson Airplane's breakup.'' He flashed her a smile. ''Yeah, I know what you're thinking. With a name like Lucky, I should have rich parents living in Bel Air. I actually went to Bel Air a few years ago and tried to talk this old couple into adopting me, but no go.''

Syd actually smiled at that one. Bingo. He *knew* she was hiding a sense of humor in there somewhere.

''Now that you know far too much about me,'' he said, ''it's your turn. You're from New York, right?''

Her eyes narrowed suspiciously. ''How did you know that? I don't have an accent.''

''But you don't need an accent when you come from New York,'' Lucky said with a grin. ''The fact that you do everything in hyperspeed gives you away. Those of us from southern California can spot a New Yorker a mile away. It's a survival instinct. If we can't learn to ID you, we can't know to take cover or brace for impact when you make the scene.''

Sydney might've actually laughed at that. But he wasn't sure. Her smile had widened though, and he'd been dead right about it. It was a good one. It lit her up completely, and made her extremely attractive—at least in a small, dark, non-blond-beauty-queen sort of way.

And as Lucky smiled back into Sydney's eyes, the answer to all his problems became crystal clear.

Boyfriend.

It was highly likely that he could get further faster if he managed to become Sydney Jameson's boyfriend. Sex could be quite a powerful weapon. And he knew she was attracted to him, despite her attempts to hide it. He'd caught her checking him out more than once when she thought he wasn't paying attention.

This was definitely an option that was entirely appealing on more than one level. He didn't have to think twice.

"Do you have plans for tonight?" he asked, slipping smoothly out of best-friend mode and into low-scale, friendly seduction. The difference was subtle, but there *was* a difference. "Because I don't have any plans for tonight and I'm starving. What do you say we go grab some dinner? I know this great seafood place right on the water in San Felipe. You can tell me about growing up in New York over grilled swordfish.''

"Oh," she said, "I don't think—"

"Do you have other plans?"

"No," she said, "but—"

"This is perfect," he bulldozed cheerfully right over her. "If we're going to work together, we need to get to know each other better. *Much* better. I just need to stop at home and pick up my wallet. Can you believe I've been walking around all day without any cash?"

Hoo-yah, this was perfect. They were literally four

blocks from his house. And what better location to initiate a friendly, low-key seduction than home sweet home?

Syd had to hold on with both hands as Lucky quickly cut across two lanes of traffic to make a right turn into a side street.

"Don't you live on the base?" she asked.

"Nope. Officer's privilege. This won't take long, I promise. We're right in my neighborhood."

Now, *that* was a surprise. This neighborhood consisted of modestly sized, impeccably kept little houses with neat little yards. Syd hadn't given much thought to the lieutenant's living quarters, but if she had, she wouldn't have imagined this.

Sure enough, he pulled into the driveway of a cheery little yellow adobe house. A neatly covered motorcycle was parked at the back of an attached carport. Flowers grew in window boxes. The grass had been recently, pristinely mowed.

"Why don't you come in for a second?" Lucky asked. "I've got some lemonade in the fridge."

Of course he did. A house like this *had* to have lemonade in the refrigerator. Bemused and curious, Syd climbed down from the cab of his shiny red truck.

It was entirely possible that once inside she would be in the land of leather upholstery and art deco and waterbeds and all the things she associated with a glaringly obvious bachelor pad. And instead of lemonade, he'd find—surprise, surprise—a bottle of expensive wine in the back of the refrigerator.

Syd mentally rolled her eyes at herself. Yeah, right. As if this guy would even consider *her* a good candidate for seduction. That wasn't going to happen. Not in a million years. Who did she think she was, anyway? Barbie to his Ken? Not even close. She wouldn't even qualify for Skipper's weird cousin.

Lucky held the door for her, smiling. It was a self-confident smile, a warm smile…an *interested* smile?

No, she had to be imagining that.

But she didn't have time for a double take, because, again, his living room completely surprised her. The furniture was neat but definitely aging. Nothing matched, some of the upholstery was positively flowery. There was nothing even remotely art deco in the entire room. It was homey and warm and just plain comfortable.

And instead of Ansel Adams prints on the wall, there were family photographs. Lucky as a flaxen-haired child, holding a chubby toddler as dark as he was fair. Lucky with a laughing blonde who had to be his mother. Lucky as an already too-handsome thirteen-year-old, caught in the warm, wrestling embrace of a swarthy, dark-haired man.

"Hey, you know, I've got an open bottle of white wine," Lucky called from the kitchen, "if you'd like a glass of that instead of lemonade…?"

What? Syd wasn't aware she had spoken aloud until he repeated himself, dangling both the bottle in question and an extremely friendly smile from the kitchen doorway.

The interest in his smile was *not* her imagination. Nor was the warmth in his eyes.

God, Navy Ken was an outrageously handsome man. And when he looked at her like that, it was very, very hard to look away.

He must've seen the effect he had on her in her eyes. Or maybe it was the fact that she was drooling that gave her away. Because the heat in *his* eyes went up a notch.

"I've got a couple of steaks in the freezer," he said, his rich baritone wrapping as enticingly around her as the slightly pink late-afternoon light coming in through the front blinds. "I could light the grill out back and we could have dinner here. It would be nice not to have to fight the traffic and the crowds."

"Um," Syd said. She hadn't even agreed to go to dinner with him.

"Let's do it. I'll grab a couple of glasses, we can sit on the deck," he decided.

He vanished back into the kitchen, as if her declining his rather presumptuous invitation was an impossibility.

Syd shook her head in disbelief. This was too much. She had absolutely no doubt about it now. Lieutenant Lucky O'Donlon was hitting on her.

His motive was frightfully obvious. He was attempting to win her over. He was trying to make her an ally instead of an adversary in this task-force-coupling from hell. And, in typical alpha male fashion, he'd come to the conclusion that the best way to win her support involved full-naked-body contact. Or at least the promise of it.

Sheesh.

Syd followed him into the kitchen, intending to set him straight. "Look, Lieutenant—"

He handed her a delicate tulip-shaped glass of wine. "Please, call me Lucky." He lifted his own glass, touching it gently to hers, as he shot her a smile loaded with meaning. "And right now I *am* feeling particularly lucky."

Syd laughed. Oh, dear God. And instead of telling him flat out that she had to go and she had to go *now,* she kept her mouth shut. She *didn't* have any plans for tonight, and—God help her—she wanted to see just how far this clown was willing to go.

He continued to gaze at her as he took a sip of his wine.

His eyes were a shade of blue she'd never seen before. It was impossible to gaze back at him and not get just a little bit lost. But that was okay, she decided, as long as she realized that this was a game, as long as she was playing, too, and not merely being played.

He set his wineglass down on the counter. "I've got to change out of my Good Humor man costume. Excuse me for a minute, will you? Dress whites and grilling dinner aren't a good mix. Go on out to the deck—I'll be there in a flash.''

He was so confident. He walked out of the kitchen without looking back, assuming she'd obediently do as he commanded.

Syd took a sip of the wine as she leaned back against the counter. It was shockingly delicious. Didn't it figure?

She could hear Lucky sing a few bars of something that sounded suspiciously like an old Beach Boys tune. Didn't that figure also? We'll have fun, fun, fun indeed.

He stopped singing as he pushed the button on his answering machine. There were two calls from a breathy-voiced woman named Heather, a third from an equally vapid-sounding Vareena, a brief "call me at home," from an unidentified man, and then a cheerful female voice.

"Hi, Luke, it's Lucy McCoy. I just spoke to Alan Francisco, and he told me about Admiral Stonegate's little bomb. I honestly don't think this is going to be a problem for you—I've met the candidates he's targeted and they're good men. Anyway, the reason I'm calling is I've found out a few more details about this case that I think you should know, and it's occurred to me that it might be a good idea for the grown-ups—assuming Bobby's part of your team—to meet tonight. I'm on duty until late, so why don't we say eleven o'clock—twenty-three hundred hours—at Skippy's Harborside? Leave a message on my machine if this works for you. Later, dude.''

There was one more call—the pool cleaner wanted to reschedule her visit for later in the week—but then the answering machine gave a final-sounding beep. There was silence for a moment, and then Syd heard Lucky's lowered voice.

"Hey, Luce. S'me. Twenty-three hundred sounds peachy keen. I haven't talked to Frisco yet—did you actually use the word *candidates?* Why do I hate this already, before I even know what the hell's going on?'' He swore softly and laughed. "I guess I just have a good imagination. See you at Skip's."

He hung up the phone without making any noise, then whistled his way into the bathroom.

Syd quietly opened the screen door and tiptoed onto the deck. She stood there, leaning against the railing, looking down into the crystal blueness of his swimming pool and the brilliantly lush flower gardens as he made his grand entrance.

He had changed, indeed. The crisp uniform had been replaced by a pair of baggy cargo shorts and a Hawaiian shirt, worn open to reveal the hard planes of his muscular, tanned chest. Navy Ken had magically become Malibu Ken. He'd run his fingers through his hair, loosening the gel that had glued it down into some semblance of a conservative military style. It now tumbled over his forehead and into his eyes, waving tendrils of sun-bleached gold, some of it long enough to tickle his nose. His feet were bare and even his toes were beautiful. All he needed was a surfboard and twenty-four hours' worth of stubble on his chin, and he'd be ready for the Hunks of the Pacific calendar photo shoot.

And he knew it, too.

Syd took little sips of her wine as Lucky gave a running discourse on his decision four years ago to build this deck, the hummingbird feeders he'd put in the garden, and the fact that they'd had far too little rain this year.

As he lit the grill, he oh-so-casually pointed out that the fence around the backyard made his swimming pool completely private from the eyes of his neighbors, and how—wink, wink—that helped him maintain his all-over tan.

Syd was willing to bet it wouldn't take much to get him to drop his pants and show off the tan in question. Lord, this guy was too much.

And she had absolutely no intention of skinny dipping with him. Not now, not ever, thanks.

"Have you tried it recently?" he asked.

Syd blinked at him, trying to remember his last conversational bounce. Massage. He'd just mentioned some really terrific massage therapy he'd had a few months ago, after a particularly strenuous SEAL mission. She wasn't sure exactly what he'd just asked, but it didn't matter. He didn't wait for her to answer.

"Here, let me show you." He set his glass on the railing of the deck and turned her so that she was facing away from him.

It didn't occur to him that she might not want him to touch her. His grip was firm, his hands warm through the thin cotton of her shirt and jacket as he massaged her shoulders. He touched her firmly at first, then harder, applying pressure with his thumbs.

"Man, you're tense." His hands moved up her neck, to the back of her head, his fingers against her skin, in her hair.

Oh. My. God.

Whatever he was doing felt impossibly good. Fabulously good. *Sinfully* good. Syd closed her eyes.

"It's been a stressful few days, hasn't it?" he murmured, his mouth dangerously close to her ear. "I'm glad we've got this chance to, you know, start over. Get to know each other. I'm…looking forward to…being friends."

God, he was good. She almost believed him.

His hands kept working their magic, and Syd waited to see what he'd do or say next, hoping he'd take his time before he crossed the line of propriety, yet knowing that it wasn't going to be long.

He seemed to be waiting for some sort of response from her, so she made a vague noise of agreement that came out sounding far too much like a moan of intense pleasure as he touched a muscle in her shoulders that no doubt had been tightly, tensely flexed for the past fifteen years, at least.

"Oh, yeah," he breathed into her ear. "You know, I feel it, too. It's crazy, isn't it? We hardly know each other and yet…" In one smooth move he turned her to face him. "I'm telling you, Sydney, I've been dying to do this from the moment we first met."

It was amazing. It was like something out of a movie. Syd didn't have time to step back, to move away. His neon-blue gaze dropped to her mouth, flashed back to her eyes, and then, whammo.

He was kissing her.

Syd had read in her massive research on Navy SEALs that each member of a team had individual strengths and skills. Each member was a specialist in a variety of fields. And Lieutenant Lucky O'Donlon, aka Navy Ken, was clearly a specialist when it came to kissing.

She meant to pull away nanoseconds after his lips touched hers. She meant to step back and freeze him with a single, disbelieving, uncomprehending look.

Instead, she melted completely in his arms. The bones in her body completely turned to mush.

He tasted like the wine, sweet and strong. He smelled like sunblock and fresh ocean air. He felt so solid beneath her hands—all those muscles underneath the silk of his shirt, shoulders wider than she'd ever imagined. He was all power, all male.

And she lost her mind. There was no other explanation. Insanity temporarily took a tight hold. Because she kissed him back. Fiercely, yes. Possessively, absolutely. Ravenously, no doubt about it. She didn't just kiss him, she inhaled the man.

She slanted her head to give him better access to her mouth as he pulled her more tightly against him.

It was crazy. It was impossibly exciting—he was undeniably even more delicious than that excellent wine. His hands skimmed her back, cupping the curve of her rear end, pressing her against his arousal and—

And sanity returned with a crash. Syd pulled back, breathing hard, furious with him, even more furious with herself.

This man was willing to take her to bed, to be physically intimate with her—all simply to control her. Sex meant so little to him that he could cheerfully use himself as a means to an end.

And as for herself—her body had betrayed her, damn it. She'd been hiding it, denying it, but the awful truth was, this man was hot. She'd never been up close to a man as completely sexy and breathtakingly handsome as Lucky O'Donlon. He was physical perfection, pure dazzling masculine beauty. His looks were movie-star quality, his body a work of art, his eyes a completely new and unique shade of blue.

No, he wasn't just hot, he was white-hot. Unfortunately, he was also insensitive, narrow-minded, egocentric and conniving. Sydney didn't like him—a fact she conveniently seemed to have forgotten when he kissed her.

The hunger in his perfect eyes was nearly mesmerizing as he reached for her again.

"Thanks but no thanks," she managed to spit out as she sidestepped him. "And while I'm at it, I'll pass on dinner, too."

He was completely thrown. If she'd felt much like being amused, she could have had a good laugh at the expression on his face as he struggled to regroup. "But—"

"Look, Ken, I'm not an idiot. I know damn well what this is about. You figure you can keep me happy by throwing me a sexual bone—no pun intended. And yes, your kisses are quite masterful, but just the same—no thanks."

He tried to feign innocence and then indignation. "You think that…? Wait, no, I would never try to—"

"What?" she interrupted. "I'm supposed to believe that crap about 'isn't it crazy? This attraction—you feel it, too?'" She laughed in disbelief. "Sorry, I don't buy it, pal.

Guys like you hit on women like me for only two reasons.
It's either because you want something—''

"I'm telling you right now that you're wrong—''

"Or you're desperate.''

"Whoa.'' It was his turn to laugh. "You don't think very
highly of yourself, do you?''

"Look me in the eye,'' she said tightly, "and tell me
honestly that your last girlfriend wasn't blond, five-foot-
ten and built like a supermodel. Look me in the eye and
tell me you've always had a thing for flat-chested women
with big hips.'' Syd didn't let him answer. She went back
into the house, raising her voice so he could hear her. "I'll
catch a cab back to the police-station parking lot.''

She heard him turn off the grill, but then he followed
her. "Don't be ridiculous. I'll give you a ride to your car.''

Syd pushed her way out the front door. "Do you think
you can manage to do that without embarrassing us both
again?''

He locked it behind him. "I'm sorry if I embarrassed
you or offended you or—''

"You did both, Lieutenant. How about we just not say
anything else right now, all right?''

He stiffly opened the passenger-side door to his truck
and stood aside so that she could get in. He was dying to
speak, and Syd gave him about four seconds before he gave
in to the urge to keep the conversation going.

"I happen to find you very attractive,'' Luke said as he
climbed behind the wheel.

Two and a half seconds. She knew he'd give in. She
should have pointedly ignored him, but she, too, couldn't
keep herself from countering.

"Yeah,'' she said. "Right. Next you'll tell me it's my
delicate and ladylike disposition that turns you on.''

"You have no idea what's going on in my head.'' He
started his truck with a roar. "Maybe it is.''

Syd uttered a very non-ladylike word.

The lieutenant glanced at her several times, and cranked the air-conditioning up a notch as Syd sat and stewed. God, the next few weeks were going to be dreadful. Even if he didn't hit on her again, she was going to have to live with the memory of that kiss.

That amazing kiss.

Her knees still felt a little weak.

He pulled into the police-station parking lot a little too fast and the truck bounced. But he remembered which car was hers and pulled up behind it, his tires skidding slightly in the gravel as he came to a too-swift stop.

Syd turned and looked at him.

He stared straight ahead. It was probably the first time he'd ever been turned down, and he was embarrassed. She could see a faint tinge of pink on his cheeks.

She almost felt sorry for him. Almost.

After she didn't move for several seconds, he turned and looked at her. "This *is* your car, right?"

She nodded, traces of feeling sorry turning into hot anger. "Well?"

"Well, what?" He laughed ruefully. "Something tells me you're not waiting for a good-night kiss."

He wasn't going to tell her. He'd had no intention of telling her, the son of a bitch.

Syd glared at him.

"What?" he said again. "Jeez, what did I do now?"

"Eleven o'clock," she reminded him as sweetly as she could manage. "Skippy's Harborside?"

Guilt and something else flickered in his eyes. Disappointment that she'd found out, no doubt. Certainly not remorse for keeping the meeting a secret. He swore softly.

"Don't make me go over your head, Lieutenant," Syd warned him. "I'm part of your team, part of this task force."

He shook his head. "That doesn't mean you need to participate in every meeting."

"Yes, it does."

He laughed. "Lucy McCoy and I are friends. This meeting is just an excuse to—"

"Exchange information about the case," she finished for him. "I heard her phone message. I would have thought it was just a lovers' tryst myself, but she mentioned what's-his-name, Bobby, would be there."

"Lovers' tryst…?" He actually looked affronted. "If you're implying that there's something improper between Lucy and me—"

Syd rolled her eyes. "Oh, come on. It's a little obvious there's something going on. I wonder if she knows what you were trying to do with me. I suppose she couldn't complain because she's married to—"

"How dare you?"

"Your…what did you call it? XO? She's married to your XO."

"Lucy and I are *friends*." His face was a thundercloud—his self-righteous outrage wasn't an act. "She loves her husband. And Blue…he's…he's the best."

His anger had faded, replaced by something quiet, something distant. "I'd follow Blue McCoy into hell if he asked me to," Luke said softly. "I'd never dishonor him by fooling around with his wife. Never."

"I'm sorry," Syd told him. "I guess… You just… You told me you never take anything too seriously, so I thought—"

"Yeah, well, you were wrong." He stared out the front windshield, holding tightly to the steering wheel with both hands. "Imagine that."

Syd nodded. And then she dug through her purse, coming up with a small spiral notebook and a pen. She flipped to a blank page and wrote down the date.

Luke glanced at her, frowning slightly. "What…?"

"I'm so rarely wrong," she told him. "When I am, it's worth taking note of."

She carefully kept her face expressionless as he studied her for several long moments.

Then he laughed slightly, curling one corner of his mouth up into an almost-smile. "You're making a joke."

"No," she said. "I'm not." But she smiled and gave herself away. She climbed out of the truck. "See you tonight."

"No," he said.

"Yes." She closed the door and dug in her purse for her car keys.

He leaned across the cab to roll down the passenger-side window. "No," he said. "Really. Syd, I need to be able to talk to Lucy and Bob without—"

"Eleven o'clock," she said. "Skippy's. I'll be there."

As she got into her car and drove away, she glanced back and saw Luke's face through the windshield.

No, this meeting wasn't going to happen at Skippy's at eleven. But the time couldn't be changed—Lucy McCoy had said she was on duty until late.

But if she were Navy Ken, she'd call Lucy and Bobby what's-his-name and move the location—leaving Syd alone and fuming at Skipper's Harborside at eleven o'clock.

Bobby what's-his-name.

Syd pulled up to a red light and flipped through her notebook, looking for the man's full name. Chief Robert Taylor. *Yes.* Bobby Taylor. Described as an enormous SEAL, at least part Native American. She hadn't yet met the man, but maybe that was a good thing.

Yeah, this could definitely work.

Chapter 4

Lucky hadn't really expected to win, so he wasn't surprised when he followed Heather into La Cantina and saw Sydney already sitting at one of the little tables with Lucy McCoy.

He'd more than half expected the reporter to second-guess his decision to change the meeting's location and track them down, and she hadn't disappointed him. That was part of the reason he'd called Heather for dinner and then dragged her here, to this just-short-of-seedy San Felipe bar.

Syd had accused him of being desperate as she'd completely and brutally rejected his advances. The fact that she was right—that he had had a motive when he lowered his mouth to kiss her—only somehow served to make it all that much worse.

Even though he knew it was foolish, he wanted to make sure she knew just how completely non-desperate he was, and how little her rejection had mattered to him, by casually showing up with a drop-dead gorgeous, blond beauty queen on his arm.

He also wanted to make sure there was no doubt left lingering in her nosy reporter's brain that there was something going on between him and Blue McCoy's wife.

Just the thought of such a betrayal made him feel ill.

Of course, maybe it was Heather's constant, mindless prattle that was making the tuna steak he'd had for dinner do a queasy somersault in his stomach.

Still he got a brief moment of satisfaction as Syd turned and saw him. As she saw Heather.

For a fraction of a second, her eyes widened. He was glad he'd been watching her, because she quickly covered her surprise with that slightly bored, single-raised-eyebrow half-smirk she had down pat.

The smirk had stretched into a bonafide half smile of lofty amusement by the time Lucky and Heather reached their table.

Lucy's smile was far more genuine. "Right on time."

"You're early," he countered. He met Syd's gaze. "And you're here."

"I got off work thirty minutes early," Lucy told him. "I tried calling you, but I guess you'd already left."

Syd silently stirred the ice in her drink with a straw. She was wearing the same baggy pants she'd had on that afternoon, but she'd exchanged the man-size, long-sleeved, button-down shirt for a plain white T-shirt, her single concession to the relentless heat. She hadn't put on any makeup for the occasion, and her short dark hair looked as if she'd done little more than run her fingers through it.

She looked tired. And nineteen times more real and warm than perfect, plastic Heather.

As Lucky watched, Syd lifted her drink and took a sip through the straw. With lips like that, she didn't need makeup. They were moist and soft and warm and perfect. He knew that firsthand after kissing her.

That one kiss they'd shared had been far more real and meaningful than Lucky's entire six month off-and-on, whenever-he-was-in-town, non-relationship with Heather. And yet, after kissing him as if the world were coming to an end, Syd had pushed him away.

"Heather and I had dinner at Smokey Joe's," Lucky told them. "Heather Seeley, this is Lucy McCoy and Sydney Jameson."

But Heather was already looking away, her MTV-length attention span caught by the mirrors on the wall and her distant but gorgeous reflection...

Syd finally spoke. "Gee, I had no idea we could bring a date to a task-force meeting."

"Heather's got some phone calls to make," Lucky explained. "I figured this wasn't going to take too long, and after..." He shrugged.

After, he could return to his evening with Heather, bring her home, go for a swim in the moonlight, lose himself in her perfect body. "You don't mind giving us some privacy, right, babe?" He pulled Heather close and brushed her silicon-enhanced lips with his. Her perfect, *plastic* body...

Sydney sharply looked away from them, suddenly completely absorbed by the circles of moisture her glass had made on the table.

And Lucky felt stupid. As Heather headed for the bar, already dialing her cell phone, he sat down next to Lucy and across from Syd and felt like a complete jackass.

He'd brought Heather here tonight to show Syd...what? That he was a jackass? Mission accomplished.

Okay, yes, he *had* taken Syd into his arms on his deck earlier this evening in an effort to win her alliance. But somehow, some way, in the middle of that giddy, free-fall-inducing kiss, his strictly business motives had changed.

He thought it had probably happened when her mouth had opened so warmly and willingly beneath his. Or it might've been before that. It might've been the very instant his lips touched hers.

Whenever it had happened, all at once it had become very, *very* clear to him that he kept on kissing her purely because he wanted to.

Desperately.

Yes, there was that word again. As he ordered a beer from the bored cocktail waitress, as he pointed out Heather and told the waitress to get her whatever she wanted—on him—he tried desperately not to sound as if he were reeling from his own ego-induced stupidity in bringing Heather here. He knew Syd was listening. She was still pretending to be enthralled with the condensation on the table, but she *was* listening, so he referred to Heather as "that gorgeous blonde by the bar, with the body to die for."

Message sent: *I don't need you to want to kiss me ever again.*

Except he was lying. He needed. Maybe not quite desperately, but it was getting pretty damn close. Jeez, this entire situation was growing stupider and stupider with every breath he took.

Syd was so completely not Lucky's type. And he was forced to work with her to boot, although he was still working on ways to shake her permanently after tomorrow's session with the hypnotist.

She was opinionated, aggressive, impatient and far too intelligent—a know-it-all who made damn sure the rest of the world knew that she knew it all, too.

If she tried, even just a little bit, she'd be pretty. In a very less-endowed-than-most-women way.

Truth was, if life were a wet T-shirt contest and Heather and Syd were the contestants, Heather would win, hands down. Standing side by side, Syd would be rendered invisible, outshone by Heather's golden glory. Standing side by side, there should have been no contest.

Except, one of the two women made Lucky feel completely alive. And it wasn't Heather.

"Hey, Lucy. Lieutenant." U.S. Navy SEAL Chief Bobby Taylor smiled at Sydney as he slipped into the fourth seat at the table. "You must be Sydney. Were my directions okay?" he asked her.

Syd nodded. She looked up at Lucky almost challengingly. "I wasn't sure exactly where the bar was," she told him, "so I called Chief Taylor and asked for directions."

So that's how she found him. Well, wasn't she proud of herself? Lucky made a mental note to beat Bobby to death later.

"Call me Bob. Please." The enormous SEAL smiled at Syd again, and she smiled happily back at him, ignoring Lucky completely.

"No nickname?" she teased. "Like Hawk or Cyclops or Panther?"

And Lucky felt it. Jealousy. Stabbing and hot, like a lightning bolt to his already churning stomach. My God. Was it possible Sydney Jameson found Bob Taylor attractive? More attractive than she found Lucky?

Bobby laughed. "Just Bobby. Some guys during BUD/S tried to call me Tonto, which I objected to somewhat...forcefully." He flexed his fists meaningfully.

Bobby *was* a good-looking man despite the fact that his nose had been broken four or five too many times. He was darkly handsome, with high cheekbones, craggy features, and deep-brown eyes that broadcast his mother's Native American heritage. He had a quiet calmness to him, a Zen-like quality that *was* very attractive.

And then there was his size. Massive was the word for the man. Some women really went for that. Of course, if

Bobby wasn't careful to keep up his PT and his diet, he'd quickly run to fat.

"I considered Tonto politically incorrect," Bobby said mildly. "So I made sure the name didn't stick."

Bobby's fists were the size of canned hams. No doubt he'd been extremely persuasive in his objections.

"These days the Lieutenant here is fond of calling me Stimpy," Bob continued, "which is the name of a really stupid cartoon cat." He looked down at his hands and flexed his hot-dog-sized fingers again. "I've yet to object, but it's getting old."

"No," Lucky said. "It's because Wes—" he turned to Syd. "Bobby's swim buddy is this little wiry guy named Wes Skelly, and visually, well, Ren and Stimpy just seems to fit. It's that really nasty cartoon that—"

"Wes isn't little," Lucy interrupted. "He's as tall as Blue, you know."

"Yeah, but next to Gigantor here—"

"I *like* Gigantor," Bobby decided.

Syd was laughing, and Lucky knew from the way the chief was smiling at her that he was completely charmed, too. Maybe that was the way to win Syd's alliance. Maybe she could be Bobby's girlfriend.

The thought was not a pleasant one, and he dismissed it out of hand. Charming women was *his* strength, damn it, and he was going to charm Sydney Jameson if it was the last thing he did.

Lucy got down to business. "You talk to Frisco?" she asked him.

Lucky nodded grimly. "I did. Do you think it's possible Stonegate doesn't really want us to apprehend the rapist?"

"Why? What happened?" Syd demanded.

"Lieutenant Commander Francisco got called in to meet with Admiral Stonegate," Lucy explained. "Ron Stonegate's not exactly a big fan of the SEAL teams."

"What'd Stonehead do this time?" Bobby asked.

"Easy on the insults," Lucky murmured. He glanced at Syd, wishing she weren't a reporter, knowing that anything they said could conceivably end up in a news story. "We've been ordered by the…admiral to use this assignment as a special training operation," he said, choosing his words carefully, leaving out all the expletives and less-than-flattering adjectives he would have used had she not been there, "for a trio of SEAL candidates who are just about to finish up their second phase of BUD/S."

"King, Lee and Rosetti," Bobby said, nodding his approval.

Lucky nodded. Bobby had been working as an instructor with this particular group of candidates right from the start of phase one. He wasn't surprised the chief should know the men in question.

"Tell me about them," Lucky commanded. He'd made a quick stop at the base and had pulled the three candidates' files after he'd talked to Frisco and before he'd picked up Heather. But you could only tell so much about a man from words on a piece of paper. He wanted to hear Bobby's opinion.

"They were all part of the same boat team during phase one," Bobby told him. "Mike Lee's the oldest and a lieutenant, Junior Grade, and he was buddied up with Ensign Thomas King—a local kid, much younger. African American. Both have IQs that are off the chart, and both have enough smarts to recognize each other's strengths and weaknesses. It was a good match. Petty Officer Rio Rosetti, on the other hand, is barely twenty-one, barely graduated from high school, struggles to spell his own name, but he can build anything out of nothing. He's magic. He was out in a skiff and the propeller snagged a line and one of the blades snapped. He took it apart, built a new propeller out of the junk that was on board. They couldn't move fast, but they could move. It was impressive.

"Rosetti's swim buddy bailed during the second day of Hell Week," Bobby continued, "and Lee and King took him in. He returned the favor a few days later, when Lee started hallucinating. He was seeing evil spirits and not taking it well, and King and Rosetti took turns sitting on him. The three of them have been tight ever since. King and Lee spend nearly all their off time tutoring Rosetti. With their help, he's managed to stay with the classroom program." He paused. "They're good men, Lieutenant."

It was good to hear that.

Still. "Turning a mission this serious into a training op makes about as much sense as sticking the team with Lois Lane, here," Lucky said.

"Twelve hours, seventeen minutes," Syd said. "Hah."

He blinked at her, temporarily distracted. "Hah? What hah?"

"I knew when you found out that I was a reporter it was only a matter of time before you used the old Lois Lane cliché," she told him. Her attitude wasn't quite smug, but it was a touch too gleeful to be merely matter-of-fact. "I figured twenty-four, but you managed in nearly half the time. Congratulations, Lieutenant."

"Lois Lane," Bobby mused. "Shoot, it's almost as bad as Tonto."

"It's not very original," even Lucy agreed.

"Can we talk about this case please?" Lucky said desperately.

"Absolutely," Lucy said. "Here's *my* late-breaking news. Four more women have come forward since Sydney's article appeared in the paper this morning. *Four*." She shook her head in frustration. "I don't know why some women don't report sexual assault when it happens."

"Is it our guy?" Syd asked. "Same MO?"

"Three of the women were branded with the budweiser. Those three attacks took place within the past four weeks. The fourth was earlier. I'm certain the same perp was responsible for all four attacks," Lucy told them. "And frankly, it's a little alarming that the severity of the beatings he gives his victims seems to be increasing."

"Any pattern among the victims as to location, physical appearance, anything?" Lucky asked.

"If there is, we can't find anything other than that the victims are all females between the ages of eighteen and forty-three, and the attacks all took place in either San Felipe or Coronado," the detective replied. "I'll get you the complete files first thing in the morning. You might as well try searching for a pattern, too. I don't think you're going to find one, but it sure beats sitting around waiting for this guy to strike again."

Bobby's pager went off. He glanced at it as he shut it off, then stood. "If that's all for now, Lieutenant…"

Lucky gestured with his head toward the pager. "Anything I should know about?"

"Just Wes," the bigger man said. "It's been a rough tour for him. Coronado's the last place he wanted to be, and he's been here for nearly three months now." He nodded at Sydney. "Nice meeting you. See you later, Luce." He turned back. "Do me a favor and lock your windows tonight, ladies."

"And every night until we catch this guy," Lucky added as the chief headed for the door. He stood up. "I'm going to take off, too."

"See you tomorrow." Syd barely even looked at him as she turned to Lucy. "Are you in a hurry to get home, detective? Because I have some questions I was hoping you could answer."

Lucky lingered, but aside from a quick wave from Lucy, neither woman gave him a second glance.

"I did some research on sex crimes and serial rapists and serial *murderers*," Syd continued, "and—"

"And you're thinking about what I said about the level of violence escalating," Lucy finished for her. "You want to know if I think this guy's going to cross the line into rape-homicide."

Oh, God, Lucky hadn't even considered *that*. Rape alone was bad enough.

Lucy sighed. "Considering the abuse the perp seems to enjoy dishing out, in my opinion, it could be just a matter of time before he—"

"Heads up," Syd said in a low voice. "Barbie's coming this way."

Barbie?

Lucky looked up to see Heather heading toward them. Her body in motion made heads turn throughout the entire room.

She *was* gorgeous, but she was plastic. Kind of like a Barbie doll. Yeah, the name fit.

He wanted to stay, wanted to hear what Lucy and Syd had to say, but he'd saddled himself with Heather, and now he had to pay the price.

He had to take her home.

With Heather, there was always a fifty-fifty chance she'd invite him up to her place and tear off his clothes. Tonight she'd made a few suggestive comments at dinner that led him to believe it was, indeed, going to be one of those nights where they engaged in a little pleasure gymnastics.

"Ready to go home?" Heather smiled at him, a smile loaded with promise. A smile he knew that Syd had not missed.

Good. Let her know that he was going to get some tonight. Let her know he didn't need her to make fireworks.

"Absolutely." Lucky put his arm around her waist.

He glanced at Syd, but she was already back to her discussion with Lucy, and she didn't look up.

As Heather dragged him to the door, Lucky knew he was the envy of every man in the bar. He was going home with a beautiful woman who wanted to have wild sex with him.

He should have been running for his car. He should have been in a hurry to get her naked.

But as he reached the door, he couldn't stop himself from hesitating, from looking back at Syd.

She glanced up at that exact moment, and their eyes met and held. The connection was instantaneous. It was cracklingly powerful, burningly intense.

He didn't look away, and neither did she.

It was far more intimate than he'd ever been with Heather, and they'd spent days together naked.

Heather tugged at his arm, pressed her body against him, pulled his head down for a kiss.

Lucky responded instinctively, and when he looked back at Syd, she had turned away.

"Come on, baby," Heather murmured. "I'm in a hurry."

Lucky let her pull him out the door.

The pickup truck was following her.

Syd had first noticed the headlights in her rearview mirror as she'd pulled out of La Cantina's parking lot.

The truck had stayed several car lengths behind her as she'd headed west on Arizona Avenue. And when she'd made a left turn onto Draper, he'd turned, too.

She knew for sure when she did a series of right and left turns, taking the shortcut to her neighborhood. It couldn't be a coincidence. He was definitely following her.

Syd and Lucy had talked briefly after Navy Ken had taken his inflatable Barbie home. She'd stayed in the bar after Lucy had left as well, having a glass of beer as she wrote her latest women's safety article on her laptop. It was far easier to write in the noisy bar than it would have been in her too-quiet apartment. She missed the chaos of the newsroom. *And* being home alone would only have served to remind her that Lucky O'Donlon wasn't.

Miss Vapid USA was, no doubt, his soul mate. Syd wondered rather viciously if they spent all their time together gazing into mirrors. Blond and Blonder.

Lucy had volunteered the information that Heather was typical of the type of women the SEAL fraternized with. He went for beauty queens who were usually in their late teens, with an IQ not much higher than their age.

Syd didn't know why she was surprised. God forbid a man like Luke O'Donlon should ever become involved with a woman who actually *meant* something to him. A woman who talked back to him, offering a differing opinion and a challenging, vivacious honest-to-God relationship....

Who was she kidding? Did she really imagine she tasted integrity in his kisses?

It was true that he'd protested admirably when she'd accused him of trying to steal his XO's wife, but all that meant was that he had a line in his debauchery that he would not cross.

He was hot, he was smooth, he could kiss like a dream, but his passion was empty. For indeed, what was passion without emotion? A balloon that, when popped, revealed nothing but slightly foul-smelling air.

She was glad she'd seen Luke O'Donlon with his Barbie doll. It was healthy, it was realistic and just maybe it would keep her damned subconscious from dreaming erotic dreams about him tonight.

Syd took a right turn onto Pacific, pulling into the right lane and slowing down enough so that anyone in their right mind would pass her, but the truck stayed behind her.

Think. She had to think. Or rather, she had to stop thinking about Luke O'Donlon and his perfect butt and focus on the fact that a sociopathic serial rapist could well be following her through the nearly deserted streets of San Felipe.

She'd written an article dealing with this very subject just minutes ago.

If you think someone is following you, she'd said, do not go home. Drive directly to the police station. If you have a cell phone, use it to call for help.

Syd fumbled in her shoulder bag for her cell phone, hesitating only slightly before she pushed the speed-dial button she'd programmed with Lucky O'Donlon's home phone number. It would serve him right if she interrupted him.

His machine picked up after only two rings, and she skipped over his sexy-voiced message.

"O'Donlon, it's Syd. If you're there, pick up." Nothing. "Lieutenant, I know my voice is the last thing you probably want to hear right now, but I'm being followed." Oh, crud, her voice cracked slightly, and her fear and apprehension peeked through. She took a deep breath, hoping to sound calm and collected, but only managing to sound very small and pitiful. "Are you there?"

No response. The answering machine beeped, cutting her off.

Okay. Okay. As long as she kept moving, she'd be okay.

And chances were, if she pulled into the brightly lit police-station parking lot, whoever was following her would drive away.

But what a missed opportunity *that* would be. If this *were* the rapist behind her, they could catch him. Right now. Tonight.

She pressed one of the other speed-dial numbers she'd programmed into her phone. Detective Lucy McCoy's home number.

One ring. Two rings. Three…

"'Lo?'' Lucy sounded as if she'd already been asleep.

"Lucy, it's Syd.'' She gave a quick rundown of the situation, and Lucy snapped instantly awake.

"Stay on Pacific,'' Lucy ordered. "What's your license plate number?''

"God, I don't know. My car's a little black Civic. The truck's one of those full-size ones—I haven't been able to see what color—something dark. And he's hanging too far back for me to see his plate number.''

"Just keep driving,'' Lucy said. "Slow and steady. I'm calling in as many cars as possible to intercept.''

Slow and steady.

Syd used her cell phone and tried calling Lucky one more time.

Nothing.

Slow and steady.

She was heading north on Pacific. She could just follow the road all the way up to San Francisco, slowly and steadily. Provided the truck behind her let her stop for gas. She was running low. Of course a little car like this could go for miles on a sixteenth of a tank. She had no reason to be afraid. At any minute, the San Felipe police were going to come to the rescue.

Any minute. Any. Minute.

She heard it then—sirens in the distance, getting louder and deafeningly louder as the police cars moved closer.

Three of them came from behind. She watched in her rear-view mirror as they surrounded the truck, their lights flashing.

She slowed to a stop at the side of the road as the truck did the same, twisting to look back through her rear window as the police officers approached, their weapons drawn, bright searchlights aimed at the truck.

She could see the shadow of the man in the cab. He had both hands on his head in a position of surrender. The police pulled open the truck's door, pulled him out alongside the truck where he braced himself, assuming the position for a full-body search.

Syd turned off the ignition and got out, wanting to get closer now that she knew the man following her wasn't armed, wanting to hear what he was saying, wanting to get a good look at him—see if he was the same man who'd nearly knocked her down the stairs after attacking her neighbor.

The man was talking. She could see from the police officers standing around him that he was keeping up a steady stream of conversation. Explanation, no doubt, for why he was out driving around so late at night. Following someone? Officer, that was just an unfortunate coincidence. I was going to the supermarket to pick up some ice cream.

Yeah, right.

As Syd moved closer, one of the police officers approached her.

"Sydney Jameson?" he called.

"Yes," she said. "Thank you for responding so quickly to Detective McCoy's call. Does this guy have identification?"

"He does," the officer said. "He also says he knows you—and that you know him."

What? Sydney moved closer, but the man who'd been following her was still surrounded by the police and she couldn't see his face.

The police officer continued. "He also claims you're both part of a working police task force...?"

Sydney could see in the dim streetlights that the truck was red. *Red.*

As if on cue, the police officers parted, the man turned his face toward her and...

It was. Luke O'Donlon.

"Why the *hell* were you following me?" All of her emotions sparked into anger. "You scared me to death, damn it!"

He himself wasn't too happy about having been frisked by six unfriendly policemen. He was still standing in the undignified search position—legs spread, palms against the side of his truck, and he sounded just as indignant as she did. Maybe even more indignant. "I was following you home. You were supposed to go home, not halfway across the state. Jeez, I was just trying to make sure you were safe."

"What about Heather?" The words popped out before Sydney could stop herself.

But Luke didn't even seem to hear her question. He had turned back to the police officers. "Are you guys satisfied? I'm who I say I am, all right? Can I please stand up?"

The police officer who seemed to be in charge looked to Syd.

"No," she said, nodding yes. "I think you should make him stay like that for about two hours as punishment."

"Punishment?" Luke let out a stream of sailor's language as he straightened up. "For doing something *nice?* For worrying so much about you and Lucy going home from that bar alone that I dropped Heather off at her apartment and came straight back to make sure you'd be okay?"

He hadn't gone home with Miss Ventura County. He'd given up a night of steamy, mindless, emotionless sex because he had been worried about her.

Syd didn't know whether to laugh or hit him.

"Heather wasn't happy," he told her. "That's your answer for 'what about Heather?'" He smiled ruefully. "I don't think she's ever been turned down before."

He *had* heard her question.

She'd spent most of the past hour trying her hardest not to imagine his long, muscular legs entangled with

Heather's, his skin slick and his hair damp with perspiration as he...

She'd tried her hardest, but she'd always had a very good imagination.

It was stupid. She'd told herself that it didn't matter, that *he* didn't matter. She didn't even like him. But now here he was, standing in front of her, gazing at her with those impossibly blue eyes, with that twenty-four-carat sun-gilded hair curling in his face from the ocean's humidity.

"You scared me," she said again.

"You?" He laughed. "Something tells me you're un-scareable." He looked around them at the three police cars, lights still spinning, the officers talking on their radios. He shook his head with what looked an awful lot like admiration. "You actually had the presence of mind to call the police from your cell phone, huh? That was good, Jameson. I'm impressed."

Syd shrugged. "It wasn't that big a deal. But I guess you just don't spend that much time with smart women."

Lucky laughed. "Ouch. Poor Heather. She's not even here to defend herself. She's not that bad, you know. A little heartless and consumed by her career, but that's not so different from most people."

"How could you be willing to settle for 'not that bad?'" Syd countered. "You could have just about anyone you wanted. Why not choose someone with a heart?"

"That assumes," he said, "that I'd even *want* someone's heart."

"Ah," she said, turning back to her car. "My mistake."

"Syd."

She turned back to face him.

"I'm sorry I scared you."

"Don't let it happen again," she said. "Warn me in advance all right?" She turned away.

"Syd."

She sighed and turned to face him again. "Quickly, Ken," she begged. "We've got a seven o'clock meeting scheduled at the police station. I'm not a morning person, and I'm even less of a morning person when I get fewer than six hours of sleep."

"I'm going to follow you home," he told her. "When you go up to your apartment, flash your light a few times so I know everything's okay, all right?"

Syd didn't get it. "You don't even like me. Why the concern?"

Lucky smiled. "I never said I didn't like you. I just don't want you on my team. Those are two very different things."

Chapter 5

"Sit on the couch—or in the chair," Dr. Lana Quinn directed Sydney. "Wherever you think you'll be more comfortable."

"I appreciate your finding the time to do this on such short notice," Lucky said.

"You got lucky," Lana told him with a smile. "Wes called right after my regular one o'clock cancelled. I was a little surprised actually—it's been a while since I've heard from him."

Lucky didn't know the pretty young psychologist very well. She was married to a SEAL named Wizard with whom he'd never worked. But Wizard had been in the same BUD/S class with Bobby and Wes, and the three men had remained close. And when Lucky had stopped Wes in the hall to inquire jokingly if he knew a hypnotist, Wes had surprised him by saying, yes, as a matter of fact, he did.

"How is Wes?" Lana asked.

Lucky was no shrink himself, but the question was just a little too casual.

She must have realized the way her words had sounded and hastened to explain. "He was in such a rush when he called, I didn't even have time to ask. We used to talk on the phone all the time back when my husband was in Team Six, you know, when he was gone more often than not—I think it was because Wes and I both missed Quinn. And after he transferred back to California, back to Team Ten, Wes kind of dropped out of touch."

"Wes is doing good—just made chief," Lucky told her.

"That's great," Lana enthused—again just a little too enthusiastically. "Congratulate him for me, will you?"

Lucky was not an expert by any means, but he didn't have to be an expert to know there was more to that story than Lana was telling. Not that he believed for one minute that Wes would've had an affair with the wife of one of his best friends. No, Wes Skelly was a caveman in a lot of ways, but his code of honor was among the most solid Lucky had ever known.

It *did* make perfect sense, though, for Wes to have done something truly stupid, like fall in love with his good friend's wife. And if that had happened, Wes *would* have dropped out of Lana's life like a stone. And Lucky suspected she knew that, psychologist that she was.

God, life was complicated. And it was complicated enough without throwing marriage and its restrictions into the picture. He was never getting married, thank you very much.

It was a rare day that went by without Lucky reminding himself of that—in fact, it was his mantra. Never getting married. Never getting married.

Yet lately—particularly as he watched Frisco with his wife, Mia, and Blue with Lucy, and even the captain, Joe Cat, who'd been married to *his* wife, Veronica, longer than any of the other guys in Alpha Squad, Lucky had felt...

Envy.

God, he hated to admit it, but he *was* a little jealous.

When Frisco draped his arm around Mia's shoulder, or when she came up behind him and rubbed his shoulders after a long day. When Lucy stopped in at the crowded, busy Alpha Squad office and Blue would look across the room and smile, and she'd smile back. Or Joe Cat. Calling Veronica every chance he got, from a pay phone in downtown Paris, from the Australian outback after a training op. He'd lower his voice, but Lucky had overheard far more than once. *Hey babe, ya miss me? God, I miss you....*

Lucky had come embarrassingly close to getting a lump in his throat more than once.

Despite his rather desperate-sounding mantra, Joe and Blue and Frisco and all of the other married SEALs made the perils of commitment look too damn good.

As Lucky watched, across the room Sydney perched on the very edge of the couch, arms folded tightly across her chest as she looked around Lana's homey office. She didn't want to be here, didn't want to be hypnotized. Her body language couldn't be any more clear.

He settled into the chair across from her. "Thanks for agreeing to this."

He could see her trepidation in the tightness of her mouth as she shook her head. "I don't think it's going to work."

"Yeah, well, maybe it will."

"Don't be too disappointed if it doesn't."

She was afraid of failing. Lucky could understand that. Failure was something he feared as well.

"Why don't you take off your jacket," Lana suggested to Sydney. "Get loose—unbutton your shirt a little, roll up your sleeves. I want you to try to get as comfortable as possible. Kick off your boots, try to relax."

"I don't think this is going to work," Sydney said again, this time to Lana, as she slipped her arms out of her jacket.

"Don't worry about that," Lana told her, sitting down in the chair closest to Sydney. "Before we go any further, I want to tell you that my methods are somewhat unconventional. But I have had some degree of success working with victims of crimes, helping them clarify the order and details of certain traumatic or frightening events, so bear with me. And again, there's no guarantee that this *will* work, but we've got a better shot at it if you try to be open-minded.''

Syd nodded tightly. "I'm trying."

She was. Lucky had to give her that. She didn't want to be here, didn't *have* to be here, yet here she was.

"Let's start with you telling me what you felt when you encountered the man on the stairs," Lana said. "Did you see him coming, or were you startled by him?"

"I heard the clatter of his footsteps," Syd told her as she unfastened first one, then two, then three buttons on her shirt.

Lucky looked away, aware that he was watching her, aware that he didn't want her to stop at three, remembering with a sudden alarming clarity the way she had felt when he'd held her in his arms. She'd tasted so sweet and hot and...

Lucky was dressed in his summer uniform, and he resisted the urge to loosen his own collar. He was overheating far too often these days. He *should* have called Heather after following Syd home last night. He should have called and groveled. Chances are she would have let him in.

But he'd gone home instead. He'd swum about four hundred laps in his pool, trying to curb his restlessness, blaming it on the fact that Alpha Squad was out there, in the real world, while he'd been left behind.

"He was moving fast," Syd continued. "He clearly didn't see me, and I couldn't get out of his way."

"Were you frightened?" Lana asked.

Syd thought about that, chewing for a moment on her lower lip. "More like alarmed," she said. "He was big. But I wasn't afraid of him because I thought he was dangerous. It was more like the flash of fear you get when a car swerves into your lane and there's nowhere to go to avoid hitting it.''

"Picture the moment that you first heard him coming," Lana suggested, "and try to flip it into slow motion. You hear him, then you see him. What are you thinking? Right at that second when you first spot him coming down the stairs?"

Syd looked up from untying the laces of her boots. "Kevin Manse," she said.

She was still leaning over, and Lucky got a sudden brief look down the open front of her shirt. She was wearing a black bra, and he got a very clear look at black lace against smooth pale skin. As she moved to untie her other boot, Lucky tried to look away. Tried and failed. He found himself watching her, hoping for another enticing glimpse of her small but perfectly, delicately, deliciously shaped, lace-covered breasts.

Sydney Jameson was enormously attractive, he realized with a jolt as he examined her face. Sure he'd always preferred women with a long mane of hair, but hers was darkly sleek and especially lustrous, and the short cut suited the shape of her face. Her eyes were the color of black coffee, with lashes that didn't need any makeup to look thick and dark.

She wasn't traditionally pretty, but whenever she stopped scowling and smiled, she was breathtaking.

And as far as her clothes…

Lucky had never particularly liked the Annie Hall look before, but with a flash of awareness, he suddenly completely understood its appeal. Buried beneath Syd's baggy, mannish clothing was a body as elegantly, gracefully feminine as the soft curves of her face. And the glimpse he'd had was sexy as hell—sexy in a way he'd never imagined possible, considering that the women he usually found attractive were far more generously endowed.

She straightened up, kicking off her boots. She wasn't

wearing socks, and her feet were elegantly shaped with very high arches. God, what was wrong with him that the sight of a woman's bare foot was enough to push him over the edge into complete arousal?

Lucky shifted in his seat, crossing his legs, praying Lana wouldn't ask him to fetch anything from her desk all the way across the room.

"Who's Kevin Manse?" the psychologist asked Sydney.

Syd sat back, crossing her legs tailor-style, tucking her sexy feet beneath her on the couch. "He was a football player I, um…" she flashed a look in Lucky's direction and actually blushed "…knew in college. I guess the sheer size of this guy reminded me of Kevin."

Wasn't that interesting? And completely unexpected. Syd Jameson certainly didn't seem the type to have dated a football player in college. "Boyfriend?" Lucky asked.

"Um," Syd said. "Not exactly."

Ah. Maybe she'd liked the football player, and he hadn't even noticed her. Maybe, like Lucky, Kevin had been too busy trying to catch the eyes of the more bodacious cheerleaders.

Lana scribbled a comment on her notepad. "Okay," she said. "Let's give this a shot, shall we?"

Syd laughed nervously. "So how do you do this? All I can think of is Elmer Fudd trying to hypnotize Bugs Bunny with his pocket watch on a chain. You know, 'You ah getting vewwy sweepy.'"

Laughing, Lana crossed the room and turned off the light. "Actually, I use a mirror ball, a flashlight and voiced suggestions. Lieutenant, I have to recommend that you step out into the waiting room for a few minutes. I've found that SEALs are highly susceptible to this form of light-induced hypnotism. My theory is that it has to do with the way you've trained yourself to take combat naps." She sat down again across from Syd. "They fall, quickly, into deep REM sleep for short periods of time," she explained before looking back at Lucky. "There may be a form of self-hypnosis involved when you do that." She smiled wryly. "I'm not sure though. Quinn won't let me experiment on him. You can try staying in here, but..."

"I'll leave the room—temporarily," Lucky said.

"Good idea. I'm sure Dr. Quinn doesn't want both of us waddling around quacking like ducks," Syd said.

Hot damn, she'd made a joke. Lucky laughed, and Syd actually smiled back at him. But her smile was far too small and it faded far too quickly.

"Seriously," she added. "If I do something to really embarrass myself, don't rub it in, all right?"

"I won't," he told her. "As long as you promise to return the same favor some day."

"I guess that's fair."

"Step outside, Lieutenant."

"You'll wait to ask her any questions until I come back in?"

Lana Quinn nodded. "I will."

"Quack, quack," Syd said.

Lucky closed the door behind him.

As he paced, he punched a number into his cell phone. Frisco picked up the phone on his office desk after only half a ring.

"Francisco."

"Answering your own phone," Lucky said. "Very impressive."

"Understaffed," Frisco said shortly. "S'up?"

"I'm wondering if you've heard anything about yesterday's diving accident."

Frisco said some choice words, none of them polite. "God, what a stupid-fest. The SEAL candidate—*former* SEAL candidate—who nearly had nitrogen bubbles turn his brain into Swiss cheese, apparently snuck out of the barracks the night before the accident. It was his birthday, and some well-meaning but equally idiotic friends flew him to

Vegas to visit his girlfriend. The flight back was delayed, and he didn't land in San Diego until oh-three-hundred. The stupid bastard made it back into the barracks without being found out, but he was still completely skunked when the training op started at oh-four-thirty.''

Lucky cringed. It was dangerous to dive any less than twenty-four hours after flying. And if this guy was diving drunk, to boot…

"If he'd spoken up then, he would've been forced out of BUD/S, but this way they're throwing the book at him," Frisco continued. "He's facing a dishonorable discharge at the very least."

The fool was lucky he was alive, but indeed, that was where his luck ended. "How many of the candidates were covering for him?" Lucky asked. An incident like this could well eliminate half of an entire class.

"Only five of 'em," Frisco said. "All officers. All gone as of oh-six-hundred this morning."

Lucky shook his head. One guy couldn't handle having a birthday without getting some from his girlfriend, and six promising careers were flushed.

The door opened, and Lana Quinn poked her head out of her office. "We're ready for you, Lieutenant."

"Whoops," Lucky said to Frisco. "I've got to go. It's hypno-time. Later, man."

He hung up on his commanding officer and snapped his phone shut, slipping it into his pocket.

"Move slowly," Lana told him. "She's pretty securely under, but no quick motions or sudden noises, please."

The blinds were down in the office and, with the overhead lights off, Lucky had to blink for a moment to let his eyes adjust to the dimness.

He moved carefully into the room, standing off to the side, as Lana sat down near Syd.

She was stretched out on the couch, her eyes closed, as

if she were asleep. She looked deceptively peaceful and possibly even angelic. Lucky, however, knew better.

"Sydney, I want to go back, just a short amount of time, to the night you were coming home from the movies. Do you remember that night?"

As Lucky sat down, Syd was silent.

"Do you remember that night?" Lana persisted. "You were nearly knocked over by the man coming down the stairs."

"Kevin Manse," Syd said. Her eyes were still tightly shut, but her voice was strong and clear.

"That's right," Lana said. "He reminded you of Kevin Manse. Can you see him, Syd?"

Sydney nodded. "He nearly knocks me over on the stairs. He's angry. And drunk. I know he's drunk. I'm drunk, too. It's my first frat-house party."

"What the—"

Lana silenced Lucky with one swift motion. "How old are you, Sydney?"

"I'm eighteen," she told them, her husky voice breathless and young-sounding. "He apologizes—oh, God, he's *so* cute, and we start talking. He's an honors student as well as the star of the football team and I can't believe he's talking to *me.*"

"Now it's more than ten years later," Lana interrupted gently, "and the man on the stairs only *reminds* you of Kevin."

"I'm so dizzy," Syd continued, as if she hadn't heard Lana. "And the stairs are so crowded. Kevin tells me his room's upstairs. I can lie down for a while on his bed. And he kisses me and…" She sighed and smiled. "And I know he doesn't mean alone."

"Oh, God," Lucky said. He didn't want to hear this.

"Sydney," Lana said firmly. "I need you to come back to the present day now."

"I pretend not to be nervous when he locks the door

behind us," Syd continued. "His books are out on his desk. Calculus and physics. And he kisses me again and…"

She made a soft noise of pleasure, and Lucky rocketed out of his seat. "Why won't she listen to you?"

Lana shrugged. "Could be any number of reasons. She's clearly strong-willed. And this could well have been a pivotal moment in her life. Whatever her reasons, she doesn't want to leave it right now."

Syd moved slightly on the couch, her head back, her lips slightly parted as she made another of those intense little sounds. Dear God.

"Why don't we see if we can get to the end of this episode," Lana suggested. "Maybe she'll be more receptive to moving into the more recent past if we let her take her time."

"What," Lucky said, "we're just going to sit here while she relives having sex with this guy?"

"I've never done this before," Syd whispered. "Not really, and— *Oh!*"

Lucky couldn't look at her, couldn't not look at her. She was breathing hard, with a slight sheen of perspiration on her face. "Okay," he said, unable to stand this another second. "Okay, Syd. You do the deed with Mr. Wonderful. It's over. Let's move on."

"He's so sweet," Syd sighed. "He says he's afraid people will talk if I stay there all night, so he asks a friend to drive me back to my dorm. He says he'll call me, and he kisses me good night and I'm…I'm so amazed at how good that felt, at how much I love him— I can't wait to do it again."

Okay. So now he knew that not only was Sydney hot, she was hot-blooded as well.

"Sydney," Lana's voice left no room for argument. "Now it's just a little less than a week ago. You're on the stairs, in your apartment building. You're coming home from the movies—"

"God." Sydney laughed aloud. "Did that movie *suck*. I can't believe I spent all that money on it. The highlight was that pop singer who used to be a model who now thinks he's an actor. And I'm not talking about his acting. I'm talking about the scene that featured his bare butt. It alone was truly worthy of the big screen. And," she laughed again, a rich, sexy sound, "if you want to know the truth, these days the movies is the closest I seem to be able to get to a naked man."

Lucky knew one easy way to change that, fast. But he kept his mouth shut and let Lana do her shrink thing.

"You're climbing the stairs to your apartment," she told Syd. "It's late, and you're heading home and you hear a noise."

"Footsteps," Syd responded. "Someone's coming down the stairs. Kevin Manse—no, he just looks for half a second like Kevin Manse, but he's not."

"Can you mentally push a pause button," Lana asked, "and hold him in a freeze-frame?"

Syd nodded. "He's not Kevin Manse."

"Can you describe his face? Is he wearing a mask? Panty hose over his head?"

"No, but he's in shadow," Syd told them. "The light's behind him. He's got a short crew cut, I can see the hair on his head sticking straight up, lit the way he is. But his face is dark. I can't really see him, but I know he's not Kevin. He moves differently. He's more muscle-bound— you know, top-heavy from lifting weights. Kevin was just big all over."

Lucky could well imagine. God, this was stupid. He was jealous of this Kevin Manse guy.

"Let him move toward you," Lana suggested, "but in slow motion, if you can. Does the light ever hit his face?"

Syd was frowning now, her eyes still closed, concentrating intensely. "No," she finally said. "He swerves around me, hits me with his shoulder. *Sorry, bud.* He turns his face toward me and I can see that he's white. His hair looks golden, but maybe it's just brown, just the reflected light."

"Are you sure he's not wearing a mask?" Lana asked.

"No. He's still moving down the stairs, but he's turning his head to look at me, and I turn away."

"*You* turn away," Lana repeated. "Why?"

Syd laughed, but there was no humor in it. "I'm embarrassed," she admitted. "He thought I was a man. It's happened to me before, and it's worse when they realize they've made a mistake. I hate the apologies. *That's* when it's humiliating."

"So why do you dress that way?" Lucky had to ask.

Lana shot him an appalled "what are you doing?" look. He didn't give a damn. He wanted to know.

"It's safe," Syd told him.

"Safe."

"*Lieutenant,*" Lana said sternly.

"Back to the guy on the stairs," Lucky said. "What's *he* wearing?"

"Jeans," Syd said without hesitating. "And a plain dark sweatshirt."

"Tattoos?" Lucky asked.

"His sleeves are down."

"On his feet?"

She was silent for several long seconds. "I don't know."

"You turn away," Lana said. "But do you look back at him as he goes down the stairs?"

"No. I hear him, though. He slams the front door on his way out. I'm glad—it sometimes doesn't latch and then anyone can get in."

"Do you hear anything else?" Lucky asked. "Stop and listen carefully."

Syd was silent. "A car starts. And then pulls away. A fan belt must be loose or old or something because it squeals a little. I'm glad when it's gone. It's an annoying sound—it's not an expensive part, and it doesn't take much to learn how to—''

"When you're home, do you park in a garage," Lucky interrupted, "or on the street?"

"Street," she told him.

"When you pulled up," he asked, "after the movie, were there any cars near your apartment building that you didn't recognize?"

Syd chewed on her lip, frowning slightly. "I don't remember."

Lucky looked at Lana. "Can you take her back there?"

"I can try, but…"

"Gina's door is open," Syd said.

"Syd, let's try to backtrack a few minutes," Lana said. "Let's go back to your car, after you've left the movie theater. You're driving home."

"Why is her door open?" Syd asked, and Lana glanced at Lucky, shaking her head.

"Her boyfriend must've left it open," Syd continued. "Figures a guy can't replace a fan belt also can't manage to shut a door and…" She sat up suddenly, her eyes wide open. She was looking straight at Lucky, but through him, or in front of him, not at him. She didn't see him. Instead, she saw something else, something he couldn't see. "Oh, my *God!*"

Her hair was damp with perspiration, and she reached up with a shaking hand to push it away from her eyes.

Lana leaned forward. "Sydney, let's go back—"

"Oh, my God, *Gina!* She's in the corner of the living room, and her face is bleeding! Her eye's swollen shut and…oh, God, oh, God. She wasn't just beaten. Her clothes are torn and…" Her voice changed, calmer, more controlled. "Yes, I need the police to come here right away." She recited the address as if she were talking on the telephone. "We'll need an ambulance, too. And a policewoman, please. My neighbor's been…raped." Her voice broke, and she took a deep breath. "Gina, here's your robe. I think it would be okay if you put it around yourself. Let me help you, hon…"

"Sydney," Lana said gently. "I'm going to bring you back now. It's time to go."

"Go?" Syd's voice cracked. "I can't leave Gina. How could you even *think* that I could just leave Gina? God, it's bad enough I have to pretend everything's going to be okay. Look at her! *Look* at her!" She started to cry; deep, wracking sobs that shook her entire body, a fountain of emotion brimming over and spilling down her cheeks. "What kind of monster could have done this to this girl? Look in her eyes—all of her hopes, her dreams, her *life*, they're *gone!* And you know with that mother of hers, she's going to live the rest of her life hiding from the world, too afraid ever to come back out again. And why? Because she left the window in the kitchen unlocked. She wasn't careful, because nobody had *bothered* to warn any of us that this son of a bitch was out there! They knew, the police *knew*, but nobody said a single word!"

Lucky couldn't stop himself. He sat next to Sydney, and pulled her into his arms. "Oh, Syd, I'm sorry," he said.

But she pushed him away, curling into herself, turning into a small ball in the corner of the couch, completely inconsolable.

Lucky looked at Lana helplessly.

"Syd," she said loudly. "I'm going to clap my hands twice, and you're going to fall asleep. You'll wake up in one minute, feeling completely refreshed. You won't remember any of this."

Lana clapped her hands, and just like that, Syd's body relaxed. The room was suddenly very silent.

Lucky sat back, resting his head against the back of the couch. He drew in a deep breath and let it out with a whoosh. "I had no idea," he said. Syd was always so strong, so in control…. He remembered that message he'd found on his answering machine last night when he'd gotten home. The way she hadn't quite managed to hide the fear in her voice when she'd called him for help, thinking she was being followed by a stranger. *You scared me to death,* she'd told him, but he hadn't really believed it until he'd heard that phone message.

What else was she hiding?

"She clearly considers her stake in this to be personal," Lana said quietly. She stood up. "I think it would be better if you were in the waiting room when she wakes up."

Chapter 6

"Where are we going?" Syd asked, following Luke down toward the beach.

"I want to show you something," he said.

He'd been quiet ever since they'd left Lana Quinn's office—not just quiet, but subdued. Introspective. Brooding.

It made her nervous. What exactly had she said and done while under the hypnotist's spell to make the ever-smiling Navy Ken *brood?*

Syd had come out of the session feeling a little disoriented. At first she'd thought the hypnosis hadn't worked, but then she'd realized that about half an hour had passed from the time she'd first sat down. A half hour of which she remembered nothing.

To Syd's disappointment, Lana told her she *hadn't* got a clear look at the rapist's unmasked face as he'd come down the stairs. They weren't any closer to identifying the man.

Luke O'Donlon hadn't said a word to her. Not in Lana's office, not in his truck as they'd headed back here to the base. He'd parked by the beach and gotten out, saying only, "Come on."

They stood now at the edge of the sand, watching the activity. And there was a great deal of activity on this beach, although there was nary a beach ball, a bikini-clad girl, a picnic basket or a colorful umbrella in sight.

There were men on the beach, lots of men, dressed in long pants and combat boots despite the heat. One group ran down by the water at a pounding pace. The other group was split into smaller teams of six or seven, each of which wrestled a huge, heavy-looking, ungainly rubber raft toward the water, carrying it high above their heads while men with bullhorns shouted at them.

"This is part of BUD/S," Luke told her. "SEAL training. These men are SEAL candidates. If they make it through all the phases of this training, they'll go on to join one of the teams."

Syd nodded. "I've read about this," she said. "There's a drop-out rate of something incredible, like fifty percent, right?"

"Sometimes more." He pointed down the beach toward the group of men that were running through the surf. "Those guys are in phase two, which is mostly diving instruction, along with additional PT. That particular class started with a hundred men and today they're down to twenty-two. Most guys ring out in the first few days of phase one, which consists mostly of intense PT—that's physical training."

"I'd kind of figured that out."

"Navyspeak contains a lot of shorthand," he told her. "Let me know if you need anything explained."

Why was he being so nice? He could have managed to sound patronizing, but he just sounded…nice. "Thanks," Syd managed.

"Anyway, this class," he pointed again to the beach, "is down to only twenty-two because they had a string of bad luck—some kind of stomach flu hit during the start of Hell Week, and a record number of men were evac-ed out.'' He smiled, as if in fond memory. ''If it was just a matter of barf and keep going, most of 'em probably would've stayed in, but this flu came with a dangerously high fever. Medical wouldn't let them stay. Those guys were rolled back to the next class—most of them are going through the first weeks of phase one again right now. To top that off, this particular class also just lost six men in the fallout from that diving accident. So their number's low.''

Syd watched the men who were running through the water—the candidates Luke had said were in the second phase of BUD/S training. ''Somehow I was under the impression that the physical training ended after Hell Week.''

Luke laughed. ''Are you kidding? PT never ends. Being a SEAL is kind of like being a continuous work in progress. You always keep running—every day. You've got to be able to do consistent seven-and-a-half-minute miles tomorrow and next month—and next year. If you let it slip, your whole team suffers. See, a SEAL team can only move as fast as its slowest man when it's moving as a unit.''

He gestured toward the men still carrying the black rubber boats above their heads. ''That's what these guys are starting to learn. Teamwork. Identify an individual's strengths and weaknesses and use that information to keep your team operating at its highest potential.''

A red-haired girl on a bicycle rode into the parking lot. She skidded to a stop in the soft sand a few yards away from Luke and Syd, and sat down, watching the men on the beach.

''Yo, Tash!'' Luke called to her.

She barely even glanced up, barely waved, so intent was she on watching the men on the beach. It was the girl Syd had met yesterday, the one who'd been at the base with Lieutenant Commander Francisco's wife. She was looking for someone, searching the beach, shading her eyes with her hand.

"Frisco's not out here right now," Luke called to her.

"I know," she said and went right on looking.

Luke shrugged and turned back to Syd. "Check out this group here." He pointed at the men with the boats. "See this team with the short guy? He's not pulling his weight, right? He's not carrying much of the IBS—the inflatable boat—because he can hardly reach the damn thing. The taller men have to compensate for him. But you better believe that the vertically challenged dude will make up for it somewhere down the road. He's light, probably fast. Maybe he's good at climbing. Or he can fit into tight places—places the bigger men can't. Shorty may not help too much when it comes to carrying something like an IBS, but, guaranteed, he'll do more than his share in the long run."

He was quiet then, just watching the SEAL candidates. The group of runners—the candidates in the second phase of BUD/S training—collapsed on the sand.

"Five minutes," Syd heard distantly but distinctly through a bullhorn. "And then, ladies, we do it all over again."

The instructor with the bullhorn was Bobby Taylor, his long dark hair pulled back into a braid.

As Syd watched, one of the candidates approached Bobby, pointing up toward the edge of the beach, toward them. Bobby seemed to shrug, and the candidate took off, running toward them through the soft sand.

He was young and black, and the short, nearly shaved hairstyle that all the candidates sported served to emphasize the sharp angles of his face. He had a few scars, one disrupting the line of his right eyebrow, the other on his cheek, and they added to his aura of danger.

Syd thought he was coming to talk to Luke, but he headed straight for the little girl on the bike.

"Are you crazy?" His less-than-friendly greeting was accompanied by a scowl. "What did I tell you about riding your bike out here alone? And that was *before* this psycho-on-the-loose crap."

"No one wanted to ride all the way out here with me." Tasha lifted her chin. They were both speaking loudly enough for Syd to easily overhear. "Besides, I'm fast. If I see any weirdos, I can get away, no problem."

Sweat was literally pouring off the young man's face as he bent over to catch his breath, hands on his knees. "You're fast," he repeated skeptically. "Faster than a car?"

She was exasperated. "No."

"No." He glared at her. "Then it's *not* no problem, is it?"

"I don't see what the big deal—"

The black man exploded. "The *big deal* is that there's some son-of-a-bitch psycho running around town raping and beating the hell out of women. The *big* deal is that, as a female, you're a potential target. As a pretty, young female who's riding her bike alone, you're an attractive, easy target. You might as well wear a sign around your neck that says *victim.*"

"I read this guy breaks into women's homes," Tasha countered. "I don't see what that has to do with me riding my bike."

Syd couldn't keep her mouth shut any longer. "Actually," she said, "serial rapists tend to do something called *troll* for victims. That means they drive around and look for a likely target—someone who's alone and potentially defenseless—and they follow her home. It's possible once they pick a victim, they follow her for several days or even weeks, searching for the time and place she's the most vulnerable. Just because all of the other attacks we know about occurred in the victims' homes doesn't mean he's not going to pull his next victim into the woods."

"Thank you, voice of reason," the young man said. He gave Tasha a hard look. "Hear that, wild thing? Uncle Lucky's girlfriend here sounds like she knows what she's talking about."

Uncle Lucky's girlfriend...? "Oh," Syd said. "No. I'm not his—"

"So, what am I supposed to do?" The girl was exasperated and indignant. "Stay home all day?"

Tasha and her friend were back to their fight, intently squaring off, neither of them paying any attention to Syd's protests.

Luke, however, cleared his throat. Syd didn't dare look at him.

"Yes," the young man answered Tasha's question just as fiercely and without hesitation. "Until this is over, *yes. Stay home.*"

She gave him an incredulous look. "But, Thomas—"

"How many times in the years that we've been friends have I ever asked you for a favor, princess?" Thomas asked, his voice suddenly quiet, but no less intense. "I'm asking for one now."

Tears welled suddenly in Tasha's eyes and she blinked rapidly. "I needed to see you. After hearing about that diving accident..."

The harsh lines of his face softened slightly. "I'm fine, baby."

"I see that," she said. "*Now.*"

Syd turned away, aware that she was watching them, afraid that her curiosity about their relationship was written all over her face. Thomas had to be in his twenties, and Tasha was only in her teens. He'd referred to them as friends, but it didn't take a genius-level IQ to see that the girl's attachment to this man was much stronger. But he was being careful not to touch her, careful to use words like *friends,* careful to keep his distance.

"How about I call you?" he suggested, kindly. "Three

times a week, a few minutes before twenty-one hundred—
nine o'clock? Check in and let you know how I'm doing.
Would that work?''

Tasha chewed on her lower lip. ''Make it five times a
week, and you've got a deal.''

''I'll try for four,'' he countered. ''But—''

She shook her head. ''*Five*.''

He looked at her crossed arms, at the angle of her tough-
kid chin and assumed the same pose. ''*Four*. But I don't
get every evening off, you know, so some weeks it might
be only three. But if I get weekend liberty, I'll drop by,
okay? In return, you've got to promise me you don't go
anywhere alone until this bad guy is caught.''

She gave in, nodding her acceptance, gazing up at him
as if she were memorizing his face.

''Say it,'' he insisted.

''I promise.''

''I promise, too,'' he said then glanced at his watch.
''Damn, I gotta go.''

He turned, focusing on Luke and Syd as if for the first
time. ''Hey, Uncle Lucky. Drive Tasha home.''

It was, without a doubt, a direct order. Luke saluted.
''Yes, sir, *Ensign* King, sir.''

Thomas's harshly featured face relaxed into a smile that
made him look his age. ''Sorry, Lieutenant,'' he said. ''I
meant, *please* drive Tasha home, *sir*. It's not safe right now
for a young woman to ride all that distance alone.''

Luke nodded. ''Consider it done.''

''Thank you, sir.'' The young man pointed his finger at
Tasha. ''I don't want to see you here again. At least not
without Mia or Frisco.''

And he was gone, lifting his hand in a farewell as he ran
back to the rest of his class.

Luke cleared his throat. ''Tash, you mind hanging for a
minute? I've got—''

The girl had already moved down the beach, out of earshot. She sat in the sand, arms around her knees, watching the SEAL candidates. Watching Thomas.

"I've got to finish this really important discussion I was having with my *girlfriend,*" Luke finished, purely for Syd's benefit.

She narrowed her eyes at him. "Not funny."

"Damn," he said with a smile. "I was hoping I could get you to squawk again. 'I'm not his girlfriend,'" he imitated her badly.

"Also not funny."

His smile widened. "Yes, it is."

"No, it's—"

"Let's call it a healthy difference of opinions and let it go at that."

Syd closed her mouth and nodded. Fair enough.

He looked out over the glistening ocean, squinting slightly against the glare. "The reason I wanted you to see this, you know, BUD/S, was to give you a look at the teamwork that takes place in the SEAL units."

"I know you think I'm going to get in your way over the next few days or weeks," Syd started. "But—"

Luke cut her off. "I *know* you'll get in my way," he countered. "When was the last time you ran a seven-and-a-half minute mile?"

"Never, but—"

"The way I see it, we can make this work by utilizing your strengths and being completely honest about your weaknesses."

"But—" This time Syd cut her own self off. Did he say *make this work?*

"Here's what I think we should do," Luke said. He was completely serious. "I think we should put you to work doing what you do best. Investigative reporting. Research. I want you to be in charge of finding a pattern, finding *some*thing among the facts we know that will bring us closer to the rapist."

"But the police are already doing that."

"We need to do it, too." The breeze off the ocean stirred his already tousled hair. "There's got to be something they've missed, and I'm counting on you to find it. I know you will, because I know how badly you want to catch this guy." He gazed back at the ocean. "You, uh, kind of gave that away in Lana Quinn's office."

"Oh," Syd said. "God." What else had she said or done? She couldn't bring herself to ask.

"We're both on the same page, Syd," Luke said quietly, intensely. "I really want to catch this guy, too. And I'm willing to have you on my team, but only if you're willing to be a team player. That means you contribute by using your strengths—your brain and your ability to research. And you contribute equally by sitting back and letting the rest of us handle the physical stuff. You stay out of danger. We get a lead, you stay back at the base or in the equipment van. No arguments. You haven't trained for combat, you haven't done enough PT to keep up, and I won't have you endanger the rest of the team or yourself."

"I'm not *that* out of shape," she protested.

"You want to prove it?" he countered. "If you can run four miles in thirty minutes while wearing boots, and complete the BUD/S obstacle course in ten minutes—"

"Okay," she said. "Good point. Not in this lifetime. I'll stay in the van."

"Last but not least," he said, still earnestly, "I'm in command. If you're part of this team, you need to remember that I'm the CO. When I give an order you say 'yes, sir.'"

"Yes, sir."

He smiled. "So are we in agreement?"

"Yes, sir."

"You obviously need to learn the difference between a question and an order."

Syd shook her head. "No," she said, "I don't."

* * *

"Okay," Syd asked, "it's ten against one. Do you fight or flee?"

"Fight. Definitely fight." Petty Officer Rio Rosetti's Brooklyn accent came and went depending on who he was talking to, and right now it was one hundred percent there. When he was with Syd, he was one hundred percent tough guy.

Lucky stood outside his temporary office, eavesdropping as Lieutenant Michael Lee added his quiet opinion.

"Depends on who the ten are," Lee mused. "And what they're carrying. Ten of Japan's elite commandos—I might choose the old 'live to fight another day' rule and run."

"What I want to know," Ensign Thomas King's rich voice chimed in, "is what I'm doing in a ten-to-one situation without the rest of my SEAL team."

Syd fit right in. For the past two days, she and Lucky and Bobby had been working around the clock, trying to find something that the police might've missed. Syd worked with the information they had on the victims, and Bobby and Lucky went through file after file of personnel records, looking for anything that connected any of the officers and enlisted men currently stationed in Coronado to any hint of a sex crime.

Admiral Stonegate's handpicked trio of SEAL candidates spent their off hours helping. They were a solid group— good, reliable men, despite their connection to Admiral Stonehead.

And after only two days, Syd was best friends with all three of them. And Bobby, too.

She laughed, she smiled, she joked, she fumed at the computers. It was only with Lucky that she was strictly business. All "yes, sir," and "no, sir," and that too-polite, slightly forced smile, even when they were alone and still working at oh-one-hundred....

Lucky had managed to negotiate a truce with her. They

had a definite understanding, but he couldn't help but wish he could've gone with the girlfriend alliance scenario. Yes, it would've been messy further down the road, but it would have been much more fun.

Especially since he still hadn't been able to stop thinking about that kiss.

"Here's another 'what if' situation for you," Lucky heard Syd say. "You're a woman—"

"What?" Rio hooted. "I thought you wanted to know about being a SEAL?"

"This is related to this assignment," she explained. "Just hear me out. You're a woman, and you turn around to find a man wearing panty hose on his head in your apartment in the middle of the night."

"You tell him, 'no darling, that shade of taupe simply doesn't work with your clothing.'" Rio laughed at his joke.

"You want me to kill him or muzzle him?" Thomas King asked.

"Rosetti, I'm serious here," Syd said. "This has happened to eleven women. There's nothing funny about it. Maybe you don't understand because you're *not* a woman, but personally I find the thought terrifying. I saw this guy. He was big—about Thomas's size."

"Flee," Mike Lee said.

"But what if you can't?" Syd asked. "What if there's no place to run? If you're trapped in your own apartment by a known rapist? Do you fight? Or do you submit?"

Silence.

Submit. The word made Lucky squirm. He stepped into the room. "Fight," he said. "How could you do anything but fight?"

The three other men agreed, Rio pulling his boots down off the table and sitting up a little straighter.

Syd glanced up at him, her brown eyes subdued.

"But we're not women," Rio said with a burst of wisdom and insight. "We're not even men anymore."

"Hey, speak for yourself," Thomas said.

"I mean, we're *more* than men," Rio countered. "We're SEALs. Well, *almost* SEALs. And with the training I've had, I'm not really afraid of anyone—and I'm not exactly the biggest guy in the world. Most women haven't got either the training or the strength to kick ass in a fight with a guy who outweighs 'em by seventy pounds."

Lucky looked at Syd. She was wearing a plain T-shirt with her trademark baggy pants, sandals on her feet instead of her boots. Sometime between last night and this morning, she'd put red polish on her toenails.

"What would you do?" he asked her, taking a doughnut from the box that was open on the table. "Fight or…" He couldn't even say it.

She met his gaze steadily. "I've been going through the interviews with the victims, looking for a pattern of violence that correlates to their responses to his attack. A majority of the women fought back, but some of them didn't. One of them pretended to faint—went limp. Several others say they froze—they were so frightened they couldn't move. A few others, like Gina, just cowered."

"And?" Lucky said, dragging a chair up to the table.

"And I wish I could say that there's a direct relationship between the amount of violence the rapist inflicted on the victim and the amount that she fought back. In the first half-dozen or so attacks, it seemed as if the more the woman fought, the more viciously he beat her. And there were actually two cases where our perp walked away from women who didn't fight back. As if he didn't want to waste his time."

"So then it makes sense to advise women to submit," Lucky figured.

"Maybe at first, but I'm not so sure about that anymore. His pattern's changed over the past few weeks." Syd scowled down at the papers in front of her. "We have eleven victims, spanning a seven-week period. During those seven weeks, the level of violence our guy is using to dominate his victims has begun to intensify.''

Lucky nodded. He'd overheard Syd and Lucy discussing this several nights ago.

''Out of the six most recent victims, we've had four who fought back right from the start, one who pretended to faint, and Gina, the most recent, who cowered and didn't resist. Out of those six, Gina got the worst beating. Yet—go figure—the other woman who didn't resist was barely touched.''

''So if you fight this guy, you can guarantee you'll be hurt,'' Lucky concluded. ''But if you submit, you've got a fifty-fifty chance of his walking away from you.''

''And a chance of being beaten within an inch of your life,'' Syd said grimly. ''Keep in mind, too, that we're making projections and assumptions based on six instances. We'd really need a much higher number of cases to develop any kind of an accurate pattern.''

''Let's hope we don't get that opportunity,'' Mike Lee said quietly.

''Amen to that,'' Thomas King seconded.

''I still think, knowing that, I would recommend zero resistance,'' Lucky said. ''I mean, if you had a shot at this guy just walking away…''

''That's true.'' Syd chewed on her lower lip. ''But actually, there's more to this—something that puts a weird spin on the situation. It has to do with, um…'' She glanced almost apologetically at the other men. ''Ejaculation.''

Rio stood up. ''Whoops, look at the time. Gotta go.''

Syd made a face. ''I know this is kind of creepy,'' she said, ''but I think it's important you guys know all the details.''

''Sit,'' Lucky ordered.

Rio sat, but only on the edge of his seat.

''Actually, Lieutenant,'' Mike said evenly, ''we've got a required class in five minutes. If we leave now, we'll be on time." He looked at Syd. "I assume you'll be writing a memo about...this for the other members of the task force...?"

Syd nodded.

"There you go," Rio said with relief. "We'll read all about it in your memo."

All three men stood up, and Lucky felt a surge of panic. They were going to go, leaving him alone with Syd, who wanted to discuss... Yikes. Still, what was he supposed to say, "no, you can't go to class?"

"Go," he said, and they all nearly ran out the door.

Syd laughed. "Well," she said, "I sure know how to clear a room, don't I?" She raised an eyebrow. "Are you sure you don't want to follow them, Lieutenant? Read about this in my memo instead?"

Lucky stood up to pour himself a cup of coffee from the setup by the door. He had to search for a mug that was clean, and he was glad for the excuse to keep his back to her. "Nothing about this assignment has been pleasant. So if you think this is something I need to hear..."

"I do."

Lucky poured himself a cup of coffee, then, taking a deep breath, he turned to face her. He carried it back to the table and sat down across from her. "Okay," he said. "Shoot."

"According to the medical reports, our man didn't... shall we say, achieve sexual completion, unless the woman fought back," Syd told him.

Oh, God.

"We need to keep in mind," she continued, "the fact that rape isn't about sex. It's about violence and power. Domination. Truth is, many serial rapists never ejaculate at all. And in fact, out of these eleven cases of rape, we've got only four instances of sexual, um, completion. Like I said, all of them occurred when the victim fought back, or—and this is important—when the victim was *forced* to fight back.''

''But wait. You said a majority of the victims fought back.'' Lucky leaned forward. ''Couldn't he have been wearing a condom the other times?''

''Not according to the victims' statements.'' Syd stood up and started to pace. ''There's more, Luke, listen to this. Gina said in her interview that she didn't resist. She cowered, and he hit her, and she cowered some more. And then, she says he spent about ten minutes trashing her apartment. I went in there. The place looked like there'd been one hell of a fight. But she *didn't fight back*.

''I'm wondering if this guy was trying to simulate the kind of environment in which the victim *has* fought back, in an attempt to achieve some kind of sexual release. When he went back to Gina after he tore the place up, he kicked the hell out of her, but she still didn't do more than curl into a ball—and, if my theory's right, she therefore didn't give him what he wanted. So what does he do? He's angry as hell and he tears at her clothes, but she still doesn't resist. So he grabs her by the throat and starts squeezing. Bingo. Instant response. She can't breathe—she starts struggling for air. She starts fighting. And that does the trick for him, maybe that plus the sheer terror he can see in her eyes, because now, you know, she thinks he's going to kill her. He achieves sexual completion, inflicts his final moment of pain upon her by burning her, then leaves. The victim's still alive—this time.''

Oh, God.

''It's really just a matter of time before he squeezes someone's throat too hard, or for too long, and she dies,'' Syd continued grimly. ''And if taking a life gives him the right kind of rush—and it's hard to believe that it won't— he'll have transitioned. Serial rapist to serial killer. We already know he's into fear. He likes terrorizing his victims. He likes the power that gives him. And letting someone know she's going to die can generate an awful lot of terror for her and pleasure for him.''

Syd carried her half-empty mug to the sink and tossed the remnants of her coffee down the drain. ''Fight or submit,'' she said. ''Fighting gives him what he wants, but gets you a severe beating. Still, submitting pisses him off. And it could enrage him enough to kill.''

Lucky threw his half-eaten doughnut into the trash can, feeling completely sick. ''We've got to catch this guy.''

''That,'' Syd agreed, ''would be nice.''

Chapter 7

Luke O'Donlon was waiting when Syd pulled up.

"Is she alive?" she asked as she got out of her car.

The quiet residential area was lit up, the street filled with police cars and ambulances, even a fire truck. Every light was blazing in the upscale house.

Luke nodded. "Yes."

"Thank God. Have you been inside?"

He shook his head. "Not yet. I took a...walk around the neighborhood. If he's still here, he's well hidden. I've got the rest of the team going over the area more carefully."

It was remarkable, really. When Syd had received Luke's phone call telling her Lucy had just called, that there'd been another attack, she'd been fast asleep. She'd quickly pulled on clothes, splashed water on her face and hurried out to her car. She felt rumpled and mismatched, slightly off-balance and sick to her stomach from exhaustion and fear that this time the attacker had gone too far.

Luke, on the other hand, looked as if he'd been grimly alert for hours. He was wearing what he'd referred to before as his summer uniform—short-sleeved, light fabric—definitely part of the Navy Ken clothing action pack. His shoes were polished and his hair was neatly combed. He'd even managed to shave, probably while he was driving over. Or maybe he shaved every night before he went to bed on the off chance he'd need to show up somewhere and be presentable at a moment's notice.

"Is the victim...?"

"Badly beaten," he said tersely.

As if on cue, a team of paramedics carried a stretcher from the house, one of them holding an IV bag high. The victim was strapped down, her neck in a brace. She was carried right past them—the poor woman looked as if she'd been hit by a truck, both eyes swollen shut, her face savaged with bruises and cuts.

"God," Luke breathed.

It was one thing to read about the victims. Even the horror of photographs was one step removed from the violence. But seeing this poor woman, a mere hour after the attack...

Syd knew the sight of that battered face had brought the reality of this situation home to the SEAL in a way nothing else could have.

"Let's go inside," she said.

Luke was still watching the victim as she was gently loaded into the ambulance. He turned his head toward Syd almost jerkily.

Uh-oh. "You okay?" she asked quietly.

"God," he said again.

"It's awful, isn't it? That's pretty much what Gina looked like," she told him. "Like she'd gone ten rounds with a heavyweight champ on speed. And what he did to her face is the least of it."

He shook his head. "You know, I've seen guys who were injured. I've helped patch up guys who've been in combat. I'm not squeamish, really, but knowing that someone did that to her and got *pleasure* from it...." He took a deep breath and blew it out hard. "I'm feeling a little...sick."

He'd gone completely pale beneath his tan. Oh, boy, unless she did something fast, the big tough warrior was going to keel over in a dead faint.

"I am, too," Syd said. "Mind if we take a minute and sit down?" She took his arm and gently pulled him down next to her on the stairs that led to the front door, all but pushing his head down between his knees.

They sat there in silence for many long minutes after the ambulance pulled away. Syd carefully kept her eyes on the activity in the street—the neighbors who'd come out in their yards, the policemen keeping the more curious at a safe distance—looking anywhere but at Luke. She was aware of his breathing, aware that he'd dropped his head slightly in an attempt to fight his dizziness. She took many steadying breaths herself—but her own dizziness was more from her amazement that he could be affected this completely, this powerfully.

After what seemed like forever, she sensed more than saw Luke straighten up, heard him draw in one last deep breath and blow it out in a burst.

"Thanks," he said.

Syd finally risked a glance at him. Most of the color had returned to his face. He reached for her hand, loosely lacing her fingers with his as he gave her a rueful smile. "That would've been really embarrassing if I'd fainted."

"Oh," she said innocently, "were you feeling faint, too? I know I'm not taking enough time to eat right these days, and that plus the lack of sleep...."

He gently squeezed her hand. "And thanks, also, for not rubbing in the fact that right now *I'm* the one slowing *you* down."

"Well, now that you mention it...."

Luke laughed. God, he was good-looking when he

laughed. Syd felt her hands start to sweat. If she hadn't been light-headed before, she sure as hell was now.

"Let's go inside," Luke said. "Find out if this guy left a calling card this time."

Syd gently pulled her hand free as she stood up. "Wouldn't that be nice?"

"Mary Beth Hollis…" Detective Lucy McCoy told Syd over the phone "…is twenty-nine years old. She works in San Diego as an administrative assistant to a bank president."

Syd was sitting in the airless office at the naval base, entering the information about the latest victim into the computer. "Single?" she asked.

"Recently married."

Syd crossed her fingers. "Please tell me her husband works here at the base…" She had a theory about the victims, and she was hoping she was right.

But Lucy made the sound of the loser button. "Sorry," she said. "He works in legal services at the same bank."

"Her father?"

"Deceased. Her mother owns her own flower shop in Coronado."

Syd didn't give up. "Brothers?"

"She's an only child."

"How about her husband. Did he have any brothers or sisters in the Navy?"

Lucy knew where she was going. "I'm sorry, Syd, Mary Beth has no family ties to the base."

Syd swore. That made her theory a lot less viable.

"But…" Lucy said.

Syd sat up. "What? You've got something?"

"Don't get too excited. You know the official police and FInCOM position—"

"That the fact that eight out of twelve victims are connected to the base is mere coincidence?" Syd said a most indelicate word. "Where's the connection with Mary Beth?"

"It's a stretch," Lucy admitted.

"Tell me."

"Former boyfriend. And I mean former. As in nearly ancient history. Although Mary Beth just got married, she's been living with her lawyer for close to four years. Way before that, she was hot and heavy with a captain who still works as a doctor at the military hospital. Captain Steven Horowitz."

Syd sighed. Four years ago. That *was* a stretch.

"Still think there's a connection?" Lucy asked.

"Yes."

Lucky poked his head in the door. "Ready to go?"

Like Syd, he'd been working nonstop since last night's late-night phone call about the most recent attack. But unlike Syd, he still looked crisp and fresh, as if he'd spent the afternoon napping rather than sifting through the remaining personal files of the men on the naval base.

"I gotta run," Syd told Lucy. "I'm going back to the hypnotist, see if I noticed any strange cars parked in front of my house on the night Gina was attacked. Wish me luck."

"Good luck," Lucy said. "If you could remember the license-plate number, I'd be most appreciative."

"Yeah, what are the odds of that? I don't even know my own plate number. Later, Lucy." Syd hung up the phone, saved her computer file and stood, trying to stretch the kinks out of her back.

"Anything new turn up?" Lucky asked as they started down the hall.

"Four years ago, Mary Beth Hollis—victim twelve—used to date a Captain Horowitz."

"Used to *date*," he repeated. He gave her a sidelong glance. "You're working hard to keep your theory alive, eh?"

"Don't even think of teasing me about this," Syd countered. "Considering all the women who lived in San Felipe and Coronado, it *couldn't* be coincidence that nine out of twelve victims were related to *someone* who worked at the base. There's a connection between these women and the base, I'm sure of it. However, what that connection is..." She shook her head in frustration. "It's there—I just can't see it. Yet," she added. "I know I'm close. I have this feeling in my..." She broke off, realizing how ridiculous she sounded. She had a *feeling*....

"In your gut?" he finished for her.

"Okay." She was resigned. "Go ahead. Laugh at me. I know. It's just a crazy hunch."

"Why should I laugh at you," Luke said, "when I believe that you're probably on to something?" He snorted. "Hell, I'd trust your hunches over FInCOM's any day."

He wasn't laughing. He actually believed her.

As Syd followed Lieutenant Lucky O'Donlon out into the brilliant afternoon, she realized that over the past few days, something most unlikely had occurred.

She and Navy Ken had actually started to become friends.

Syd opened her eyes and found herself gazing up at an unfamiliar ceiling in a darkened room. She was lying on her back on a couch and...

She turned her head and saw Dr. Lana Quinn's gentle smile.

"How'd I do?" she asked.

Lana made a slight face and shook her head. "A 'dark, old-model sedan' was the best you could come up with. When I asked you what make or model, you said *ugly*. You didn't see the plates—not that anyone expected you to— but I have to confess I'd hoped."

"Yeah, me, too." Syd tiredly pulled herself up into a

sitting position. "I'm not a car person. I'm sorry—" She looked around. "Where's Luke?"

"Waiting room," Lana said as she pulled open the curtains, brightening up the room. "He fell asleep while he was out there—while I was putting you under. He looked so completely wiped out, I couldn't bring myself to wake him."

"It's been a tough couple of days," Syd told the doctor.

"I heard another woman was attacked last night."

"It's been frustrating," Syd admitted. "Particularly for Luke. We haven't had a whole lot of clues to go on. There's not much to do besides wait for this guy to screw up. I think if Luke had the manpower, he'd put every woman in both of these cities in protective custody. I keep expecting him to start driving around with a bullhorn warning women to leave town."

"Quinn's in DC this week," Lana said. "He's worried, too. He actually asked Wes Skelly to check up on me. I left for work earlier than usual this morning, and Wes was sitting in his truck in front of my house. It's crazy."

"Luke keeps trying to get me to stay overnight at the base," Syd told her, "and for the first time in his life, it's for platonic reasons."

Lana laughed as she opened the door to the waiting room. "I'm sorry to have to kick you out so soon, but I've got another patient."

"No problem. Dark, old-model sedan," Syd repeated. "Thanks again."

"Sorry I couldn't be of more help."

Syd went into the waiting room, where a painfully thin woman sat as far away as possible from Luke, who lay sprawled on the couch, still fast asleep.

He was adorable when he slept—completely, utterly, disgustingly adorable.

The skinny woman went into Lana's office, closing the door tightly behind her as Syd approached Luke.

"Time to go," she announced briskly.

No response.

"O'Donlon."

He didn't even twitch. His eyes remained shut, his lashes about a mile long, thick and dark against his perfect, tanned cheeks.

No way was she going to touch him. She'd read far too many books where professional soldiers nearly killed the hapless fool who tried to shake them awake.

She clapped her hands, and still he slept on. "Damn it, Luke, wake up."

Nothing. Not that she blamed him. She was exhausted, too.

All right. She wasn't going to touch him, but she *was* going to poke him from a safe distance. She took the copy of *Psychology Today* that was on the end table, rolled it up and, trying to stay as far back from him as possible, jabbed him in the ribs.

It happened so fast, she wasn't completely sure she even saw him move. One moment, his eyes were closed, the next he had her pinned to the waiting-room floor, one hand holding both of her wrists above her head, his other forearm heavy against her throat.

The eyes that gazed into hers were those of an animal—soulless and fierce. The face those eyes belonged to was hard and severe and completely deadly, his mouth a taut line, his teeth slightly bared.

But then he blinked and turned back into Luke O'Donlon, aka Lucky, aka her own living Navy Ken.

"Jeez." He lifted his arm from her throat so that she could breathe again. "What the hell were you trying to do?"

"Not this," Syd said, clearing her throat, her head starting to throb from where it had made hard contact with the floor. "In fact, I was trying to do the exact opposite of this. But I couldn't wake you up."

"Oh, man, I must've…" He shook his head, still groggy. "Usually I can take a combat nap and wake up at the least little noise."

"Not this time."

"Sometimes, if I'm really tired, and if I know I'm in a safe place, my body takes over and I go into a deep sleep and—" his eyes narrowed slightly. "You're supposed to be hypnotized," he remembered. "How come you're not hypnotized?"

As Syd stared up into the perfect blueness of his eyes, she wasn't sure she *wasn't* hypnotized. Why else would she just lie here on the floor with the full weight of his body pressing down on top of her without protesting even a little?

Maybe she'd gotten a concussion.

Maybe that was what had rendered her so completely stupid.

But maybe not. Her head hurt, but not that much. Maybe her stupidity was from more natural causes.

"Dark, old-model sedan," she told him. "Lana didn't want to wake you, and it's just as well. I'm an idiot when it comes to cars. That and calling it ugly was the best I could do."

Was he never going to get off her ever again? She could feel the muscular tautness of his thigh pressed between her legs. She could feel… Oh, God.

"Are you okay?" he asked, rolling away from her. "Last time you were hypnotized it was something of an emotional roller coaster. I'm sorry I fell asleep. I really wanted to be there, in case…" He laughed sheepishly, giving her what she thought of as his best Harrison Ford self-deprecating smile. It was as charming on Luke as it was on Harrison. "Well, this sounds really presumptuous, but I wanted to be there in case you needed me."

She would have found his words impossibly sweet—if she were the type to be swayed by sweet words. And she would've missed the warmth of his body if she were the type to long for strong arms to hold her. And if she were the type to wish he'd pull her close again and kiss her and kiss her and kiss her...

But she wasn't. She *wasn't.*

Having a man around was nice, but not a necessity.

Besides, she never took matters of the heart and all of their physical, sexual trappings lightly. Sex was a serious thing, and Luke, with his completely unplastic, extremely warm body, didn't do serious. He'd told her that himself.

"I *was* okay," she said, desperately trying to bring them back to a familiar place she could handle—that irreverent place of friendly insults and challenges, "until you hit me with a World Wrestling Federation-quality body slam, Earthquake McGoon."

"Ho," he said, almost as if he were relieved to be done with the dangerously sweet words and their accompanying illusion of intimacy himself, as if he were as eager to follow her back to the outlined safety of their completely platonic friendship. "You're a fine one to complain, genius, considering you woke me up by sticking a gun barrel into my ribs."

"A *gun* barrel!" She laughed her disbelief. "Get real!"

"What the hell was that, anyway?"

Syd picked up the magazine and tightly rolled it, showing him.

"It felt like a gun barrel." He pulled himself to his feet and held out his hand to help Syd up. "Next time you want to wake me, and calling my name won't do it," he said, "think Sleeping Beauty. A kiss'll do the trick every time."

Yeah, right. Like she'd ever try to kiss Luke O'Donlon awake. He'd probably grab her and throw her down and...

And kiss her until the room spun, until she surrendered her clothes, her pride, her identity, her very soul. And probably her heart, as well.

"Maybe we shouldn't leave," she said tartly, as she followed Luke out the door. "It seems to me that the safest place for a Navy SEAL who fantasizes that he's Sleeping Beauty is right here, in a psychologist's waiting room."

"Ha," Luke said, "ha."

"What's on the schedule for this afternoon?" Syd asked as Luke pulled his truck into the parking lot by the administration building.

"I'm going to start hanging out in bars," Luke told her. "The seedier the better."

She turned to look at him. "Well, *that's* productive. Drinking yourself into oblivion while the rest of us sweat away in the office?"

He turned off the engine but didn't move to get out of the truck. "You know as well as I do that I have no intention of partying."

"You think you'll single-handedly find this guy by going to bar after bar?" she asked. "You don't even know what he looks like."

He ran his hands through his hair in frustration. "Syd, I've got to do something before he hurts someone else."

"His pattern is four to seven days between attacks."

Luke snorted. "That's supposed to make me feel better?" He swore, hitting the steering wheel with the heel of his hand. "I feel like I'm sitting on a time bomb. What if this guy goes after Veronica Catalanotto next? She's home all alone, with only a toddler in her house. Melody Jones is out of town with her baby, thank God." He ticked them off on his fingers—the wives of his teammates in Alpha Squad. "Nell Hawken lives over in San Diego. She's safe—at least until this bastard decides to widen his target area. PJ Becker works for FInCOM. Both she and Lucy are best qualified to deal with this. They're both tough but, hell, no one's invincible. And there's you."

He turned to look at her again. "You live alone. Doesn't that scare you, even a little bit?"

Syd thought about last night. About that noise she thought she'd heard as she was brushing her teeth. She'd locked herself in the bathroom, and if she'd had the cell phone with her, she would have called Luke in a complete panic.

But she hadn't had her phone—in hindsight she could say thank God—and she'd sat, silently, fear coursing through her veins, for nearly thirty minutes, barely breathing as she waited, listening to hear that noise outside the bathroom door again.

Fight or submit.

She'd thought about little else for all thirty of those minutes.

And fight pretty much won.

There was nothing in the bathroom that could be used as a weapon except for the heavy ceramic lid to the back of the toilet. She'd brandished it high over her head as she'd finally emerged from the bathroom to find she was, indeed, alone in her apartment. But she'd turned on every lamp in the place, checked all the window locks twice, and slept—badly—with the lights blazing.

"Nah," she said now. "I'm just not the type that scares easily."

He smiled as if he knew she was lying. "What, did you get spooked and sleep with all the lights on last night?" he asked.

"Me?" She tried to sound affronted. "No way."

"That's funny," he said. "Because when I drove past your place at about 1:00 a.m. it sure looked as if you had about four million watts of electricity working."

She was taken aback. "You drove past my apartment…?"

He realized he'd given himself away. "Well, yeah…I was in the neighborhood.…"

"How many nights have you been spending your time

cruising the streets of San Felipe instead of sleeping?'' she asked.

He looked away, and she realized she'd collided with the truth. ''No wonder you nearly fainted last night,'' she said. No wonder he'd looked as if he hadn't been pulled from bed.

''I wasn't going to faint,'' he protested.

''You were *so* going to faint.''

''No way. I was just a little dizzy.''

She glared at him. ''How on earth do you expect to catch this guy if you don't take care of yourself—if you don't get a good night's sleep?''

''How on earth can I get a good night's sleep,'' he said through gritted teeth, ''*until* I catch this guy?''

He was serious. He was completely serious. ''My God,'' Syd said slowly. ''It's the real you.''

''The real me?'' he repeated, obviously not understanding. Or at least pretending that he didn't understand.

''The insensitive macho thing's just an act,'' she accused him. She was certain of that now. ''Mr. Aren't-I-Wonderful? in a gleaming uniform—a little bit dumb, but with too many other enticements to care. Most people can't see beyond that, can they?''

''Well,'' he said modestly, ''I don't have *that* much to offer....''

The truth was, he was a superhero for the new millenium. ''You're a great guy—a really intriguing mix of alpha male and sensitive beta. Why do you feel that you have to hide that?''

''I'm not sure,'' he said, ''but I think you're insulting me.''

''Cut the crap,'' she commanded. ''Because I also know you've got a beta's IQ, smart boy.''

''Smart boy,'' he mused. ''Much better than Ken, huh, Midge?''

Syd tried not to blush. How many times had she slipped

and actually addressed him as Ken? Too many, obviously. "What can I say? You had me fooled with the ultraplastic veneer."

"As long as we're doing the *Invasion of the Body-Snatchers* thing and pointing fingers at the non-pod people, I'd like to do the same to you." He extended his arm so that his index finger nearly touched her face, and let out an awful-sounding squawk.

Syd raised one eyebrow as she gazed silently at him.

"There," he said, triumphantly. "That look. That disdained dismay. You hide behind that all the time."

"Right," she said. "And what exactly is it that I'm bothering to hide from you?"

"I think you're hiding," he paused dramatically, "the fact that you cry at movies."

She gave him her best "you must be crazy" look. "I do not."

"Or maybe I should just say *you cry*. You pretend to be so tough. So…unmovable. Methodically going about trying to find a connection between the rape victims, as if it's all just a giant puzzle to be solved, another step in the road to success which starts with you writing an exclusive story about the capture of the San Felipe Rapist. As if the human part of the story—these poor, traumatized women—doesn't make you want to cry."

She couldn't meet his gaze. "Even if I were the type of person who cried, there's no time," she said as briskly as she possibly could. She didn't want him to know she'd cried buckets for Gina and all of the other victims in the safety and privacy of her shower.

"I think you're secretly a softy," he continued. "I think you can't resist giving to every charity that sends you a piece of junk mail. But I also think someone once told you that you'll be bulldozed over for being too nice, so you try to be tough, when in truth you're a pushover."

Syd rolled her eyes. "If you really need to think that about me, go right a—"

"So what are *you* doing this afternoon?"

Syd opened the door to the cab, ready to end this conversation. How had it gotten so out of hand? "Nothing. Working. Learning all there is to know about serial rapists. Trying to figure out what it is I'm missing that ties the victims together."

"Frisco told me you asked his permission to bring Gina Sokoloski onto the base."

Busted. Syd shrugged, trying to downplay it. "I need to talk to her, get more information. Find out if there's anyone connecting her to the Navy—anyone we might have missed."

"You could have done that over the phone."

Syd climbed out of the truck, slamming the door behind her. Luke followed. "Yeah, well, I thought it would be a good idea if Gina actually left her mother's house. It's nearly been two weeks, and she still won't open her bedroom curtains. I may not even be able to convince her to come with me."

"See?" he said. "You're nice. In fact, that's not just regular nice, that's *gooey* nice. It's prize-winning nice. It's—"

She turned toward him, ready to gag him if necessary. "All right! Enough! I'm nice. Thank you!"

"Sweet," he said. "You're sweet."

"Grrrr," said Syd.

But he just laughed, clearly unafraid.

Lucky stood on the beach, about a dozen yards behind the blanket Syd had spread on the sand. She'd brought wide-brimmed hats—one for Gina and one for herself, no doubt to shade the younger woman's still-battered face from the hot afternoon sun. Syd had bought sunglasses, too. Big ones that helped hide Gina's bruised eyes. Together they looked like a pair of exotic movie stars who'd filtered through some time portal direct from the 1950s.

Syd had brought a cooler with cans of soda, one of which she was sipping delicately through a straw. No doubt Syd had thought of the straws on account of Gina's recently split lips.

Gina clutched her soda tightly, her legs pulled in to her chest, her arms wrapped around them, her head down. It was as close to a fetal position as she could get. She was a picture of tension and fear.

But Syd was undaunted. She sprawled on her stomach, elbows propping up her chin, keeping up a nearly continuous stream of chatter.

Down on the beach, the phase-one SEAL candidates were doing a teamwork exercise with telephone poles. And, just for kicks, during a so-called break, Wes and Aztec and the other instructors had them do a set of sugar-cookie drills—running into the surf to get soaked, and then rolling over and over so that the white powdery sand stuck to every available inch of them, faces included. Faces in particular. Then it was back to the telephone poles.

Syd gestured toward the hard-working, sand-covered men with her cola can, and Lucky knew she was telling Gina about BUD/S. About Hell Week. About the willpower the men needed to get through the relentless discomfort and physical pain day after day after day after day, with only four blessed hours of sleep the whole week long.

Perseverance. If you had enough of that mysterious quality that made you persevere, you'd survive. You'd make it through.

You'd be wet, you'd be cold, you'd be shaking with fatigue, muscles cramping and aching, blisters not just on your feet, but in places you didn't ever imagine you could get blisters, and you'd break it all down into the tiniest segments possible. Life became not a day or an hour or even a minute.

It became a footstep. Right foot. Then left. Then right again.

It became a heartbeat, a lungful of air, a nanosecond of existence to be endured and triumphed over.

Lucky knew what Syd was telling Gina, because she'd asked him—and Bobby, and Rio, Thomas and Michael—countless questions about BUD/S, and about Hell Week in particular.

As he watched, whatever precisely Syd was saying caught Gina's attention. As he watched, the younger woman lifted her head and seemed to focus on the men on the beach. As he watched, Syd, with her gentle magic, helped Gina take the first shaky steps back to life.

Gina, like the SEAL candidates in BUD/S, needed to persevere. Yeah, being assaulted sucked. Life had given her a completely unfair, losing hand to play—a deal that was about as bad as it could get. But she needed to keep going, to move forward, to work through it one painful step at a time, instead of ringing out and quitting life.

And Syd, sweet, kind Syd, was trying to help her do just that.

Lucky leaned against Syd's ridiculous excuse for a car, knowing he should get back to work, but wanting nothing more than to spend a few more minutes here in the warm sun. Wishing he were on that blanket with Syd, wishing she had brought a soda for him, wishing he could lose himself in the fabulously textured richness of her eyes, wishing she would lean toward him and lift her mouth and...

Ooo-kay.

It was definitely time to go. Definitely time to...

Over on the blanket, Syd leapt to her feet. As Lucky watched, she danced in a circle around Gina, spinning and jumping. Miracle of miracles, Gina was actually laughing at her.

But then Syd turned and spotted him.

Yeesh. Caught spying.

But Syd seemed happy to see him. She ran a few steps toward him, but then ran back to Gina, leaning over to say something to the young woman.

And then she was flying toward him, holding on to that silly floppy hat with one hand, her sunglasses falling into the sand. Her feet were bare and she hopped awkwardly and painfully over the gravel at the edge of the parking area to get closer to him.

"Luke, I think I've found it!"

He immediately knew which *it* she was talking about. The elusive connection among the rape victims.

"I've got to take Gina back home," she said, talking a mile a minute. "I need you to get some information for me. The two other women who had no obvious ties to the base? I need you to find out if they have or *had* a close relationship with someone who was stationed here four years ago."

She was so revved up, he hated to be a wet blanket, but he didn't get it. She looked at the expression on his face and laughed. "You think I'm nuts."

"I think it's a possibility."

"I'm not. Remember Mary Beth Hollis?"

"Yeah." He was never going to forget Mary Beth Hollis. The sight of her being carried to the ambulance was one he'd carry with him to his dying day.

"Remember she dated Captain Horowitz four years ago, before she was married?"

He remembered hearing about the woman's romantic connection to the navy doctor, but he hadn't committed the details to memory.

"Gina just told me that her mother's second husband was a master chief in the regular Navy," Syd continued. "Stationed where? Stationed *here*. He was transferred to the east coast when he and Gina's mom were divorced—when? Four years ago. Four. Years. Ago."

Understanding dawned. ''You think all these women are connected in that they know someone who was stationed here—''

''Four years ago,'' she finished for him, her entire face glowing with excitement. ''Or maybe it's not exactly four years ago, maybe it's more or less than that. What we need to do is talk to the two victims who've got no obvious connection to the base, see if they *had* a connection, past tense. Call Lucy McCoy,'' she ordered him. ''What are you waiting for? Go. Hurry! I'll meet you in the office as soon as I drive Gina home.''

She started hopping back over the rocks, and Lucky couldn't resist. He scooped her up and carried her the few feet to the soft sand. Problem was, once he had her in his arms, he didn't want to put her down. Especially when she looked up at him with such surprised laughter in her eyes.

''Thank you,'' she said. ''Actually, my *feet* thank you.''

She squirmed, and he released her, and then it was *his* turn to be surprised when she threw her arms around his neck and gave him an exuberant hug.

''Oh, baby, this is it,'' she said. ''This is the connection! It's going to help us identify and protect the women this guy is targeting.''

Lucky closed his eyes as he held her tightly, breathing in the sweet scent of her sunblock.

She pulled free far too soon. ''Hurry,'' she said again, pushing him in the direction of the administration building.

Lucky went, breaking into an obedient trot, even though he was far from convinced they'd find anything new. He hoped with all of his heart that Syd wouldn't be too disappointed.

Of course, if she was, he could always comfort her. He was good at providing comfort—particularly the kind that slid neatly into seduction.

God, what was he thinking? This was *Syd*.

Syd—who'd kissed him as if the world were coming to

an end. Syd—whose body had felt so tempting beneath his just this morning. Syd—whose lit-up windows he'd stared at for nearly an hour last night, dying to ring her bell for more reasons than simply to make sure she was safe.

Okay. True confession time. Yes, it was Syd, and yes, he wanted to seduce her. But he liked her. A lot. Too much to trade in their solid friendship for his typical two-week, molten-lava, short-term fling.

He wasn't going to do it.

He was going to stay away from her, keep it platonic.

Yeah. Right.

Chapter 8

"Another former boyfriend and a father who's since died," Luke said to Syd as she hurried into the office.

She stopped short. "Oh, my God, I'm *right?*"

"You're amazingly, perfectly, *brilliantly* right." He grabbed her and danced her around the room.

It was a lot like this morning in Lana Quinn's waiting room. One minute she was standing there and the next she was in motion. She clung to him for dear life as he spun her around and around.

"Finally," he said, "something that we might be able to go on."

She looked up at him breathlessly. "Only *might?*"

"I'm trying to be restrained." He narrowly avoided a head-on collision with a file cabinet.

She had to laugh at that. "This is you, *restrained?*"

Luke laughed, too, as he finally slowed to a stop, as he once more let her feet touch the ground. "This is me, *extremely* restrained."

He was still holding her as tightly as she was holding

him, and suddenly, as he gazed into her eyes, he wasn't laughing anymore.

She was pressed against him from her shoulders to her thighs and the fit felt impossibly good. He was warm and solid and he smelled good, too.

He was looking down at her, her face tipped up to his, his mouth mere inches from hers, and for several long, heart-stopping moments, Syd was certain that he was going to kiss her.

Like the last time he'd kissed her, she saw it coming, but this go-round seemed so much more unrehearsed. The shift of emotions and the heightened awareness in his eyes couldn't possibly be an act, could it? Or the way his gaze dropped for just an instant to her lips, the way his own lips parted just a tiny bit, the tip of his tongue wetting them slightly in an unconscious move.

But then, instead of planting a big knee-weakening one on her, he released her. He let her go and even stepped back.

Whoa, what just happened here?

Luke grabbed her hand and pulled her over to the main computer. "Check *this* out. Show her the thing," he commanded the SEAL candidates.

Thomas was at the keyboard with Rio hovering over his shoulder, and they both moved slightly to the side so that Syd could see the screen. As if her eyes could focus on the screen.

She still felt completely disoriented. Luke hadn't kissed her. Of course, this was an office in a building on a U.S. naval base, she told herself, and he was the team's commanding officer. This was the U.S. Navy and there were probably rules about kissing.

Restrained, he'd said, indeed. Syd had to smile. Funny, she wouldn't have thought he'd have had it in him.

Thomas was talking to her, explaining what they'd done on the computer. "We pulled up the personnel files of all twelve of the servicemen and women—living and dead, active duty and retired—who're connected to the victims.''

''All twelve,'' Rio chimed in, ''were stationed here in Coronado during the same eight-week period in 1996.''

Eight weeks, four years ago. That *couldn't* be a coincidence, could it? Syd leaned closer to look at the numbers on the screen for herself.

''According to the information we've been given directly from the women who were attacked, the servicemen and woman also all knew their corresponding victim during that time,'' Thomas pointed out.

''We've pulled a complete list of personnel who were here during that eight-week period,'' Luke said handing her a thick tome that was stapled together with what looked like a railroad spike. ''Even if they were only here for a day during that time, their name's on this list. Mike's out delivering a copy to Lucy McCoy. She's going to run these names through the police computer, see if anyone left the service and ended up with a police record—particularly one that includes charges of sexual assault.''

''We already have ten good candidates,'' Bobby added. ''Ten of the men on that list were given dishonorable discharges either at that time or later in their careers.''

''Basically, that means they were kicked out of the Navy,'' Luke explained.

Syd was overwhelmed. ''I can't believe you did all this so quickly—that you actually managed to figure out the connection.''

''*You* figured out the connection,'' Luke told her. ''We just filled in the blanks.''

She looked down at the enormous list of names she still held in her hands. ''So now what do we do? Contact all these men and women and warn them that they or someone they love—or used to love—is in danger of being attacked?''

"Only a percentage of those men and women are still living in this area," Bobby said.

"A percentage of a billion is still a huge number," Syd countered.

"There's not a billion names on that list," Luke told her. She hefted the list. "It feels as if there is."

"Most of Alpha Squad's in there," Bobby told her. "The squad came to Coronado for a training op, I remember, and ended up pulling extra duty as BUD/S instructors. There was this one class, where the dropout rate was close to zero. I think three guys rang out, total. It was the most amazing thing, but as they went into Hell Week, we were completely understaffed."

"I remember that," Luke said. "Most of us had done a rotation assisting the instructors, so we ended up shanghaied into helping take these guys through their paces."

"Most of Alpha Squad," Syd echoed, realizing just what that meant. Anyone female and connected to anyone on this list was a potential target for attack. She looked at Luke. "Have you called—"

"Already done," he said, anticipating her question. "I've talked to all the guys' wives except Ronnie Catalanotto, and I left a pretty detailed message on her machine and told her to call me on my cell phone ASAP."

"You know, Lieutenant Lucky, sir," Rio said, "one way to catch this guy might be to set Syd here up as bait, make it look like she's your girlfriend and—"

"Uh-uh," Luke said. "No way."

Well, wasn't he vehemently opposed to *that*?

"I'm not talking about sending her out into the bad part of San Felipe in the middle of the night," Rio persisted. "In fact, she'll be safer than she is right now, considering we'll be watching her whenever she's alone."

"She lives on the third floor of a house in a neighborhood that's more concrete and asphalt than landscaping,"

Luke argued. "How are you going to watch her? Unless you're hiding someplace in her apartment—"

"We can plant microphones," Thomas suggested. "Set up a surveillance system, have a van down on the street."

"We can bring the skel's attention to you, too." Rio was really excited about this. Syd could tell he'd watched too many episodes of "NYPD Blue." Skel. Oh, brother. "You could go on TV, do an interview, insult him in some way. Claim that there's no way in hell he could be a SEAL. Obviously he's trying to make *some*body believe he's one—maybe he's trying to make himself believe it. Throw some reality into his face. Tick him off, then appear in public with Syd, do some kissy-face stuff and—"

"No. This is crazy."

Syd sat down at the conference table, trying to look unaffected and even slightly bored, as if she hadn't just realized that she'd completely misinterpreted that almost-kiss that she and Luke hadn't shared not quite five minutes ago. He'd spun her around, and she'd latched onto him. He hadn't looked at her as if he wanted to kiss her. No, she'd probably been looking at him that way. And he'd stopped laughing because he felt awkward. He wasn't being restrained because they were at his place of work. He simply wasn't interested.

How could she have thought he'd be even remotely interested in her?

Bobby cleared his throat. "You know, this *could* work."

"Yeah, but think of his reputation," Syd said dryly, "if he were seen in public with *me*."

Luke turned to look at her, the expression on his face unreadable. "You actually want to *do* this?" His voice cracked with disbelief. "Are you completely insane? Your job is research, remember? We had an agreement. You're supposed to be the one in the surveillance van, not the one used as bait. *Bait.* Dear Lord, save me from a conspiracy of fools!"

"Hey, what happened to brilliant?" Syd asked sharply.

He glared at her. "You tell me! You're the one who's lost your mind!"

"Maybe we could get Detective McCoy to pretend she's your girlfriend," Thomas volunteered.

"Oh, that would work," Syd rolled her eyes. "Clearly this guy pays attention to details. You don't think he'd notice that Luke sends out this 'come and get me and mine' message, and then starts getting chummy with the wife of one of his best friends? Oh, and she's a police detective, too. Anyone notice that not-too-fresh smell? Could that possibly be the stench of a *setup?*"

"Do you have *any* idea at all how much damage this dirtwad could do to you in the amount of time it would take the fastest SEAL team in the world to get from a van on the street to your third-floor apartment?" Luke asked hotly. "Do you know that this son of a bitch broke Mary Beth Hollis's cheekbone with his first punch? Do you really want to find out what that feels like? My God, Sydney! Think about *that,* will you *please?*"

"So maybe the setup should be at your house," she countered. "We can make like I move in with you, and set up a pattern where you come home extremely late—where there's a repeated block of time when I'm there alone. The team can hide in your backyard. Shoot, they can hide in your basement."

"No, they can't. I don't have a basement."

She nearly growled at him in exasperation. "Luke, think about this! If we can guarantee that the team will be close, then, yes, *yes,* I'm willing to do this to catch this guy. I really, *really* want to catch this guy. As far as I can see, the only real objection is that you and I will have to spend more time together, that we'll have to put on a show of a relationship in public. But, shoot, I can stomach that for the greater good of mankind, if *you* can."

Luke laughed in disbelief. If she didn't know better,

she'd think his feelings were hurt. "Well, gee, that's big of you."

Syd stood there, staring at him, both wanting him to give in, and praying that he'd refuse. God, how on earth was she going to play boyfriend-girlfriend with this impossible, incredible man for any length of time? How was she going to share a house with him? If she were a gambler, she'd bet big money that she'd end up in his bed within a day or two. No, make that an hour or two. It was a sure thing—except for one little important detail. He didn't want her in his bed.

"I think this could really work," Bobby said, his calm voice breaking the charged silence.

"I do, too," Mike said, speaking up for the first time. "I think we should do it."

Luke said something completely, foully unrepeatable—something having to do with barnyard animals, something that implied that he was out of his mind, then stomped out of the room.

Bobby smiled at Syd's confused expression. "That was a green light," he interpreted. "A go-ahead. Why don't you use those media contacts you have and set up whatever kind of interview for the lieutenant that you can? TV's best, of course. Oh, and Syd—let's keep this to ourselves. The fewer people who know this relationship between you and Luke isn't real, the better."

Syd rolled her eyes. "Anyone who knows him will take one look at me and realize something's up."

"Anyone who knows him," Bobby said, "will take one look at you, and think he's finally found someone worthy of his time."

Lucky couldn't remember the last time he'd felt this nervous because of a woman.

He had to park his truck three houses down from the Catalanottos'. Veronica's "little" cookout had turned into a full-blown party, judging from all the cars and trucks parked on the street. Bobby's truck and Wes's bike were there. PJ Becker's lime-green Volkswagen bug. Frisco's Jeep. Lucy McCoy's unassuming little subcompact.

"We'll just stop in so I can talk Veronica into leaving town for a week or so," he told Syd as they walked down the driveway toward the little house. "We can use this party as a dress rehearsal for when we go into town later. If we can fool this group of people into thinking we're together, we can fool anyone."

Syd looked over at him, one perfect eyebrow slightly raised. "Do you really think we can fool them? We don't look like we're together."

She was right. In fact, they looked about as un-together as a man and woman could. "What do you think I...? Should I put my arm around your shoulders?"

Yeesh, he hadn't sounded this stupidly uncertain since that eighth-grade dance he'd been invited to as a sixth-grader.

"I don't know," she admitted. "Would you put your arm around my shoulders if we really were together?"

"I'd..." He put his arm around her waist, tucking her body perfectly alongside his. He didn't mean for it to happen, but his hand slipped up beneath the edge of her T-shirt and his fingers encountered satiny smooth skin.

Uh-oh.

He braced himself, waiting for her to hit him, or at least to pull away and assault him with a severe scolding. But she didn't. In fact, she slipped her arm around him, tucking her own hand neatly into the back pocket of his shorts, nearly sending him into outer space.

Lucky had to clear his throat before he could speak. "You think this is okay?" With his hand where it was against her bare skin, it was far more intimate and possessive than an arm thrown around her shoulders.

Syd cleared her throat, too. Hah, she wasn't as matter-of-fact as she was pretending to be.

"God, this is weird." She lifted her head to look up at him. "This *is* weird, isn't it?"

"Yes."

"Are you as nervous about this as I am?"

"Yes," Lucky said, glad to be able to admit it.

"If you have to kiss me," Syd told him, "try not to kiss me on the mouth, okay?"

Have to?

"Oh," he said, "well, sure. I mean, that's good. You tell me what you don't want me to do and I'll make sure I don't cross those boundaries—"

"No!" She sounded completely flustered. "It's not about boundaries. It's just…I had about a ton of garlic on my pizza for lunch yesterday, and I still have Dominic's Italian Café-breath. I just…I didn't want to gross you out."

Lucky laughed—it was such a lame excuse. "There's no way you could still have garlic-breath more than twenty-four hours later."

"You've obviously never had one of Dominic's deluxe garlic pizzas."

"Look, Syd." He stopped about ten feet from the Catalanottos' front steps, pulling her to face him. "It's okay. You don't need to make up reasons why I shouldn't kiss you."

"I'm not making up reasons," she insisted.

"So then, if I don't mind about the alleged garlic-breath, *you* don't mind if I kiss you?"

The early evening shadows played artfully across Syd's face as she laughed. "I can't believe we're having this conversation."

And standing there, looking down at her, with his arm still around her waist, Lucky wanted to kiss her about as badly as he'd ever wanted to kiss anyone.

And damn it, as long as they were playing this pretend

girlfriend game, he might as well take advantage of the fact that it would only *help* their cover if he *did* kiss her.

But how the hell did one go about kissing a friend? He knew all there was to know about how to kiss a stranger, but this was different. This was far more dangerous.

And suddenly he knew exactly what to do, what to say.

"You've got me dying to find out if you really do taste like garlic," he said.

"Oh, believe me, I do."

"Do you mind…?" He tipped her chin up to his. "For the sake of scientific experimentation…?"

She laughed. That was when he knew he had her. That was when he knew he *could* kiss her without having her get all ticked off at him. She might pull away really fast, but she wasn't going to hit him.

So he lowered his head those extra inches and covered her mouth with his.

And, oh, my. Just like when he'd kissed her on that deck just off his kitchen, she turned to fire in his arms. Just like when he'd kissed her on his deck, she wrapped her arms around him and pulled him closer, kissing him just as hungrily as he kissed her.

It was the kind of kiss that screamed of pure sex, the kind that lit him up pretty damn instantly, the kind that made him want to tear her clothes from her body so he could take her, right here and right now—on his captain's front lawn.

It was the kind of kiss that made him instantly aware that it had been forty-nine long days, seventeen agonizing hours and twelve very impatient minutes since he'd last had sex. It was the kind of kiss that made him instantly forget whomever it was he'd last had sex with. Hell, it made him forget every other woman he'd ever known in his entire women-filled life.

It was the kind of kiss he might normally have ended only to spend the rest of the evening actively plotting ways he could get away with kissing this woman again. But— ha! He laughed as well as he could, considering he was still kissing her. They were playing the pretend girlfriend game. He *could kiss her whenever he wanted!*

Oh, my, she tasted hot and sweet and delicious. And yes, he thought just maybe he could taste the slightest, subtlest spicy hint of garlic, too.

Syd pulled back, and he let her come up for air, ready to protest that he thought he needed to kiss her again just to make sure he wasn't imagining the garlic, ready to give her a mile-long list of reasons why he should probably kiss her again, ready to…

He realized belatedly that the light had gone on next to the Catalanottos' front door. He turned his head, and sure enough. Veronica was standing there, laughing at him.

"You," she said. "Figures it would be you."

Lucky saw that they'd drawn a crowd. PJ Becker was behind Veronica. And Mia Francisco peeked through the front window, Frisco right behind her. Frisco gave him a smile and a thumbs-up.

Syd jettisoned herself from his arms, but he caught her hand and reeled her back in.

"It's okay," he murmured to her. "I knew someone would be bound to notice us. We're together, remember? You're my new girlfriend—I'm allowed to kiss you."

"Sorry," Veronica called through the screen in her crisp British accent. "Frankie came out onto the back deck, insisting that a man and a lady were making a baby in the front yard, and we just had to see for ourselves."

"Oh, my God," Syd said, her face turning bright pink.

"I obviously need to discuss the details of conception with him again," she said, laughter in her voice. "I'd thought we'd been over that 'kissing doesn't make a baby' stuff, but apparently it didn't stick. I suppose it's all right— he's only four."

"Do you want to come in?" PJ called out, "or should

we just all go away? Give you some privacy—close the door and turn off the light?''

Lucky laughed as he pulled Syd to the door.

The introductions took no time, and then Veronica was pulling Syd through the house to the back deck. ''You've got to see the view we've got of the ocean,'' she said, as if she'd known Syd for years, ''and I've got to check the chicken that's on the grill.''

''Bobby already checked the chicken,'' about four voices called out.

''Everyone here is convinced I can't cook,'' Veronica told Syd as she opened the slider. She made a face. ''Unfortunately they're right.''

''Hey, Syd,'' Bobby said serenely from his place at the grill.

He was wearing only a bathing suit, and with all his muscles gleaming, his long hair tied back in a braid, he looked as if he belonged on the cover of one of those historical romances. Syd did a major double take, and Lucky poked her in the side, leaning close to whisper, ''Don't stare—you're with me, remember?''

''You know Lucy McCoy,'' Veronica said to Syd. ''And Tasha Francisco, and Wes Skelly—''

''Actually, we've never met,'' Wes said. He didn't stand up from where he was sprawled in a lounge chair. ''See, I'm not allowed to help with this op,'' he told Veronica, his voice tinged with sarcasm and coated with perhaps just a little too much beer. ''I'm not a member of the team because I'm a potential suspect, right, Lieutenant?''

Lucky kept his voice cheerful. ''Come on, Skelly, you know I didn't have anything to do with picking my team. Admiral Stonehead did it for me.''

''Hi, everyone. Sorry, I'm late—I was held up at the office, and then it was such a nice evening I couldn't resist walking over.''

Lucky turned to see Lana Quinn climbing the stairs that led from the beach.

Bobby greeted her with a hug. "Where's Wizard, the mighty Quinn? I thought he was coming home today."

She made a face. "Team Six has been sidetracked. What else is new? He's going to be away at least another few weeks. I know, I know—I should feel lucky he even got a chance to call."

Wes lurched to his feet, knocking over the little plastic table next to him, spilling pretzels across the deck. He swore sharply. "I'm sorry," he said. "Ron, I'm sorry, I forgot I… I have to go…do something. I'm sorry."

He vanished into the house, nearly knocking Syd over on his way. Lucky turned to Bobby, making the motion of keys turning in the ignition, silently asking if Wes was okay to drive.

Bobby shook his head no, then pulled his hand out of his bathing-suit pocket, opening it briefly—just long enough so that Lucky could see he'd already claimed possession of his friend's keys. Bobby made a walking motion with his fingers. Wes would walk back to the base.

On the other side of the deck, Syd helped Lana Quinn clean up the spilled pretzels.

"So. Does the new GF know you're a jerk?"

Lucky turned to see PJ Becker grinning at him, but he knew her words were only half in jest. Which, of course, made them half-serious, as well. This woman *still* hadn't forgotten the way he'd hit on her back when they'd first met. She'd forgiven, sure, but she'd probably never forget. It was one of the things he liked best about her. She'd never, ever let him get away with anything.

"Yeah," he said. "She knows. She likes me anyway." It wasn't entirely a lie. Syd *did* like him. Just not in the way PJ meant.

Senior Chief Harvard Becker's wife gazed at Syd with her gorgeous, liquid-brown eyes—eyes that never missed

anything. "You know, O'Donlon, if you're smart enough
to have hooked up with someone like Syd Jameson, maybe
I seriously underestimated you. She's a good writer—she
had a weekly column in the local paper about a year ago,
you know. I tried never to miss it. There's a good brain—
a thinking brain—in that girl's head." She gave him another brilliant smile and a kiss on the cheek. "Who knows?
Maybe you're not such a jerk after all."

As Lucky laughed, PJ went to give her best evil eye to
the extremely pregnant Mia, who looked as if she were
thinking about helping pick up pretzels.

Lucky sidled up to Bobby. "What's up with Wes?"

Bobby shrugged. "It hasn't been his year."

"Is he gonna be okay?"

"The walk will do him good. I'll throw his Harley into
the back of my truck."

"Anything I can do to help?" Lucky asked.

"Nope."

"Let me know if that changes."

"Yep."

Lucky grabbed Veronica's arm as she went past carrying
a broom. "Got a sec?"

She looked down at the broom. "Well…"

He took it from her and tossed it gracefully to PJ, who
caught it with one hand. Show off.

"Yes, I suppose I do have a sec now," Veronica said
cheerfully. "What's up?"

"I need you to go to New York," he said.

"How's a 10:00 a.m. flight tomorrow sound?"

He kissed her, relief flooding through him. "Thank
you."

"Lucy was pretty persuasive. This monster you're trying
to catch sounds awful. However, I've noticed that neither
she nor PJ are planning to come with me."

"Lucy's SFPD and PJ's FInCOM."

"And you're convinced they can take care of themselves?'' She searched his eyes, her concern written plainly on her face.

He tried to make it a joke. ''Can you imagine the fallout if I even so much as *implied* PJ couldn't handle this on her own? And as for Lucy...'' he glanced across the deck to where the detective was leaning against the railing, talking to Lana Quinn and Syd ''...I'm going to strongly encourage her to bunk down at the police station until this is over.''

Veronica followed his gaze. ''You make sure Syd is careful, too.''

''Oh, yeah,'' Lucky said. ''Don't worry about that. She's, uh...she's moving in with me.''

It was the weirdest thing. It was all part of the pretend girlfriend game, designed to catch the rapist, but as he said the words aloud—words he'd never before uttered, not ever in his entire life—it felt remarkably real. He felt a little embarrassed, a little proud, a little terrified, and a whole hell of a lot of anticipation.

Syd *was* moving in with him. She was going to go home with him tonight. It was true that she was going to sleep in the guest bedroom, but for the first time in God knows how long he wouldn't have to worry about her safety. Maybe, just maybe, he'd get some sleep tonight.

On the other hand, maybe not, considering she was going to be in the next room, and considering he was *still* half-aroused from that incredible kiss.

Veronica's eyes widened, and then filled with tears. She threw her arms around his neck and hugged him. ''Oh, Luke, I'm so happy for you!'' She pulled back to gaze into his eyes. ''I was so certain you were just going to bounce from Heather to Heather for the rest of your life.'' She raised her voice. ''Everyone, Lucky's finally living up to his nickname! He just told me Syd's moving in with him!''

There was a scramble for cans of beer—soda for Frisco and Mia and Tash—as Veronica made a toast. Lucky didn't dare look at Syd directly—he could feel her embarrassment from all the way across the room. And he could feel Frisco's eyes on him, too. His swim buddy and temporary CO was smiling, but there were questions in his eyes. Like, wow, didn't *this* happen incredibly fast? And, why didn't you mention this to me before now?

Tomorrow he'd sit down with Frisco and fill him in on the details—tell him the truth.

But right now...

He had to get Syd out of there before she died of embarrassment.

He put down the beer someone had thrust into his hand and rescued her from PJ, Mia, Lana and Veronica. "I hate to drop a bomb and run," he said.

"Speech!" someone said. It was Bobby, the bastard. He knew it was just a setup and he was probably having a good laugh behind that inscrutable calm.

"Speech," PJ echoed. "This is too good. No way are we going to let you get away without telling us at least *some* of the juicy details. Where'd you guys meet? How long have you been seeing each other?" She approached Lucky and gazed hard into his eyes from about four inches away. "Who are you really, and what have you done with our commitment-shy friend Lucky?"

"Very funny," Lucky said, tugging Syd past PJ and over to the door.

"Oh, come on," PJ said. "At least tell us how she managed to talk you into sharing a house. I mean, that's a major step. A grown-up decision." She smiled at Syd. "I'm proud of you. Good job! Way to make him follow *your* rules."

"Actually, *I* was the one who talked her into moving in with me," Lucky lied. "I'm finally in love." He shrugged. "What can I say?"

"Who knows?" Syd asked as they got into his truck.

"That this is just an act? Only Bobby. And Lucy Mc-

Coy,'' Luke admitted. ''I had to tell Lucy, especially considering she's supposed to be informed of my team's every move. She called this afternoon, mad as hell about that TV interview. She was ready to wring my neck.'' He started the engine, switched on the headlights and pulled out into the street, turning around in a neighbor's driveway. ''Officially, she's pissed, but unofficially, she hopes this works. She knows we'll keep you as safe—safer—than the police would.''

He glanced at her in the dimness of the cab. ''I'm going to tell Frisco tomorrow, but I'm going to ask him not to tell Mia. I think Bobby's right. The fewer people who know, the better.''

Syd sat as far away from him as she possibly could on the bench seat, trying desperately not to think about the way he'd kissed her. About the way she'd kissed him. At the words he'd said so casually as they left the party: *I'm finally in love....*

Yeah, like that would ever happen. Syd had figured Luke O'Donlon out. He wasn't ever going to fall in love. At least not all the way. He thought he was safe as long as he kept himself surrounded by the beautiful, intelligent, exceptional and *already married* wives of his best friends. He could cruise through life, half in love with Lucy and Veronica and PJ and Mia, never having to worry about getting in too deep. He could have meaningless sexual relationships with self-absorbed, vacuous young women like Heather—again, without risking his heart.

But what if he was wrong? Not about Heather—Syd didn't think for one instant that Luke would ever lose his heart to her. But Lucy McCoy was an entirely different story. As was that outrageously beautiful African American woman she'd met just tonight—PJ Becker. It would be too tragic if Luke actually fell in love with a woman he couldn't have.

"So how long have you had a thing for PJ Becker?" she asked him.

He managed to pull off a completely astonished look. *"What?"*

"Don't play dumb," she told him. "And don't worry, I don't think everyone knows. It's just I've learned to read you pretty well, and you reacted differently to her than you did to Veronica or Lana."

He was embarrassed and rather vehement. "I don't have a thing for her."

"But you *did,*" she guessed.

He gave it to her, but grudgingly. "Well, yeah, like a million years ago, before she even hooked up with the senior chief."

"And let me guess, *a million years ago,* you did something really dumb, like, oh, say, you hit on her?"

He was silent, and she just waited. He finally glanced at her out of the corner of his eyes, and then couldn't keep his lips from curling up into a rueful smile. "Don't you hate being right *all* the time?"

"It's not that I'm right all the time," she countered, "it's that you're so predictable. Why don't you surprise everyone next time you meet an attractive woman—and *not* hit on her first thing?"

"What," Luke said, "you mean, if this moving-in-together thing doesn't work out and I don't end up married to you?"

She had to laugh. As if.

"Sorry about Veronica's announcement," he continued. "I honestly had no idea she was going to do that."

Syd shrugged. "It's okay. It was a little strange—all your friends looking at me sideways, wondering what type of alien mind control I was using to make you want to live with me."

"That's not what they were thinking," Luke scoffed.

Yes, it most certainly was. Syd kept her mouth closed.

"After seeing that kiss," he said with a laugh, "they think they *know* why I want to live with you."

That kiss.

For many, many pounding heartbeats, Syd had stood on the front walk of that cute little beach house with her arms wrapped around Luke O'Donlon, her lips locked on his. For many pounding heartbeats, she had dared to imagine that that kiss was real, that it had nothing to do with their game of pretend.

She'd thought she'd seen something warm, something special, deep in his eyes, right before he lowered his mouth to hers.

Okay, face it, she'd thought she'd seen his awareness of his genuine attraction, based on genuine liking and genuine respect.

She'd seen awareness, all right—awareness of the fact that they were being watched through the window. He'd known they were being watched. *That* was why he'd kissed her.

They drove in silence for several long minutes. And then he glanced at her again.

"Maybe you should scoot over here—sit closer to me. If this guy does start following us…"

Syd gave him a look. "Scoot?" she said, trying desperately to keep things light. If she moved next to him, and if he put his arm around her shoulders, she just might forget how to breathe. Unless she could somehow keep him laughing. "I'm sorry, but I never, ever *scoot* anywhere."

Luke laughed. Jackpot. "That's what I love most about you, Sydney, dear. You can pick a fight about *any*thing."

"Can not."

He laughed again and patted the seat next to him. "Come on. Move your skinny butt down here."

"Skinny?" she said, sidling a little bit closer, but nowhere near close enough to touch him. "Excuse me. Have you even *looked* at my butt? It's double wide."

"What, are you nuts?" He reached for her, pulling her so that she was sitting with her thigh pressed firmly against his, his arm draped across her shoulders. "You have a great butt. A classic butt."

"Thanks a million. You know, these days *classic* means old. Classic Coke, Classic Trek. *Old.*"

"It doesn't mean old, it means *incomparable*," he countered. "How old are you, anyway?"

"Old enough to know better than to sit this close to someone who's driving. Old enough to know I should have my seat belt on," she grumbled. "Older than you."

"No way."

"Yes way," she said, praying as he braked to a red light that he wouldn't look down at her. "I'm one year older than you."

If he looked down at her, his mouth—that incredible, amazing mouth—would be mere inches from hers. And if his mouth was mere inches from hers, she would be able to think of nothing but kissing him again.

She wanted to kiss him again.

He turned and looked down at her.

"Where are we going now?" she asked, not that she particularly cared. But she figured maybe if she used her mouth to talk, she wouldn't be tempted to use it for other things.

Like kissing Luke O'Donlon.

"There's a seafood shack down by the water here in San Felipe," he told her. "It's usually packed this time of night. I figured we'd go get some steamed clams. And maybe after that, we could do a little barhopping."

"I've never been barhopping," she admitted, mostly to fill the pause in the conversation. "I always thought it sounded so exotic."

"Actually, it can be pretty depressing," Luke told her as the light turned green and he focused on the road again, thank God. "I've been barhopping with the other single guys from Alpha Squad. Mostly Bobby and Wes. Although occasionally their buddy Quinn would come along. The Wizard. He's married—you know, to Lana—which never sat quite right with me, because our goal was to cruise the clubs, looking to pick up college girls. But I didn't really know him, didn't really know Lana—I figured it was none of my business."

"God," Syd said. "Did she know?"

Luke shook her head. "No. Quinn used to say that they had an arrangement. He wouldn't tell her and she wouldn't find out. Wes used to get so mad at him. One night he actually broke Quinn's nose."

"Wes is Bobby's swim buddy, right?" Syd thought about the SEAL she'd met for the first time tonight. He was bigger than she'd imagined from the way Luke had described him. Something about him had been disturbingly familiar. When he'd slammed into her on his way out of the party…

"Bob and Wes are the best example of a two-man team I've ever seen," Luke told her, the muscles in his thigh flexing as he braked to make a right turn into a crowded restaurant parking lot. "They're good operators separately, but together—it's like instead of getting two regular guys, you're getting two super men. They know each other so well, they play off of each other perfectly—they anticipate each other's every move. They're remarkably efficient."

"Bobby knows Wes really well, then, I guess," Syd said.

"Probably better than Wes knows himself."

"And Bobby's certain Wes couldn't be—" She cut herself off, realizing how awful her words sounded. Just because he was broad-shouldered and wore his hair exactly like the man they were looking for….

Luke parked his truck, then pushed her slightly away from him, turning to face her, to look penetratingly into her eyes. "What aren't you telling me?"

"It was weird," she admitted. "When he bumped into me… It was like déjà vu."

"Wes isn't our guy." Luke was adamant.

She couldn't help herself. "Are you sure? Are you *absolutely* positive?"

"Yes. I know him."

"There was *some*thing about him.…" And then she knew. "Luke, he smelled like the guy on the stairs."

"Smelled?"

"Yeah, like stale cigarettes. Wes is a smoker, right?"

"No. Last year Bobby made Wes quit. He *used* to be a smoker, but—"

"Sorry, he's smoking again. Maybe not in front of anybody, but he's definitely smoking, even if it's only on the sly. It was faint, but I could smell it. He smelled just like the man we're looking for."

Luke shook his head. "Wes isn't our guy," he said again. "No way. I can't—I *won't* accept that."

"What if you're wrong?" she asked. "What if you find out that all this time he's been right here, right under our noses?"

"I'm not wrong," Luke said tightly. "I know this man. You didn't see him at his best tonight, but I know him, all right?"

It wasn't all right, but Syd wisely kept her mouth shut.

Chapter 9

"So here's the scenario," Syd said as Luke opened the door, letting her into the quiet coolness of his house. "You're the only man inside an enemy stronghold when a battle, what do you call it, a firefight starts. Your team is being pushed back. You're outnumbered and outgunned. Do you fight or flee?"

He locked the door behind them, the sound of the dead-bolt clicking into place seeming to echo around them.

They were here.

Together.

Alone.

For the night.

Syd's lips were still warm from the last time he'd kissed her—at a bar called Shaky Stan's. He'd kissed her at the Mousehole, too, and at Ginger's, and at the Shark's Run Grill as well. In fact, they'd kissed their way pretty much clear across San Felipe's waterfront district.

Syd had tried to keep the kisses short. She'd tried desperately to keep from melting in his arms. But far too often, she'd failed.

If they *were* truly moving in together, after that series of temperature-raising kisses, there was no way in hell either of them would still have their clothes on within five seconds of Luke's locking that door.

Aware of that fact, with her clothes firmly on, Syd kept talking, posing one of her military scenarios. She wasn't allowed to ask any of the SEALs specific questions about their operations, but she *could* pose hypotheticals. And she did, as often as possible.

"What's inside this hypothetical stronghold?" he asked, tossing his keys onto a small table near the front door. "Is this a rescue mission or an info-gathering op?"

"Rescue mission," she decided. "Hostages. There are hostages inside. Hostaged *children.*"

He gave her a comically disbelieving look as he moved to the thermostat and adjusted the setting so that the air conditioning switched on. That was good. It was too still in here, too warm. The AC would get the air moving, make it a little less stuffy. A little less...sultry.

"Make it impossibly difficult, why don't you?" he said.

He went into the kitchen, and she followed. "I'm just trying to provide a challenge."

"Okay, great." He opened the refrigerator and scowled at the cluttered shelves. "If we've been sent in to rescue hostaged children, you better believe we've been given a direct order not to fail." He reached in behind a gallon of milk and pulled out a container that looked as if it held iced tea. "Want some?"

Syd nodded, leaning against the door frame. "Thanks."

She watched as he took two tall glasses from a cabinet and filled them with ice.

"So," she said, mostly to fill the silence. "What do you do in that situation?"

He turned to look at her. "We don't fail."

She had to laugh. "You want to be a *little* more specific?"

"I'm inside, right?" he said, pouring the tea over the ice in the glasses. "Alone. But I've got radio contact with my men outside. I guess what I do is, I use stealth and I find the enemy's points of vulnerability from inside. And then I let my team know when and where to attack. Then I find and protect the hostages, and wait for the rest of my team to come get us all out." He handed her the glass. "Lemon? Sugar?"

"Black is fine," she said. "Thanks."

God, this was weird. This man leaning against the counter in his kitchen had spent a good portion of the evening exploring the inside of her mouth with his tongue. And now they were having a refreshing glass of iced tea and a casual, impersonal chat about military strategies.

She wondered if he knew how badly she was dying for him to kiss her again. For real, this time. Inwardly she rolled her eyes. Like that would ever happen.

It was amazing really. It had only been a matter of days since Luke had first kissed her, just a few feet away from where they were standing, on the deck outside this very kitchen. They'd stood there as virtual strangers, and he'd made the wrong choice. Instead of trying to win her friendship, he'd tried to control her through his powerful sexual appeal. Little did he know that would almost entirely ruin his chances at ever becoming her friend.

Almost, but not entirely.

And somewhere, somehow, over the past few days, Luke had redeemed himself.

So now they stood here as friends. And now Syd actually *wanted* him to kiss her.

Except now that they were friends, he had no reason to kiss her.

"So," she said, trying desperately to fill the silence. "Tell me...why did you join the SEALs?"

Luke didn't answer right away. He finished stirring lemon and a small mountain of sugar into his iced tea, rinsed the spoon in the sink and put it neatly into the dishwasher. Then he picked up his glass, and went back into the living room, gesturing with his head for Syd to follow.

So she followed him. Right over to a wall that was filled with framed photographs. She'd noticed them the last time she was here. Pictures of Luke as a child, his sun-bleached hair even lighter than it was now. Pictures of young Luke with his arms around a chubby, dark-haired little girl. Pictures of Luke with a painfully thin blond woman who had to be his mother. And pictures of young Luke with a dark-haired, dark complexioned man.

He pointed now to the pictures of the man.

"This," he said, "is Isidro Ramos. He's why I joined the SEALs."

Syd looked more closely at the photograph. She could see the warmth in the man's eyes, one arm looped around young Luke's shoulder. She could see the answering adoration on the boy's smiling face. "Who is he?" she asked.

"Was," he told her, sitting down on the couch, taking a sip from his iced tea and stretching his legs out on the coffee table.

Syd knew him well enough by now to know his casualness was entirely feigned. In truth he was on edge. But was it the topic of conversation he was having trouble with—or her presence here?

"Isidro died when I was sixteen," he said. "He was my father."

His…? Syd did a double take. No way could a man that dark have had a son as fair as Luke.

"Not my biological father," he added. "Obviously. But he *was* my father far more than Shaun O'Donlon ever bothered to be."

Syd sat down on the other end of the couch. "And he's why you joined the SEALs?"

He turned and looked at her. "You want the long or the short story?"

"Long," she said, kicking off her sandals and tucking her feet up underneath her. "Start at the beginning. I want to hear it all. Why don't you start when you were born. How much did you weigh?"

As long as they kept talking, they wouldn't have to deal with such awkward topics as where she should sleep. Or rather, where she should *pretend* to sleep. She couldn't imagine being able to sleep at all, God help her, knowing Luke was in bed in the next room.

"You're kidding, right?" She shook her head and he laughed.

"Nine pounds, fourteen ounces. My mother was five feet two. She used to tell me I was nearly as big as she was at the time." He paused for a moment, looking up at the photographs. "My mother was pretty fragile," he said quietly. "You can't really tell from these pictures, because she was so happy with Isidro. The day he died, though, she pretty much gave up. She pretended to keep going, to try to fight her bad health for Ellen's—my sister's—sake. But it was a losing battle. Don't get me wrong," he added. "I loved her. She just...she wasn't very strong. She'd never been strong."

Syd took a sip of her tea, waiting for him to continue.

"Nineteen sixty-six wasn't a good year for her," he said, "considering her choices were to marry Shaun O'Donlon or have a baby out of wedlock. She was living in San Francisco, but she didn't quite have the 'flowers in her hair' thing down—at least not in '66. So she married Shaun in the shotgun wedding of the year, and I got the dubious honor of being legitimate. And—" he turned slightly so that he was facing her on the couch. "Are you really sure you want to hear *all* of this?"

"I'm interested," she told him. "A lot can be revealed

about a person simply by listening to them talk about their childhood.''

"If that's the case, then where did *you* grow up?'' he asked.

"New Rochelle, New York. My father is a doctor, my mother was a nurse before she quit to have us. Four kids, I'm the youngest. My brothers and sister are all incredibly rich, incredibly successful, with perfect spouses, perfect wardrobes and perfect tans, cranking out perfect grandkids for my parents right on schedule.'' She smiled at him. "Note that I don't seem to be on the family track. I'm generally spoken of in hushed tones. The black sheep. Serves them right for giving me a boy's name.''

Luke laughed. She really liked making him laugh. The lines around his eyes crinkled in a way that was completely adorable. And his mouth…

She looked down into her tea to avoid staring at his mouth.

"Actually,'' she confessed, "my family is lovely. They're very nice—if somewhat clueless. And they're quite okay and very supportive about my deviation from the norm. My mother keeps trying to buy me Laura Ashley dresses, though. Every Christmas, without fail. 'Gee, thanks, Mom. In *pink?* Wow, you shouldn't have. No, you *really* shouldn't have,' but next year, the exact same thing.''

Syd risked another glance at Luke. He was still laughing.

"So come on, finish up your story. Your father was a jerk. I think I know how it probably goes—he left before you turned two—''

"I wish,'' Luke said. "But Shaun stayed until I was eight, sucking my mother dry, both emotionally and financially. But the year I turned eight, he inherited a small fortune from old Great-Uncle Barnaby, and he split for Tibet. My mother filed for divorce and actually won a substantial amount in the settlement. She bought a house in

San Diego, and with the mortgage paid, she started working full time for a refugee center. This was back when people were leaving Central America in droves. That's where she met Isidro—at the center.

"We had an extra apartment over our garage, back behind our house, and he was one of about six men who lived there, kind of as a temporary thing. I remember I was a little afraid of them. They were like ghosts, just kind of floating around, as if they were in shock. I realize now that they probably were. They'd managed to escape, but their families had all been killed—some right in front of their eyes. Isidro later told me he'd been out trading for gasoline on the black market, and when he came home, his entire town had been burned and everyone—men, women and children, even infants—had been massacred. He told me he was one of the lucky ones, that he actually was able to identify the bodies of his wife and children. So many people never knew, and they were left wondering forever if maybe their families were still back there, maybe their kids were still alive."

His eyes were distant, unfocused. But then the condensation from his glass of iced tea dripped onto his leg, and he looked down and then over at Syd and smiled. "You know, it's been a long time since I've talked about Isidro. Ellen used to like to hear about him, but I didn't tell her too much of this darker stuff. I mean, the guy essentially had an entire life back in Central America before he even met my mother. He married her—my mother, I mean—so that he wouldn't be deported. If he'd been sent back to his own country, he would've been killed.

"My mother sat the two of us—me and Isidro—down at the kitchen table and told us she was going to marry him." Luke laughed, remembering. "He was completely against it. He knew she'd had to get married before, when she was younger. He told her she'd gotten married for the wrong reasons the first time, and that he wasn't going to let her do that again. And she told him that marrying him so that he wouldn't die was the best reason she could imagine. I think she was in love with him, even back then. She convinced him that she was right, they got married, and he moved out of the apartment over the garage and into our house.''

His mother had been pretty damn shrewd. She'd known what she wanted, and she'd gone about getting it. She'd known if she could get Isidro into her home, it wouldn't be long before their marriage was consummated. And she'd been right on the money.

It was funny the way life seemed to go in circles, Lucky mused as he gazed at Syd, who was way, *way* down on the other end of the couch, as far away from him as she could possibly sit. Because here he was, playing the same game his mother had played. Pretending that he was acting out of some big-picture necessity, rather than from his own personal need.

Pretending that, oh, yeah, jeez, if he really *had* to, he'd cope with the *inconvenience* of having Sydney around all day and all night.

Yeah, right. Like he didn't hope—the way his mother had hoped with Isidro—that the pressure from being with Syd constantly would trigger some kind of unavoidable and unstoppable sexual explosion. That sooner or later—if not tonight, then maybe tomorrow or the next day—Syd would push open his bedroom door with a crash and announce that she couldn't stand it another minute, that she had to have him right now.

He laughed. Yeah, like *that* was really going to happen.

"What's so funny?" she asked.

He almost told her. Somehow he managed to shrug instead. "Ellen was born just about a year after their wedding. Their marriage turned pretty real pretty fast."

She nodded, understanding, glancing up at the wall, at his mother's picture. "The proximity thing. She was beautiful, and if she was in love with him...he probably didn't stand a chance.''

''He used to talk to me about his other family,'' Lucky remembered. ''I think he probably didn't say much about them to my mother, but I asked, and he needed to talk about them. I used to go with him to meetings where he would tell about these horrible human rights violations he'd witnessed in his home country. The things he saw, Syd, the things he could bear witness to...'' He shook his head. ''He told me to value my freedom as an American above all else. Every day he reminded me that I lived in a land of freedom, every day we'd hang an American flag outside our house. He used to tell me that he could go to sleep at night and be certain that no one would break into our house and tear us from our beds. No one would drag us into the street and put bullets in our heads simply for something we believed in. Because of him, I learned to value the freedom that most Americans take for granted.

''Isidro taught me a lot of things, but that was something that really stuck. Because he'd lived with that fear. Because his other family *had* been murdered.''

Syd was silent, just watching him.

''He became a naturalized citizen when I was thirteen years old,'' he told her, letting himself lose himself a little bit in the softness of her eyes. ''That's one day of my life I'll never forget. He was so proud of becoming a real American. And God!'' He laughed. ''That November, on election day! He took me and Ellen to the polls with him, so we could watch him vote. And he made us both promise—even though El could barely talk—that we would vote every chance we got.''

''So your stepfather is why you became a SEAL.''

''Father,'' he corrected gently. ''There was nothing step about him. And, yeah, the things he taught me stuck.'' Lucky shrugged, knowing that a cynical newspaper journalist probably wouldn't see it the same way he—and Isidro—had. Knowing that she would probably laugh, hoping she wouldn't, wanting to try to explain just the same. "I know there's a lot wrong with this country, but there's also a lot right. I *believe* in America. And I joined the Navy—the SEAL teams in particular—because I wanted to give something back. I wanted to be a part of making sure we remained the land of the free and the home of the brave. And I stayed in the Navy for longer than I'd ever dreamed of because I ended up getting as much as I gave."

She laughed.

He tried to hide his disappointment. "Yeah, I know. It sounds so hokey."

"Oh—" she sat up "—no! I wasn't laughing because of what you said. God, you've just impressed the hell out of me—please don't think I'm laughing at you."

"I have?" Lucky tried to sound casual. "Impressed you? Really?" Yeesh, he sounded like a dork, pathetically fishing for more compliments.

She didn't seem to notice, caught up in her own intensity. Man, when she got serious, she got *serious*. "I was laughing because back when I first met you, I thought I had you all figured out. I thought you were one of those testosterone-laden types who'd joined the SEALs purely because they liked the idea of blowing stuff up."

"Well, yeah." Lucky needed her to stop looking at him like that, with those blazing eyes that seemed able to look right through him and see his very soul. He needed her to lighten up so that he wouldn't do something really stupid like pull her into his arms and kiss her. "What do you think I mean when I talk about getting something back from being a SEAL? What I get is to blow stuff up."

Syd laughed. Thank God.

"Tell me," she said, "about your sister. Ellen. She's getting married, right?"

"In about a week," he told her. "You better put it on your calendar. It'll look really weird if we're supposedly living together but you don't attend my only sister's wedding.''

"Oh, no." She made a face. "That really stinks. You can't possibly want to drag me along to your sister's wedding.''

"I suppose we can make up some excuse for why you're not there," Lucky said. "I mean, if you really don't want to go.''

"I'd love to go," she countered, "but I know what an important day this is for you. Bobby told me how you turned down a…what did he call it? A silver bullet assignment—something you really, really wanted—just so you could be in town.''

"If I'm not there," he said, "who's going to walk her down the aisle? Look, just plan to go with me, okay? And if you could plan to wear a dress—something formal—while you're at it…''

"God." She gazed at him in mock horror. "You must think I'm a complete idiot. What did you think I'd wear to a formal wedding? A clean pair of jeans?''

"Well, yeah," he admitted. "Either jeans or your khakis. I've noticed a certain…repetitiveness to your attire.''

"Great," she said. "First I'm an idiot, and then I'm *boring?*''

She was laughing, so he knew she wasn't completely serious, but he still felt the need to try to explain. "That's not what I meant—''

"Quit while you're ahead," she told him. "Just tell me about your sister.''

It was nearly oh-one hundred hours, but Lucky wasn't tired. Syd didn't look tired either.

So he told her about his sister, ready and willing to talk all night if she wanted him to.

He wished she wanted more than conversation from him. He wanted to touch her, to take her to his bedroom and make love to her. But he wasn't going to risk destroying this quiet intimacy they shared.

She liked him. He knew that. But this was too new and far too fragile to gamble with.

He wanted to touch her, but he knew he shouldn't. Tonight he was going to have to settle for touching her with his words.

"Blade," Rio Rosetti said. "Or Panther."

"How about Hawk?" Thomas suggested, tongue firmly in cheek.

"Yeah, Hawk's good, too."

Rio was unhappy with his current nickname and was trying to talk his friends into calling him something else.

"Personally, I think we should be developing a kinder, gentler group of SEALs, with kinder, gentler nicknames," Michael Lee said with a completely straight face. "How about Bunny?"

The look on Rio's face was comical.

Thomas cracked up. "I like it," he said. "Bunny."

"Whoa," Rio said. "Whoa, whoa, whoa—"

"Works for me," Lucky said.

They were sitting in the office, waiting for Lucy's electronic transmission of a list she'd got from the police computer.

Out of all the many men and women who had served at the Navy base during the same few-month period four years ago, nearly thirty of them—all men—had gotten into trouble with law. Twenty-three had served time. Five were still incarcerated.

The police computer had spat out names, aliases and last-known addresses for all of them. They were going to cross-reference this list again with the information they had in the navy's personnel files.

"Lucky," Rio said. "Now *there's* a nickname I'd love."

"It's taken," Mike pointed out. "Whoops, here we go. List's in. I'll print out a couple of hard copies."

"It's not as if the luck comes with the name," Thomas told Rio. "According to legend, the lieutenant here has led a charmed existence, *hence* the name."

"Charmed indeed," Rio agreed. He glanced at Lucky, who'd gone to look over Mike's shoulder at the computer screen.

The list contained name, aliases, last-known address, and a short rap sheet of charges, convictions and jail time served—their criminal resumé, so to speak.

"I couldn't help but notice that Sydney came to work this morning wearing one of your Hawaiian shirts, sir," Rio continued. "I guess your little sleepover last night went… well."

Lucky looked up to find Thomas and Bobby waiting for him to comment, too. Even Michael Lee had lifted his eyes from the computer screen. He laughed. "You guys are kidding, right? You know as well as I do that this is just a ruse to try to trap the rapist. Sure, Syd stayed over, but…" he shrugged, "…nothing happened. I mean, there's really nothing going on between us."

"She *is* wearing one of your shirts," Bobby said.

"Yeah, because last night, in a genius move, I insulted her wardrobe."

He'd fallen asleep on the couch last night and woken to the scent of coffee brewing. He'd thrown off the blanket Syd must've put over him and staggered into the kitchen to find her already showered and dressed—and wearing one of his shirts. It was weird—and a little scary. It was his full-blown morning-after nightmare, in which a woman he barely knew and didn't particularly like would move in and make herself completely at home, right down to stealing from his closet. Except in this case, there had been no night before. *And* in this case, it wasn't a nightmare.

The coffee smelled great, Syd looked amazing in his

shirt, and, as she smiled at him, his stomach didn't twist with anxiety. It twisted, all right, but in anticipation.

He liked her, liked having her in his house, liked having her be a part of his morning.

And maybe, if he were really lucky, if he lived up to this nickname of his, he'd wake up tomorrow with her in his bed. Mike handed him three copies of the printed list, and he handed one to Bobby, the others to Thomas and Rio.

Rio was now looking at him as if he were mentally challenged. "Let me get this straight. You had Syd alone. Syd. One of the most incredibly fascinating and sexy women in the world. And she's alone with you, all night. And instead of taking advantage of that incredible opportunity, you spent your time insulting her clothes?"

"Hey, guys, I went to Starbuck's. Who wants coffee?"

Syd breezed in carrying a cardboard tray filled with paper coffee cups before Lucky could tell Rio to mind his own business. "Oh, good, the list finally came in?"

"Hot off the press," Lucky told her.

She smiled as she set a cup down in front of him. "Special delivery. Extra sugar. I figured you could use it after last night."

Rio cleared his throat pointedly. "Excuse me?"

Syd smacked him lightly on the shoulder. "Don't you dare think that—that's not what I mean, dirt brain. Luke and I are friends. I kept him up all night *talking*. He fell asleep on the living-room couch at about 3:30. He's running on way too little sleep and it's all my fault."

Rio shot Lucky a disbelieving look. "You fell asleep on the living-room couch...?"

"Hey," Thomas said, "Here's a guy who got out of prison in Kentucky four weeks before the first attack was reported."

"First known attack," Lucky reminded him, giving him a grateful look for changing the subject. He rolled his chair closer to the young ensign, to look over his shoulder at the list. "Kentucky's a stretch. He'd have to be motivated to reach San Diego with the amount of money he had on him."

"Yeah, but check this out. He's already wanted again," Thomas said, "in connection with a liquor store robbery in Dallas. That happened a week after his release."

Syd leaned over Lucky's shoulder. "Can a convict just leave the state like that? Doesn't he have to check in with a parole officer?"

He turned his head to look at her and found himself eye to eye with her breasts. He looked away, his mind instantly blank. What was he just about to say?

Bobby answered for him. "As far as I understand it, parole is for when a prisoner is released early. If he serves out his full sentence, there's usually no parole."

"What's this guy's name?" Syd asked. "Where is he on the list?"

"Owen Finn." Lucky pointed to the list and she leaned even closer to read the small print. She was wearing his deodorant. It smelled different on her. Delicate and femininely fresh.

Damn, he *was* nuts. He should have at least said something to Syd last night. *So, hey, like, what do you say we get it on?* Well, maybe not that. But certainly something in between that and the great big nothing he'd uttered. Because what if this attraction was mutual? What if she'd spent all night wishing they could get physical, too? What could it hurt to be honest?

They were, after all, friends—by her own admission. As his friend, she would appreciate his honesty.

Wouldn't she?

"Finn was convicted of burglary," Syd said, straightening up. "I thought we were looking for someone with a record of sexual assault or some other violent crime."

"Finn," Bobby reported from the Navy Computer's personnel files. "Owen Franklin. Son of a medal of honor winner, entered the U.S. Naval Academy even though his grades weren't quite up to par. Rang out of BUD/S in '96, given a dishonorable discharge four months later, charged and convicted of theft. Yeah, this guy definitely has sticky fingers. No mention of violence, though.''

"How about this one?" Thomas pointed to the list, and Syd leaned over Lucky again. "Martin Taus. Charged with four counts of sexual assault but never convicted. Got off on a technicality. Never served time but paid fines and did community service for damage done in a street fight back in '98. His last-known address is a post-office box in San Diego.''

"How do we find these guys?" Syd asked. "Can't we just bring in everyone on this list?''

She sat down next to him, and he resisted the urge to put his arm around her. If they were out in public, he could've gotten away with it. But here in the office they didn't need to play the girlfriend game.

It was too bad.

"Most of them aren't local," Lucky told her. "And their last-known addresses are probably out of date. But FInCOM's definitely looking to have them all brought in for questioning.''

"Some of them aren't going to be easy to find," Thomas pointed out. "Like this Owen Finn who's wanted in Texas. He's clearly on the move.''

"When are we going to start dangling me out there as bait?" Syd asked. "We need to establish a pattern of time that I'm home alone.''

"We'll start tonight," Lucky told her. "I spoke to Frisco this morning. The phase-one SEAL candidates are going to be doing a series of night swims over the next week. I'm going to be visible at the base from the time the exercise starts at about twenty-three hundred, right up until the point I put on my gear. Then one of the other instructors will take over for me—masked and suited up, anyone who's watching won't know it's not me. I'll leave the base covertly and join Bobby and our junior frogmen, who will have concealed themselves strategically around the outside of our house. *My* house,'' he quickly corrected himself.

Alan Francisco had been disappointed—he'd said as much—when Lucky'd admitted his relationship with Syd was just an act. But he didn't say anything more, except that he was there to talk, if Lucky wanted someone to talk to. About what, Lucky'd asked. Yeah, he was a little worried about Syd putting herself in danger, but this way at least he could keep an eye on her. Everything was cool. There was nothing to talk about.

''I'll be going over to Luke's in about an hour to set up interior microphones,'' Bobby said.

''So, I'm going to be alone in the house starting at about seven until…two or three in the morning?'' she guessed.

''No, we'll have time before the exercise starts,'' Lucky told her. ''We can have dinner downtown. We'll leave here together at about eighteen hundred—six o'clock. After dinner, we'll go to my place, and around twenty-two-thirty, after Bobby and the guys have moved into position, I'll make a big show of kissing you goodbye, and I'll come here. You'll be alone from then until around oh-two-hundred. About three and a half hours.''

Syd nodded. ''Maybe if we're lucky, FInCOM will round up most of the suspects on our list before tonight. And if we're *really* lucky, one of them will be our guy.''

Lucky nodded, hoping the golden luck for which he'd been nicknamed would, indeed, shine through.

Chapter 10

The meltingly perfect lobster and the hundred-dollar bottle of wine had been completely wasted on Syd.

What with the blazing sunset, the incredible outdoor patio, the million-dollar view of the Pacific, and—last but certainly not least—the glowing golden good looks of the man sitting across the restaurant table from her, Syd had barely noticed the gourmet food or drink.

It might as well have been peanut butter sandwiches and grape juice for all the attention she gave to it.

She spent most of the meal wishing Luke would hold her hand. And when he finally did, reaching across the table to intertwine their fingers, she spent the rest of the meal wishing he'd kiss her again.

He'd kissed her outside the restaurant after giving the valet his keys. Slow, lingering kisses that rendered her speechless.

He'd kissed her in the bar, too, as they'd waited for a table. Delicate kisses. Elegant kisses. Five-star restaurant kisses.

She wasn't dressed for this place, but no one besides her seemed to care. The maitre d' was attentive, the waiters were respectful, and Luke...

Well, he'd nearly had *her* believing they were completely, totally, thrillingly in love.

"You're so quiet," he said now, his thumb tracing circles on the palm of her hand as they waited for the waiter to return with Luke's credit card, sitting beneath that perfect, color-streaked sky. The way he was looking at her, the quiet timbre of his voice—his behavior was completely that of an attentive lover. He was remarkably good at playing this part. "What are you thinking about?"

"Kissing you," she admitted.

For an eighth of a second, his guard dropped, his thumb stopped moving and she saw real surprise in his eyes. He opened his mouth to speak, but the waiter returned. And all Luke did was laugh as he gently reclaimed his fingers and signed the bill. He pocketed his receipt and stood, holding out his hand to her.

"Let's walk on the beach."

They went down the wooden steps hand in hand, and when they reached the bottom, he knelt in the sand and took off her sandals, then carried them for her, along with his own shoes. The sand was sensuously cool between her toes.

They walked in silence for about a minute, then Luke cleared his throat. "So, when you were thinking about kissing me, was it a good thought or...?"

"It was more of an amused thought," she admitted. "Like, here I am, with the best-looking man in the state of California, and oh, just in case that's not thrilling enough, he's going to kiss me a few dozen more times before the night is through. You kiss like a dream, you know? Of course you know."

"You're pretty good at it yourself."

"I'm an amateur compared to you. I can't seem to do

that thing you do with your eyes. And that little 'I'm going to kiss you now' smile. Only someone with a face like yours can pull that off.''

His laughter sounded embarrassed. "Oh, come on. I'm not—"

"Don't be coy," she reprimanded him. "You know what you look like. All you need to do is smile, and every woman within a hundred feet goes into heavy fantasy mode. Walk into any room and flash those teeth, and women start lining up for a chance to go home with you."

"Gee, if I'd only known that was all it would take…" He gave her his best smile.

She yawned. "Doesn't work on me. Not since I heard you snore last night."

"I do *not* snore."

Syd just smiled.

"I *don't*."

"Okay," she said, clearly just humoring him.

"You try to pick fights," he said, realization in his voice, "even these silly, teasing ones, because you're afraid to have a serious conversation with me."

That was *so* not true. "We had a very serious conversation last night," she argued.

"Yeah, but I did most of the talking. That was *my* serious conversation."

"I told you about my family," she protested.

"Barely."

"Well, they're boring. None of them have run off to Tibet. I mean, if anyone's Tibet-bound, it's probably *me.*"

"There you go," he said. "Trying to get me to argue with you about whether you would or wouldn't actually go to Tibet if you had the cash."

Tibet no, but New York, *yes.* Or Boston or Philly. She wanted to return to the east coast, she reminded herself. That's what all this was about. It was about helping catch a serial rapist, and then writing the best, most detailed, most emotionally connected yet factual article about a city-wide task force ever written.

She wasn't here simply to kiss this man in the moonlight.

The last of the dusk was fading fast, and the moon was just a sliver in the sky. Syd could hear the party sounds from the Surf Club farther down the beach—the echo of laughter and distant rock and roll.

Luke's face was entirely in shadow. "I like you, Syd," he told her softly. "You make me laugh. But I want to *know* you. I want to know what you want, who you really are. I want to know where you see yourself in fifty years. I want to…" He laughed, and she could've sworn it was self-consciously, that is, if it was possible that Luke O'Donlon could be self-conscious. "I want to know about Kevin Manse. I want to know if you're still in love with him, if you still measure every man you bump into against him."

Syd was so completely surprised, it very nearly qualified as stunned. Kevin *Manse?* What the…? She wished she could see Luke's eyes in the darkness. "What do…*how* do you know about Kevin Manse?"

He cleared his throat. "He, um, came up in some detail when Lana Quinn first hypnotized you."

"*Some* detail…?"

"You, um, flashed back to the first time you, uh, met him."

Syd said a very impolite word. "*Flashed back?* What do you mean, *flashed back?*"

"Um, I guess *relived* is more accurate."

"*Relived?*" Her voice went up several octaves. "What is that supposed to mean?"

"You, um, partly told us what happened, partly talked to Kevin as if he were in the room. You told us you bumped into him on the stairs at some frat party, and that he took you up to his room. We kind of tried to rush through the 'oh, Kevin, yes, Kevin' part, but—"

Syd said another equally impolite word and sat down in the sand, covering her face with her hands. God, how mortifying. "I suppose you also heard how that pitiful story ended?"

"Actually, no, I don't know how it ended." She felt more than heard Luke sit down beside her. "Syd, I'm sorry. I wasn't trying to embarrass you. I was just... I've been thinking about it a lot lately, wondering..."

She peeked out at him through her fingers. He *didn't* know how the story ended. She was saved from complete and total mortification.

"Do you, um, still love him?"

Syd laughed. She laughed and laughed and laughed, lying back on the sand, staring up at the vastness of the sky and gasping for air.

She laughed, because if she didn't laugh, she'd cry. And there was no way she would *ever* cry in front of this man. Not if she could help it.

Luke laughed, too, mostly because laughter was contagious, partly because he was confused. "I didn't mean for that to be such a funny question."

"No," she said when she finally could talk, drawing in a deep breath and letting it out in a shudder of air. "No, I *definitely* don't still love him. In fact, I never loved him."

"You said you did. While you were hypnotized."

"I was eighteen," she said. "I lost my virginity to the bastard. I temporarily confused sex with love."

As she gazed at the sky, the stars slowly appeared.

He sighed. "It was only a one-nighter, huh?"

Syd turned her head to look at him, a darker lump of a shadow against the darkness of the night. "A one-night stand. How many times have *you* done that?"

He answered honestly. "Too many."

"You're probably someone's Kevin Manse," she said.

He was silent.

"I'm sorry," she said. "That was harsh."

"But probably true. I've tried to stay away from the eighteen-year-old virgins, though."

"Oh," Syd said. "Well. Then that makes it *all* better."

Luke laughed ruefully. "Man, you are unmerciful."

"I'll cut you down, but not yet—I like seeing you twisting in the wind, baby." Syd laughed. "You want serious? I'll give you the whole pathetic story—that'll really make you squirm. But if you repeat it to *any*one, our friendship is over, do you understand?"

"I'm going to hate this, aren't I?"

"It's pretty hateful." Syd sat up and looked out over the water. "I've never told this to anyone. Not my college roommate, not my sister, not my mother, not anyone. But I'm going to tell you, because we're friends, and maybe you'll learn something from it."

"I feel like I'm approaching a car wreck. I'm horrified at the thought of the carnage, but unable to turn away."

She laughed. "It's not *that* bad."

"No?"

"Well, maybe it was at the time." She hugged her knees close to her chest and sighed. Where to start...? "Kevin was a big football star."

"Yeah," Luke said. "You mentioned that. You said he was a scholar, too. Smart as hell. And probably handsome."

"On a scale from one to ten..." Syd squinted as she thought about it. "A twelve."

"Whoa!"

On that same scale, Luke was a fifty. But she wasn't going to tell *him* that.

"So I ran into him, the big, famous football hero, on the stairs of this frat-house party," she said, "and—"

"Yeah," he interrupted. "I know that part. You went upstairs with him, and I know *that* part, too. That's the part where you started going 'oh, Kevin, yes, Kevin—'"

"Wow, you are really the funniest man in the world. Oh, wait—no, you're not! You just *think* you are."

Luke laughed softly. "I'm sorry, I'm just…being a jerk. I'm really anxious about where this is going, and I was just trying to…" he exhaled noisily. "Truth is, when you were doing that in Lana's office, it was really incredibly sexy. It was kind of hard to sit through."

She closed her eyes. "God, I'm sorry. I hope I didn't offend you."

"Yeah, right. It's always offensive to find out that the woman I'm going to be working closely with for the next few weeks is completely *hot.*"

She snorted. "Yeah, right. That's me. One hot chick."

"You steam," he told her.

"And I suppose the fact that you now know I had sex with some guy about an hour after I met him had nothing to do with your decision to hit on me?"

"I hit on you before you were hypnotized."

He was right. That *had* happened the day before—on the first day they'd met. And *after* she'd been hypnotized…

"After the session with Lana Quinn," he said, "was when I asked you to join the team, as a team player, remember?"

Syd was completely confused. "I'm not even going to *try* to make any sense out of that."

"Just finish the story," he told her. "You told me and Lana that Kevin had one of his friends drive you back to your dorm, later that night."

"Yeah," she said. "He said he thought my staying all night would be bad for my reputation. Ha." She rested her chin on her knees, still holding on to herself tightly. "Okay. Next day. Act Two. It's Sunday. There's a big game. And me, I'm a genius. I'm thinking about the fact that thanks to the bottle of Jack Daniel's we put a solid dent in up in Kevin's room, I managed to leave without giving my new soul mate my telephone number. So I spend the morning writing him a note. I think I went through about a hundred drafts before I got it right. 'Dear Kevin, Last night was truly wonderful…'''

She had to swallow to clear away the sudden, aching lump that formed in her throat. God, she was such a sap. All these years later, and Kevin Manse could *still* make her want to cry, damn him.

She felt Luke touch her, his fingers gentle in her hair, light against her back.

''You really don't have to tell me any more of this,'' he said quietly. ''I already feel really bad, and if you want, right now I'll swear to you that I'll never do a one-nighter again. I mean, it's been years since I have anyway, and—''

''I went to the football game,'' she told him. ''With my pathetic little note. And I sat there in the stands and I watched my lover from the night before play a perfect game. After it was over, I tried to get into the stadium locker rooms, but there were security guards who laughed at me when I told them I was Kevin's girlfriend. I didn't get upset. I just smiled. I figured they'd have plenty of time to get to know me—the season was just starting. They told me that Kevin always came out the south entrance after a game to greet his fans. They told me I should wait there if I wanted to see him. So I waited.''

''Oh, God,'' Luke said. ''I know exactly where this is going.''

''I waited by the south gate, with a crowd of about fifty people, for over an hour,'' Syd continued.

She remembered the smell of the spilled beer, the sweat, and the humid afternoon heat. She remembered that nervous feeling in her stomach, that anticipation at the thought of seeing Kevin again. She'd stood there, fantasizing, wondering what he'd do when he saw her. Would he laugh and hold out his arms to her? Would he get that soft look in his eyes, just as he had the night before, when they'd done those things that still made her blush? Would he pick her up and spin her around in a victory dance, and then kiss her? Syd remembered thinking that the crowd would cheer at that kiss, the way crowds always did at the end of romantic movies, when the hero and heroine were together at last.

"He finally came out," she told Luke, "and started signing autographs. It took me forever, but I made my way to the front of the crowd. And he turned to me and..."

The lump was back, damn it, and she had to clear it out of her throat.

"And he didn't remember me," she whispered. "He looked right into my eyes, and he didn't even recognize that I was the girl he'd had sex with the night before. He gave me his high-voltage, football-star smile, and took my note right out of my hand. He asked me what my name was, asked me how to spell it, and he signed his autograph on that piece of paper and gave it back to me. 'To Sydney— Stay happy, Kevin Manse.'"

Lucky sat in the sand and stared up at the now slightly hazy sky. "Can I try to find him?" he asked. "Can I track him down and beat the hell out of him?"

Syd managed a shaky laugh.

He wanted to touch her again, to put his arms around her and hold her close, but it seemed like the wrong thing to do, given the circumstances.

"I'm so sorry," he said, and his words seemed so inadequate.

Especially since he'd spent nearly all of dinner planning exactly how he was going to talk Syd into his bed tonight. Late tonight. After oh-two-hundred. In the small hours of the night, when she would be at her most vulnerable. He'd turn off the microphones, send the rest of his team home. And in the privacy of his living room...

He'd told himself that it would be good for him to be honest with her. To tell her he was attracted, admit that he was having trouble thinking about much else besides the fact that he wanted her. He was planning to move closer and closer as they sat on the couch, closing in on her until she was in his arms. He was planning to kiss her until she lost all sense of direction. He was planning to kiss her until she surrendered.

But in truth, he wasn't really being honest. He was merely calculating that this feigned honesty would get him some.

He hadn't given much thought at all to tomorrow. He hadn't considered Syd's feelings. Or her expectations.

Just like Kevin Manse, he'd thought only about his own immediate gratification. God, he was such a jerk.

Syd drew in a deep breath and let it out in a rush. "We should probably go. It's getting late. You have to head over to the base, and I've…I've got to go tattoo the word *victim* on my forehead, just to be sure our bad guy gets the right idea."

She stood up and stretched, then turned and offered Lucky a hand. He took it, and she helped him up. He'd known all along that she was strong, but she was much, much stronger than he'd ever imagined.

He held on to her hand, suddenly afraid that she didn't really like him, afraid that she was simply enduring his company, afraid of what she'd write about him in her article after this was all over. And, he was afraid that after it was over, he'd never see her again. "Syd, do you hate me?"

She turned toward him and touched his face, her fingers cool against his cheek. "Are you kidding?" Her husky voice was filled with amusement and something else. Something warm that wrapped around him and brought him more than mere relief. "I know it sounds crazy, but I think you're probably the best friend I've ever had."

Chapter 11

Syd woke to the shrill sound of the telephone ringing.

The clock on the bedside table in Luke's guest room read 3:52. It was nearly four in the morning. Who could possibly be calling now?

She knew instantly, sitting up, her heart pounding.

The rapist hadn't taken the bait. Instead, some other poor woman had been attacked.

She could hear the low murmur of Luke's voice from the other room.

His voice got louder, and, although she couldn't make out the words, she could pick up his anger loud and clear. No, this wasn't good news, that was for sure.

Luke had come home just after two. He'd been unnaturally quiet, almost pensive, and very, very tired. He'd made a quick circuit of the house, making sure all the doors and windows were securely locked, and then he'd gone into his bedroom and shut the door.

Syd had climbed into the narrow bed in this room that

had probably once been Luke's sister's, and had tried to sleep.

Tried and failed. It seemed as if she'd just drifted off when the sound of the phone jerked her back to consciousness.

From the other side of the wall, she heard a crash from Luke's room as something was noisily knocked over. She stood up, uncertain as to whether she should go make sure he was all right, when her door opened with a bang.

Luke stood there, wearing only a pair of boxers, breathing hard, backlit by the light from the hallway. "Get your clothes on. Fast. We're going to the hospital." His voice was harsh, his face grim. "Lucy McCoy's been attacked."

Syd had to run to keep up with Luke as she followed him down the hospital corridor.

Lucy McCoy. God, not Lucy....

Whoever had called Luke to give him the news hadn't known any details. How badly had she been hurt? Was she even alive?

Bobby appeared at the end of the hallway, and Luke moved even faster.

"Sit-rep," he ordered the chief as soon as they were close enough to talk without shouting.

Bobby's face was somber. "She's alive and she wasn't raped," he told them as they continued down the hall. "But that's where the good news ends. They've got her in ICU— intensive care. I...persuaded a doctor to talk to me, and he used words like *massive head injury* and *coma*. She's got a broken collarbone, broken arm, and a broken rib that punctured her lung, as well."

"Who's with her?" Luke's voice was tight.

"Wes and Mia," Bobby reported. "Frisco's taking care of the paperwork."

"Has someone tried to reach Blue?"

"Yeah, I've tried, Frisco's tried, but we're both getting a lot of static. Wherever Alpha Squad is, they're in deep. I can't even get anyone to tell me which hemisphere they're on."

"Call Admiral Robinson," Luke ordered as they stopped outside the entrance to the intensive care unit. "If anyone can get word to Alpha Squad, he can."

Bobby moved briskly off as Mia Francisco pushed open the door and stepped out of ICU.

"I thought I heard your voice." She gave Luke a hug, her eyes red from crying.

"Should you be here?" Luke asked her, putting a hand on her enormous belly.

Mia hugged Syd, too. "How could I not be here?" she said. Her lip trembled. "The doctor says the next few hours are critical. If she makes it through the night—" Her voice broke.

"Oh, God," Syd said. "It's that bad?"

Mia nodded.

"Can I see her?" Luke asked.

Mia nodded again. "She's in room four. There's usually a family-members-only rule with patients in ICU, but with Blue out of the country, the doctors and nurses are letting us sit with her. I called Veronica and Melody. They're both flying in in the morning. And Nell and Becca should be here in about an hour. PJ's already over at the crime scene."

Luke pushed open the door to the intensive care wing, and Syd followed him in.

Nighttime didn't exist in ICU. It was as brightly lit and as filled with busy doctors and nurses as if it were high noon.

Luke stopped outside room four, just looking in. Syd took his hand.

Lucy looked impossibly small and fragile lying in that hospital bed. She was hooked up to all kinds of machines and monitors. Her head was swathed in bandages, her face pale—except for where it was savagely bruised. She had an angry-looking row of stitches above her left eyebrow, and her mouth looked scraped and raw, her lips swollen and split. Her left eye was purple and yellow and completely swollen shut.

Wes sat next to her bed, head bowed as he held her hand.

He looked up as Luke slowly went into the room, Syd following him to the foot of Lucy's bed.

Wes's eyes were as red as Mia's had been. He was crying.

Wes—whom Syd still thought of as a potential suspect. God, wasn't that an awful thought? Was it possible Wes could have done this to Lucy and then come here to sit by her bed—to make sure that she died? It was like something out of a bad movie.

"Hey, Luce," Luke said, trying his best to sound cheerful, but barely able to do more than whisper. "I don't suppose you want to wake up and tell me what happened, huh?"

Lucy didn't move. On the wall, the screen monitoring her heart continued its steady beeping.

Wes gave no guilty starts. His eyes didn't move shiftily. He didn't start to sweat or shake at the thought of Lucy opening her eyes and giving out information. He just sat there, crying, holding Lucy's hand, occasionally wiping his eyes with his T-shirt sleeve.

"Well, you know what?" Luke said to her. "I'm going to come back later and we can talk then, okay?"

Nothing.

Luke was holding Syd's hand so tightly, her fingers were starting to ache from lack of blood.

"Just…hang on, Lucy," he said, his voice thick with emotion. "Blue will be here soon, I promise. Just…hang on."

* * *

Lucky stood in Blue and Lucy McCoy's second-floor bedroom, grimly taking in the crushed and twisted lamps, the knocked-over rocking chair, the mattress half off its frame, the blood smeared on the sheets and the pale yellow wall, and the broken bay window that had looked out over the McCoys' flower-filled backyard.

Dawn was sending delicate, fairy-like light into the yard and, as he stepped closer to the window, the bits and pieces of broken glass glittered prettily on the grass below.

Syd stood quietly by the door. He'd heard her slip into the bathroom after they'd first arrived and seen the evidence of the violent and bloody fight that had taken place in this very room. He'd heard her get sick. But she'd come out almost right away. Pale and shaking but unwilling to leave.

PJ Becker came into the room, followed by one of the FInCOM agents who'd been assigned to the task force. PJ's recent promotion had pushed her way high up in FInCOM's chain of command, and the agent who was with her looked a little dazed at her presence.

"Dave, you already know Lieutenant O'Donlon and Sydney Jameson. Lieutenant, Dave Sudenberg's one of our top forensics experts," PJ said. "I thought you'd be interested in hearing his take on what happened here last night, since Detective McCoy's not yet able to give us a statement."

Lucky nodded and Dave Sudenberg cleared his throat. "As far as I can tell, the perpetrator entered the premises through a downstairs window," he told them. "He managed to bypass a portion of the security system without shutting the whole thing down, which was good, since the system's lights and alarms later played a large part in saving the detective's life."

He pointed to the door that Syd was still standing near. "He entered this room through that door, and from the pattern of blood on the sheets, we can assume that Lucy was in bed at the time, and probably asleep when he landed the first blow—probably the one that broke her nose. He struck her with his fists—there would have been far more blood had he used something other than his hands.

"Lucy came up swinging. She was probably trying to get to the weapon she kept just under the bed, but he wouldn't let her near it. She hit him with this lamp," he said, pointing to the twisted wreckage of what had once been a tall, freestanding halogen. "Preliminary tests already show that the blood on this thing isn't Lucy's.

"So she clobbers him, and he goes ballistic, throws her against this wall, battering the hell out of her, and delivering what I believe was the worst of Lucy's head injuries, and wrapping his hands around her neck. But somehow, she breaks free. Somehow she doesn't lose consciousness right away. And she does the one thing that I think saved her life. She dives out the window, right through the glass, setting off the alarm system, waking the neighbors. Perp runs, and the police come and find her, half dead in the backyard."

Lucky met Syd's eyes. Dear God, now *he* was going to be sick. Lucy had to have known that a fall like that could have killed her. Had she thought she'd have zero chance of survival by staying in the room with the attacker? Fight or submit. Had she believed either would have gotten her killed, and opted to flee, despite the health risks of jumping out a second-story window?

There was a real chance he'd never find out, that Lucy wouldn't live through the night, or that, even if she did, she'd never awaken from the coma she'd slipped into.

There was a real chance Blue would come home to bury his wife.

PJ moved to the window and looked all the way down at the yard below. "Dave thinks her broken collarbone and arm were from the dive she took out the window," she said grimly. "But the broken rib, broken nose, bruised throat and near-fatal head injuries were from your guy."

"We've got enough of his DNA to see if it matches the semen and skin samples he left behind with his other victims," Sudenberg told them. "I've already sent samples to the lab."

"What's it gonna take," Lucky asked, his chest and his throat both feeling so tight he had to push to squeeze his voice out, "to get the police or FInCOM to actually pick up the likely suspects on the list Lucy helped compile?"

"It's getting done, but these things take time," PJ told him as she headed for the door. She motioned for Sudenberg to follow her. "I'll see that you're given updated status reports as they come in."

Lucky nodded. "Thanks."

"See you back at the hospital," PJ said.

Lucky stood in his kitchen, his vision blurring as he stared out the window over the sink.

Lucy had made it through the night but still showed no signs of waking.

Blue could not be reached, not even with the help of Admiral Robinson. The admiral had known where Alpha Squad was though, and had been willing to break radio silence to contact them, but the mountains and rocky terrain were playing havoc with the signal. Lieutenant Mitch Shaw, one of the Admiral's Gray Group operatives, had volunteered to go in after them. To find Blue, to send him back out and to take his place on this critical mission.

Best-case scenario had Shaw taking a record four days to walk into the hostile and nearly impenetrable countryside and find Alpha Squad almost right away—another highly unlikely possibility. Another four days for Blue to get out. Best-case scenario didn't have him reaching his wife's side in fewer than nine or ten days.

Nine or ten *days.*

Damn it. *Damn* it.

He heard Syd in the doorway, but he didn't turn around.

"Maybe I should go," she said quietly. "You probably want to be alone, and—"

He spun around, interrupting her with a very salty version of no. "Where would you go? To your apartment? I don't want you even to *think* of going back there alone, do you understand? Not unless I'm with you. From now on, you don't make a move on your own, is that absolutely clear?"

He was shouting at her, he realized. He was standing in his kitchen, blasting her for being considerate.

But she didn't shout back at him. She didn't recoil in horror. She didn't spin on her heels and walk away in a huff. Instead, she took a step toward him, reaching out her hand for him. "Luke, this isn't your fault. You know that, right?"

There was a solid lump in his throat, and no matter how hard he tried he couldn't swallow it. He couldn't push it down past the tightness in his chest. "I should have made her listen to me," he whispered. "I tried to talk her into staying at the police station, but she had such faith in her damned security system."

Syd was gazing at him with such compassion in her eyes. He knew that if she touched him, he'd be lost. If she touched him, everything he was fighting so hard to keep inside would break free, all the guilt and the anger and the fear—God, he was so afraid. It would escape, like water pouring over a dam.

He took a step back from her. "I don't want you doing this anymore. This bait thing. Not after this. No way. All bets are off. You're going to have to stay away from me from now on. I'll make sure Bobby's with you, 24-7."

She kept coming. "Luke. That doesn't make sense. This could well be the only way we'll catch this guy. I *know* you want to catch this guy."

He laughed, and it sounded sharp and brittle. "Understatement of the year."

"Maybe we should both get some sleep. We can talk about this later, after we've had time to think it through."

"There's nothing more to think about," he said. "There's too much that could go wrong. In the time it would take us to get inside the house, even from the back-yard, you could be killed. You're smaller than Lucy, Syd. If he hit you the way he hit her—" His voice broke and he had to take a deep breath before he could go on. "I won't let you risk your life that way. The thought of you being alone with that guy even for one second…"

To Lucky's complete horror, the tears he was desperately fighting welled in his eyes, and this time he couldn't force them back. This time they escaped. He wiped at them savagely, but even that didn't stop them from coming.

Ah, God, he was crying. He was standing in front of Syd and crying like a two-year-old.

It was all over. He was completely unmanned.

Except she didn't laugh. She didn't give him one of those "wow, you are both lame *and* stupid" looks that she did so well.

Instead, she put her arms around him and held him tightly. "It's okay if you cry," she told him softly. "I won't tell anyone."

He had to laugh at that. "Yeah, but you'll know."

She lifted her head to look up at him, gently pushing his hair back from his face, her eyes so soft. "I already knew."

The constriction in his chest got even tighter. God, it hurt. "I'd die if anything happened to you."

His voice broke as he thought about Blue, out there in some jungle somewhere, being told that the woman he loved more than life itself was lying in a hospital bed, maybe dying, maybe already dead.

And then Lucky wasn't just crying anymore. He was experiencing emotional meltdown. He was sobbing the way he hadn't done since Isidro had died, clinging tightly to Syd as if maybe she could save him.

His knees gave out and he crumpled, sliding down to sit on the kitchen floor.

And still Syd held on to him. She didn't say a word, didn't try to make him stop. She just sat next to him, rocking him gently.

Even if Lucy woke up, even if she opened her eyes tomorrow, she would have only *survived.* Blue could never go back and erase the trauma of what she'd been through. He could never take away the fear she must've known in what should have been the sanctuary of her bedroom, as she'd fought for her life, all alone with a man who wanted to violate her, to kill her. There would always, for the rest of their lives, be a permanent echo of that fear in her eyes.

And that was if she survived.

If she died…

How would Blue live, how would he even be able to breathe, with his heart ripped from his chest?

Would he spend the rest of his life haunted by the memory of Lucy's eyes? Would he be forever looking for her smile on a crowded street? Would the scent of her subtle perfume make him turn, searching for her, despite knowing full well that she was gone?

Lucky wasn't ever going to let himself be in that place where Blue was right now. He wasn't ever getting married. Never getting married. It had been his mantra for years as he'd struggled with the concept of commitment, yet now it held special meaning.

He didn't want to walk around feeling the fear that came with loving someone. He didn't want that, damn it!

Except look at him.

He was reduced to this quivering bowl of jelly not simply out of empathy for Blue. A solid part of the emotion that had reduced him to these stupid tears was this god-awful fear that tightened his chest and closed up his throat.

The thought of Syd spending even one single second

with the man who had brutalized Lucy made him crazy. The thought of her being beaten into a coma was terrifying.

But the thought of Syd walking out of his life, after they'd caught and convicted the San Felipe Rapist, was nearly as frightening.

He loved her.

No! Dear God, where had *that* thought come from? An overdose of whatever bizarre hormones his emotional outburst had unleashed.

Lucky drew in a deep, shuddering breath and pulled free from Syd's arms. He didn't love her. That was insane. He was Lucky O'Donlon. He didn't *do* love.

He wiped his eyes, wiped his face, reached up for a napkin from the holder on the kitchen table and blew his nose. He lived up to his nickname by tossing the napkin directly into the trash container all the way on the other side of the room with perfect aim, then sat leaning back, exhausted, against the kitchen cabinets.

No, he didn't love her. He was just a little confused, that's all. And, just to be safe, until he was able to sleep off this confusion, it would be smart for him to put a little distance between them.

Now was definitely not the time to act on his raging physical attraction for this woman. As much as he would have given for the comfort of losing himself in some highly charged sex before slipping into mind-numbing sleep, he wasn't going to do it.

Of course, there was also the not-so-small matter of his taking advantage of her.

Assuming that she'd even *let* him take advantage of her after he'd revealed just how completely pathetic a wimp he was.

Syd was silent as she sat beside him. He couldn't bring himself even to glance at her as he attempted an apologetic smile. "Sheesh. I'm sorry about that."

He sensed more than saw her turn so that she was sitting on her knees, facing him.

But then she touched him. Her fingers were cool against the heat of his face as she gently pushed his hair back from his forehead. He looked at her then—he couldn't really avoid it, she'd leaned forward and her face was about two inches from his.

Her eyes were so warm, he had to close his, for fear he'd start crying all over again.

And with his eyes closed, he didn't see her lean even farther forward. But she must have, because she kissed him.

She kissed him.

Here in his kitchen, where no one was watching, where no one could see.

It was such a sweet kiss, such a gentle kiss, her lips featherlight against his. It made his knees go even weaker, made him glad he was already sitting down.

She kissed him again, and this time he was ready for her. This time he kissed her, too, catching her mouth with his, careful to be as gentle, tasting the salt of his tears on her lips with the very tip of his tongue.

He heard her sigh and he kissed her again, longer this time, deeper. She opened her mouth to him, slowly, exquisitely meeting his tongue with hers, and Lucky threw it all away. Everything that he'd been trying to convince himself about putting distance between them went right out the window.

To hell with his confusion. He liked confusion. He *loved* confusion. If this was confusion, then damn it, give him more.

He reached for her, and she slid into his arms, her fingers in his hair, on his neck, on his back, her body so supple against him, her breasts so soft.

He'd kissed her before, but never like this. It had never been this real. It had never held this promise, this achingly pure glimpse of attainable paradise.

He kissed her again and again, slowly, lazily losing himself in the soft sweetness of her mouth, deliberately taking his time, purposely not pressuring her for anything more.

These kisses were enough. He wanted her, sure, but even if they only spent the next four hours just kissing, that would be good enough. Kissing her for four hours wouldn't be taking advantage, would it?

But Syd was the one who pushed them over the line.

She moved onto his lap, straddling him. She started unfastening the buttons on his shirt. She kissed him possessively—long, hard, deep, hungry kisses that lifted him up and made him tumble with her into a breathless, passionate, turbulent place. A place where the entire world disappeared, where nothing existed but the softness of her eyes, the warmth of her body.

She pushed his shirt off his shoulders, still kissing him.

He reached to unbutton her Hawaiian shirt—his shirt—and was completely sidetracked by the softness of her body beneath the silk, by the way her breasts fit perfectly in his hands, by the desire-tightened tips of her nipples.

She moved forward on his lap, pressing the heat between her legs against his arousal, nearly making him weep all over again.

She wanted him as badly as he wanted her.

And still she kissed him, fierce kisses now, kisses that stole his breath from his lungs, that made his heart pound in his chest.

He gave up trying to unfasten her shirt and yanked it up and over her head.

She unfastened the black lace of her bra, and then her bare breasts were in his hands, in his mouth. He kissed her, tasted her, pulling back to gaze at her. Small but perfect, she was quite possibly the most exquisitely feminine woman he'd ever seen. Her shoulders were so smooth, so slender. Her collarbone and the base of her throat were works of art. And her breasts…what on earth had she been thinking to keep all that covered up all the time?

He pulled her close and kissed her again, his arms wrapped around all that amazing satiny skin, her breasts cool against his chest.

She reached between them for the buckle on his belt. It wasn't easy to get open, but she had it unfastened and his zipper undone in a matter of seconds.

Lucky's fingers fumbled at the button on her jeans, and she pulled out of his arms to kick off her sandals, to skim her pants down her legs. He did the same with his own pants, kicking off his shoes.

"Where do you keep your condoms?" she asked huskily.

"Bathroom. In the medicine cabinet."

For some reason that surprised her. "Really?" she said. "Not in the top drawer of your bedside table, next to your water bed?"

He had to laugh. "I hate to break it to you, but I don't have a water bed."

"No lava lamp?"

He shook his head, grinning at her like an idiot. "And nary a single black light, either. My apologies. As a bachelor pad, it's definitely lacking."

She took it in stride. "I suppose not having a water bed is better than not having any condoms." She was naked and so incredibly beautiful as she stood there, looking down at him. "As appealing an idea as it is to get it on right here on the kitchen floor, do you suppose if I went into your bedroom via a quick stop in the bathroom, I could convince you to follow me?"

The bedroom. The bedroom suddenly made this all so real. Lucky had to ask. "Syd, are you sure…?"

She gave him her 'I don't believe you' look. "I'm standing here naked, Luke, about to fetch a condom from your bathroom so that you and I can have raw, screaming sex. If that's not an unequivocal yes, I don't know what is."

"Raw, screaming sex," he repeated, his mouth suddenly dry.

"Wildly passionate, deliriously orgasmic, exquisitely delicious, savage, pounding, rapture-enducing, sweaty, nasty, scorchingly ecstatic, heart-stopping, brain-meltingly raw, screaming sex." She gave him a very innocent smile. "You up for it?"

Lucky could only nod yes. His vocal chords had seized up. But his legs were working.

Somehow she managed to beat him into his bedroom. She tossed the condom on his bedside table and knelt on his bed, her gaze skimming his nearly naked body. She looked rather pointedly at his briefs. "Are you planning to keep those on?"

"I didn't want to scare you," he said modestly.

She laughed, just as he'd hoped she would.

"Come here," she said.

He did, and she kissed him as she pulled him back with her onto his bed.

The sensation of her naked body beneath his, of the silkiness of her legs intertwined with his was one he'd fantasized about often. Lucky had been with many, many women and found fantasy better than reality. But that wasn't so with Syd. In his fantasies about her, he hadn't even scratched the surface of how good it would feel to be with her this way, because it went so far beyond mere physical pleasure.

He loved the way her eyes lit up, the way she smiled at him as if making love to him was the most fun she'd ever had in her entire life.

He ran his hands down her back to the curve of her rear end. She was all his, and he laughed aloud as he touched her. He couldn't get enough of touching her.

He parted her legs with gentle pressure from his thighs, and as he kissed her, he ran his hand from her breasts to her stomach and lower, cupping her, touching her lightly at first. She was so slick and hot, it was dizzying. She opened herself to him, lifting her hips and pushing his exploring fingers more deeply inside her.

"I think now would be a very good time for you to lose the briefs," she breathed, tugging at his waistband.

He helped her peel them off, and she sighed her approval. He shut his eyes as her hand closed around him.

"I guess you don't scare easily," he murmured.

"I'm terrified," she told him, lowering her head and kissing him.

Her mouth was warm and wet and so soft, and sheer pleasure made fireworks of color explode behind his closed eyes.

And Lucky couldn't wait. He pulled her beneath him, cradling himself between her legs, his body so beyond ready for her that he was trembling.

Condom. Man, he'd nearly forgotten the condom. He reached for it on the bedside table, where she'd put it, tearing open the wrapper as he rolled off her and quickly covered himself.

But he didn't get a chance to roll back on top of her, because Syd straddled him. With one smooth move, she drove him deeply inside her.

If he'd been prone to heart attacks, he'd be a dead man.

Fortunately, his heart was healthy despite the fact it was going at about four hundred beats per minute.

Wild, she'd said. Passionate. Delirious…

Lucky couldn't tell where he ended and Syd began. They moved together, perfectly in sync, kissing, touching, breathing.

Delicious, savage, pounding…

He rolled them both over so that he was on top, so that he had control of their movement. He moved faster and harder and she liked it all, her body straining to meet him, to take him even more deeply inside her, her kisses feeding his fire.

He was slick with sweat, her body plastered exquisitely to him as they rolled once more, bringing Syd back on top. She pushed herself up so she sat astride him, her breasts glistening with perspiration, her damp hair clinging to her face as she threw her head back and laughed.

She looked down at him. "Is it just me, or is this amazingly, incredibly good?"

"Good," he managed to say. "Amazingly..."

She was moving slowly now, and each stroke took him closer and closer to the edge.

She was smiling at him, and he reached up and touched her, her face, her throat, her breasts, and he felt the start of her release. She held his gaze and breathed his name on a low, throaty sob of air that was without a doubt the sexiest sound he'd ever heard.

He pulled her close and kissed her as his own release rocketed through him.

It was heart-stopping. It *was* brain-melting. It was rapture and ecstasy.

But it wasn't sex.

It was making love, because, damn it, he was in love with her.

Chapter 12

"Nothing's changed," Luke said, tracing circles around her belly button, head propped up on one elbow as he and Syd lay among his rumpled sheets.

They'd slept for about five hours, and the sun was high in the sky. Luke had put in a call to the hospital—nothing had changed with Lucy's condition, either.

"I really don't want to use you as bait," he continued. "I honestly don't think I can do it, Syd."

His hair was charmingly rumpled, and for the first time since they'd met, he was in need of a shave. It was amazing, really, but not entirely unexpected—even his stubble was golden.

She touched his chin, ran her thumb across his incredible lips. "So what do we do?"

"Pretend to break up."

"Pretend?" she asked, praying that he wouldn't be able to tell that her heart was in her throat. She couldn't bear to look at him.

"I don't want this to end," he told her. "But I need you to be safe."

It was an excuse. Had to be. Because, like he'd said, nothing really had changed. Breaking up with him wouldn't make her any safer.

"Look," she said, pulling away from him and covering herself with the sheet. She tried hard to keep her voice light. "I think it's pretty obvious that neither of us expected this to happen. We've had a tough couple of days and things just kind of got out of hand and—"

Luke laughed in disbelief. "Is that really what you think this was? Things getting out of hand?"

Syd staunchly forced herself to meet his gaze. "Wasn't it?"

"No," he said flatly. "And as far as neither of us expecting this, well, *I* sure as hell did. I planned for it. I counted on it. I *wanted* it." He kissed her hard, on the mouth. "I wanted you. I *still* want you. But more than that, I want you to be safe."

Syd was dizzy. "You *planned*..."

"I've been hot for you for weeks, baby cakes."

"We've only known each other a few weeks."

"Exactly."

Syd was looking into his eyes, and she believed him. My God, she really believed him. *I've been hot for you for weeks....* She had no idea. Except for all the times he'd kissed her. Playing the pretend girlfriend game, he'd called it. Those kisses had seemed so real.

"I thought you were making up some stupid excuse to break up because you didn't want me around," she admitted. "I thought..."

He knew what she'd thought. "That this was just a one-nighter?" He flopped back on the pillows, staring up at the ceiling. "You honestly thought I'd do that to you? After you told me about...the football player who shall remain nameless because the mere mention of his name enrages me?''

''Well...''

He lifted his head to look at her, his eyes suddenly sharp. ''Did *you* mean for this to be a one-nighter?''

''I didn't think it would ever really happen,'' she told him honestly. ''I mean, until it was happening, and then...'' She didn't know what to tell him. ''We probably shouldn't have done this, because it's really going to screw up our friendship. You know, I really like you, Luke. I mean, as a friend...''

Oh, brother, could she sound any more stupid? And she was lying, too, by great big omission. Yeah, she really liked him as a friend, but she loved him as a lover, too.

Loved.

L-O-V-E-D.

As in, here, take my heart and crush it into a thousand tiny pieces. As in, here, take my heart and leave me here, emotionally bleeding to death as you move on to bigger and better things. As in, here, take my heart even though you don't really want it.

It was stupid, really. *She* was stupid. She'd realized it when she was having sex with the guy. The fact that she *was* having sex with the guy should have been a dead giveaway that she'd fallen for him in the first place. But, no, she had been too dumb to realize that those warm feelings she felt every time she looked at Luke O'Donlon were far more than feelings of friendship.

She'd gone and let herself fall in love with a Ken doll. Except, Luke wasn't really plastic. He was real, and he was perfect. Well, not *perfect* perfect, but perfect for *her.* Perfect except for the fact that he didn't do serious—he'd warned her about that himself—and that his usual girl-friends had had larger bra sizes back when they were twelve than Syd had now.

Perfect except for the fact that, if she let him, he *would*

crush her heart into a thousand tiny pieces. Not intention-
ally. But it didn't have to be intentional to hurt.

"I like you, too," he told her quietly. "But as more than
a friend. *Way* more."

When he said things like that, lying back in his bed,
naked and gorgeous, all blue eyes and golden hair and tan
skin, it was like playing her older sister's Mystery Date
game and opening the door to the picture of the perfect,
blond, tuxedo-clad young Mr. Right. It was like finding the
"win a free year's supply" coupon in her bag of M&M's.
It was like living the perfect Hollywood movie, the kind of
romantic comedy that ended with two complete opposites
in each other's arms, locked in a kiss. The kind of romantic
comedy that ended way before the divorce two years later.

Divorce. God, what was she thinking? It wasn't as if
Luke had asked her to marry him. There was a long, long
road between, "Honey, I like you as more than a friend,"
and "Will you marry me?"

Syd cleared her throat. "It won't make any difference if
we pretend to break up," she told him, "because our guy
has gone after ex-girlfriends, too, remember? He's not
picky. I wouldn't be any safer."

"You would be if you left town," he countered.

She was dumbstruck. "You want me to leave town?"

"Yeah." He was serious.

"No. No way. Absolutely not." Syd couldn't sit still, so
she leapt out of bed. "I'm part of this task force, part of
your team, remember?"

She was standing there naked, glaring at him, and she
grabbed the sheet from the bed and wrapped it around herself.

Luke was trying not to smile. "I don't know," he said.
"The argumentative stance worked better for me without
the sheet."

"Don't change the subject, because I'm not leaving."

"Syd, baby, I've been trying to think of another way this could work and—"

"Don't you dare *baby* me! Sheesh, sleep with a guy once, and he thinks he's got the right to tell you what to do! Sleep with a guy once, and suddenly you're in Patronizing City! I'm *not* leaving town, *Luke, baby,* so just forget about it!"

"All right!" His temper snapped, too, and he sat forward, the muscles in his shoulders taut as he pushed himself up. "Great. I'll forget about it. I'll forget about the fact that the thought of you ending up in a hospital bed in a coma like Lucy is making me *freaking crazy!*"

He was serious. He really was scared to death for her. As Syd gazed into his eyes, her anger instantly deflated. She sat on the edge of the bed, wishing she could compromise, but knowing that this was one fight she had to win.

"I'm sorry," she said, reaching for him. "But I can't leave, Luke. This story is too important to me."

"Is it really worth risking your life?"

She touched his hair, his shoulder, traced the definition of the powerful muscles in his arm. "You're a fine one to talk about risking your life and whether a job is worth it."

"I'm trained for it," he said. "You're not. You're a writer."

She met his gaze. "And what if I never wrote anything that I thought was important? What if I always played it safe? I could be very safe, you know, and write copy for the back of cereal boxes. Do you really think that's what I should do for the rest of my life?"

It was hard for him, but he shook his head, no.

"I have a great opportunity here," she told him. "There's a job I really, really want as an editor and staff writer of a magazine I really, *really admire. Think* Magazine."

"I've never heard of it," Luke admitted.

"It's targeted to young women," Syd told him, "as kind

of an alternative to all those fashion magazines that tell you that you need to make yourself beautiful and thin if you want to win Mr. Right's heart—and also send you the message that you'll never be beautiful enough or thin enough.''

''Is that your dream job?'' he asked. ''To write for this magazine?''

''My *dream* job is to write a book. I'd love to be able to afford to take a year or two and try writing fiction,'' she admitted. ''But at the rate I'm saving, I'm going to be ninety before that happens. I either have to win the lottery or find a patron. And the odds of either of those things happening is like four billion to one. This job with *Think* is the next best thing.'' They'd somehow gotten off the topic. ''This story,'' Syd said, steering them back onto track, ''when I write it, is going to help me get that job. But that's just part of why I don't want to leave, Luke. You need to understand—the other part is intensely personal. The other part comes from knowing that I can help catch this guy. *I can help!*''

''You've already helped,'' he told her.

''If I leave, you're back to square one. You've got to start from scratch. Establish a new relationship—with whom, Luke? Some policewoman? You don't think that would look really suspicious? You don't think this guy pays attention to things like that? A guy who probably follows his victim around for days, searching for patterns, learning her schedule, watching for times when she's all alone…?''

She had him, and she knew it, as he flopped back onto the bed, put his arm over his eyes and swore.

''He's probably too smart, too suspicious to come near me anyway,'' she told him.

He lifted his arm to look at her. ''You don't believe that any more than I do.'' He reached for her, pulling her close, holding her tightly. ''Promise me you won't go *any*where by yourself. Promise you'll always make sure someone from the team is watching you."

"I promise," Syd said.

"I'm talking about running down to the convenience store for some milk. It doesn't happen until we catch this guy, do you understand? I'm either right here, right next to you, or Bobby's breathing down your neck."

"I got it," Syd said. "Although, personally, I'd prefer *you* breathing down my neck."

"That can definitely be arranged." He kissed her, hard. "You *will* be safe. I'm going to make *damn* sure of it."

He kissed her again—her throat, her breasts, her stomach, moving even lower, his breath hot against her skin. That wasn't her neck he was breathing down, but Syd didn't bother to tell him. She figured he probably knew.

She closed her eyes, losing herself in the torrents of pleasure that rushed past her, over her, through her. Pleasure and emotion—thick, rich, *deep* emotion that surrounded her completely and made her feel as if she were drowning.

When it came to the things Luke O'Donlon could make her feel, she was in way over her head.

Sounds of laughter rang from Lucy McCoy's hospital room.

Hope expanded inside Lucky as he ran the last few steps and pushed open the door and...

He stopped short, and Syd, who was right behind him, bumped into him.

Lucy still lay motionless in her hospital bed, breathing with the help of a respirator.

But she was surrounded by her friends. The room was filled with women. Veronica Catalanotto sat by Lucy's bed and held her hand. Mia Francisco sat nearby, using her enormously rounded belly as a table for a bowl of raw vegetables, her legs propped up on another chair. Melody Jones, Cowboy's wife, was perched on the windowsill, her feet bare, next to Mitch Shaw's wife, Becca, who'd kept on her cowboy boots. It figured they'd sit together, be close friends. They both looked like something out of a very wholesome country music video.

Melody waved at him. "Hey, Lucky. I was just telling Wes that my sister, Brittany, came out here with me. She and Andy, my nephew, are watching the kids, so that Ronnie and I can both be here. I was just suggesting that as long as Brittany's in town, we try to set her up with Wesley."

Lucky realized that Wes Skelly was in the room, too, sitting on the floor by Lucy's bed, next to Nell Hawken, Crash's wife. They both had their backs to the wall.

Wes rolled his eyes. "Why is it always me?" he complained. "Why don't you women torment Bobby for a change?"

"For a change?" Bobby deadpanned. He was there, too, sitting cross-legged in front of young Tasha, who was putting his long black hair into dozens of braids of varying sizes.

There was more laughter, and Veronica leaned over Lucy, as if she were hoping for something. A smile. A movement. A twitch. She looked up, caught Lucky watching her and shook her head. Nothing. The strain that was just below the surface on all of their faces showed through at the tight edges of her mouth.

But she forced a smile. "Hey, Lucy, Lucky's here with Syd." She looked around the room. "Who here hasn't met Sydney Jameson? Brace yourself, ladies, no fainting please, I know we all thought it would never happen, but our Luke has been smitten at last. Syd's moving in with him."

The noise of all those female voices talking at once as introductions were made and congratulations given—along with hugs and kisses—should have been enough to wake the dead, but Lucy still didn't move.

And Syd was embarrassed. Lucky met her eyes, and

knew exactly what she was thinking. The moving in to-gether thing wasn't real. It was part of the girlfriend game. Despite the fact that their relationship had become intimate, he *hadn't* asked her to move in with him.

And she hadn't accepted.

He tried to imagine asking such a thing. How did a man go about it? It wasn't a marriage proposal, so there wasn't any need to get down on your knees, was there? Would you do it casually? While you were making dinner? Or maybe over breakfast? "Hey, babe, by the way…it's oc-curred to me that as long as you're here all the time…"

It didn't seem very romantic, far more like a convenience than a commitment.

PJ Becker stuck her head in the door. "O'Donlon. About time you graced us with your appearance. Anyone in here given him a sit-rep yet?"

"Situation report," Tasha told Syd. "They talk in code, but don't worry. You'll learn it in no time."

"Well, I found out that Melody wants to set Wes up with her sister," Lucky said to PJ, "but I doubt that's what you meant."

"Mitch left last night," Mitch's wife Becca said quietly. "As soon as Admiral Robinson called. He's going to find Blue, and send him back here, but it's probably going to take some time."

"We've decided to take turns sitting with Lucy," Ve-ronica reported. "One of us is going to be here around the clock until Blue gets back. We've worked out a schedule."

"Her doctor said it was good if we talked to her and held her hand—tried to establish some kind of contact," Nell Hawken, Crash's wife, blond and delicately pretty, added. "We thought we'd try getting together—all of us, like this—in the early evening, right before dinnertime. We figured we'd have sort of a party, tell stories and talk—see if maybe Lucy would want to wake up and join us."

"So far it hasn't worked," Mia said, "but we've just got

to be patient. The doctor said the procedure they did to relieve the pressure from the subdural injury has made the swelling go down significantly. That's a good sign.''

It was amazing. Lucky was standing in a room filled with beautiful women—the wives of some of his best friends in the world. He'd had crushes on most of them at one time or another, and he'd never dated anyone—even the illustrious Miss Georgia—that he didn't compare to them and find lacking.

Until now.

Until Syd, with her sleek dark hair, and her heart-shaped face. He'd made her wear another of his shirts today—one that was missing the top two buttons, and the collar gapped open, revealing her throat and her incredibly delicate collarbones.

But the truth was, it wasn't her body that put her into the same league as these incomparable women he adored. It was her sense of humor, her sharp wit, her brilliance—all of which shone clearly through in her incredible smile and her amazing brown eyes.

Across the room, Melody Jones slid down off the windowsill, slipping her feet into a pair of sneakers. ''I better get back. Tyler's probably driving my sister nuts.'' She looked at Veronica. ''Take your time coming over, Ron. Frankie will be fine. In fact, he can just spend the night in the baby's room, if you want.''

''Thanks,'' Veronica said. ''That would be great.''

Melody turned to Becca. ''You don't need a ride, right? You've got your own car…?''

On the other side of the room, Nell stood up and stretched. ''I've got to go, too. I'll be back tomorrow, Lucy.''

''Whoa,'' Lucky said, blocking the door. ''Wait a minute. Where are you going?''

''Home,'' they said in unison.

''No, you're not,'' he said. ''There's no way in *hell* I'm

letting *any* of you just go home. You're all potential targets. You're not walking out of here without protection."

Melody looked at Veronica. Veronica looked at Nell and Becca. Mia stood up gracefully—no small feat—and they all turned to look at her.

"He's right," she said.

God, it was a logistical nightmare. All these women going in all these different directions....

Melody didn't look convinced. "It's not like I'm alone at home. My sister and the kids are there."

"And *I* certainly don't need protection," PJ added.

"My ranch is *way* out of town," Becca said. "I'm not really worried."

Mutiny. No way was he going to let them mutiny. Lucky bristled, ready to let them know in no uncertain terms that they were *all,* star FInCOM agent PJ Becker included, going to follow the law that he was about to lay down.

But Syd put her hand on his arm.

"*I'm* worried," she said to the other women. She looked down at Lucy, lying there so still and silent in that bed. "And I'm betting that if Lucy really can hear everything we're saying, that *she's* worried, too."

She leaned over the bed. "This would be a really perfect time for you to wake up, detective," she continued, "because your friends need a crash course in exactly who this monster is we're all up against. Of course, if you don't mind, I can speak for you. I saw the way he came into your house through a locked living-room window—the way he bypassed your fancy alarm system."

Syd looked up, looked directly at Melody. "I saw the blood in your bed and on your bedroom wall—your blood."

She looked at Becca and her voice shook. "I saw the second-story window you dove through, risking a broken neck from the fall, because you knew that if he got his hands around your throat again, he *would* kill you."

She looked at PJ through the tears that brimmed in her eyes. Her voice was just a whisper now. "And I saw the gun you kept just under your bed, thinking that it—and your training as a police detective—made you safe. The gun you never even got a chance to use."

The room was dead silent.

Syd looked around at all of them. "If you're still not worried, think about your husbands. Think about the men who love you receiving the same awful message that Blue McCoy's going to get in just a few days, in just a few hours. Think about Blue, finding out that he may have lost Lucy forever."

"Oh, my God," Veronica breathed. "Lucy just squeezed my hand!"

Chapter 13

Syd paced.

And when she looked at the clock again, it was only six minutes past one—just two minutes later than it had been the *last* time she'd looked.

Luke's house was so silent.

Except, that is, for the booming sound of her pounding heart.

This must be the way it felt to be a worm, stuck on the end of a fishing hook. Or a mouse slipped into a snake trap.

Of course, Luke and Bobby and Thomas and Rio and Mike were hidden in the yard. They were watching all sides of the house, and listening in via strategically placed microphones.

"Damn," she said aloud. "I wish these mikes were two-way. I could use a little heated debate right about now, guys. Fight, flee or surrender. I realized there was an option we haven't discussed—hide. Anyone for *hide?* I'm telling you, those are some really tough choices. Right now it's all I can do to choose between Rocky Road or Fudge Ripple.''

The phone rang.

Syd swore. ''All right,'' she said as it rang again. ''I know.'' She wasn't supposed to watch TV or listen to music. Or talk. They couldn't hear potential sounds of forced entry if she was talking. ''Roger that, Lieutenant O'Donlon. I'll behave, I promise.''

The phone stopped right in the middle of the third ring.

And Syd was alone once again with the silence.

The past few days had been crazy. Luke had worked around the clock to set up a safe house for the wives of the SEALs who were out of town. He and PJ Becker had organized teams of security guards and drivers who would take the women to and from the hospital and wherever else they needed to go. After Syd's little speech at the hospital, no one was complaining.

Luke also rode the police and FInCOM, trying to get them to work faster in picking up the men who were on the likely suspects list Lucy had helped compile. So far, they'd only picked up six of the men on the list—most of whom had had strong alibis for a good number of the attacks. The others had willingly volunteered to submit DNA samples, and so far, none had matched.

Luke also gave interviews to TV reporters, looking splendid in his gleaming white Navy Ken uniform, saying things guaranteed to enrage—or at least annoy—the man they were after. Come and get me, he all but said. Just *try* to come and get me or mine.

He sat by Lucy's bed and held her hand, hoping that Blue would be found soon, and praying with the rest of them that that single hand-squeeze hadn't been just a muscle spasm—the explanation the doctors had offered.

At night, he'd kiss Syd goodbye with real trepidation in his eyes and he'd leave her alone, pretending to help with BUD/S training, but in truth sneaking back to help guard her as she sat here in silence and alone—as serial rapist bait.

At 1:30 or 2:00 a.m., he'd return through the front door and fell into bed, completely exhausted.

But never too exhausted to make exquisite love to her.

The phone rang. Syd nearly jumped through the roof, then instantly berated herself. It wasn't as if the San Felipe Rapist were going to call her on the phone, was it?

She glanced again at the clock. It was quarter after one in the morning. It had to be Lucky. Or Bobby. Or maybe it was Veronica, calling from the hospital with news about Lucy.

Please, God, let it be good news.

It rang again, and she picked it up. "Hello?"

"Syd." The voice was low and male and unrecognizable.

"I'm sorry," she said briskly. "Who's—"

"Is Lucky there?"

The hair on the back of her neck went up. Dear God, what if it *were* the rapist, calling to make sure she was alone?

"No, sorry." She kept her voice steady. "He's teaching tonight. Who's calling?"

"It's Wes."

Chief Wes Skelly. That information didn't make her feel any better. In fact, it made her even more tense. Wes—who smelled just like the man who'd nearly run her down on the stairs after brutally attacking Gina. Wes—who had the same hair, same build, same accentless voice. Wes, who was—according to Bobby—having a rough year.

How rough, exactly?

Rough enough to completely lose it? Rough enough to turn into a homicidal maniac?

"Are you safe there, all by yourself?" Wes asked. He sounded odd, possibly drunk.

"I don't know," she said. "Maybe you should tell me."

"No," he said. "No, you're not safe. Why don't you go to this safe house thing and stay with Ronnie and Melody?"

"I think you probably know why I'm not there." Syd's heart was pounding again. She knew Luke didn't believe Wes could be the attacker, but she didn't have years of camaraderie to go on. Frankly, Wes Skelly spooked her, with his barbed-wire tattoo and his crew-cut hair. Whenever she saw him, he was grimly quiet, always watching, rarely smiling.

"What?" he said. "You *wanna* go one on one with this guy?" He laughed. "Figures a woman who thinks she's going to get any kind of commitment from Lucky O'Donlon's a little wacky in the head."

"Hey," she said indignantly. "I resent that—"

He hung up abruptly, and she swore. So much for keeping her cool, keeping him talking, for coaxing a confession out of him.

"Luke, that was Wes on the phone," she told the listening microphones as she dropped the receiver into the cradle on the wall. "He was looking for you, and he sounded really strange."

Silence.

The entire house was silent.

The phone didn't ring again, nothing moved, nothing made a sound.

If this were a movie, Syd thought, the camera would cut to the outside of the house, to the places where Luke and Bobby and the SEAL candidates were completely hidden. And the camera would reveal their unconscious faces and the ropes that bound them—that would keep them from coming to her rescue when she needed them.

And she *would* need them.

The camera would pull back to show the shadowy shape of a very muscular man with Wes's short hair, with Wes's wide shoulders, creeping across the yard, toward the house.

Bad image. *Bad* image. Syd shook her head, cleared her throat. "Um, Luke, I'm a little spooked, will you please call me?"

Silence.

The phone didn't ring. She stared at it, and it *still* didn't ring.

"Luke, I'm sorry about this, but I'm serious," Syd said. "I just need to know that you're out there and—"

She heard it. A scuffling noise out back.

Flee.

The urge to run was intense, and she scurried for the living room. But the front door was bolted shut—for her own protection—and she didn't have the key. Last night that bolt had made her feel safe. Now it didn't. Now she was trapped.

"I hear a noise outside, guys," she said, praying that she was wrong, that Luke was still listening in. "Out back. Please be listening."

The front windows were painted shut, and the glass looked impossibly thick. How had Lucy managed to break through her bedroom window?

She heard the noise again, closer to the back door this time. "Someone's definitely out there."

Fight.

She turned around in a full circle, looking for something, *any*thing with which to arm herself. Luke didn't have a fireplace, so there were no fireplace pokers. There was nothing, *nothing.* Only a newspaper she could roll up. Perfect—provided the attacker was a bad dog.

"Any time, Luke," she said. *"Please."*

Baseball bat. Luke had told her he'd played in high school, that he still sometimes went over to the batting cages on the west side of San Felipe.

He didn't have a garage, didn't have a basement. Where would a guy without those things keep a baseball bat?

Front closet.

Syd scrambled for the closet, threw open the door.

It was filled with U.S. Navy-issue overcoats of all weights and sizes. She pushed through to the back and found...

Fishing poles.

And lacrosse sticks.

A set of lawn darts.

And three different baseball bats.

She grabbed one as she heard the kitchen door creak open.

Hide.

Hiding suddenly seemed the most intelligent option, and she slipped into the closet, silently closing the door behind her.

Her palms were sweating, and her mouth was dry, and her heart was beating so loudly she couldn't hear anything else.

She gripped the baseball bat as tightly as she could and prayed. Please God, whatever happened to her, don't let Luke be badly hurt. Don't let them find him hidden in the backyard, with his throat slit, staring sightlessly up at the sky and...

Whoever was inside the house wasn't trying to be quiet anymore. Footsteps went down the hall toward the bedroom, and then faster, heading back. She heard the bathroom door slam open, heard, "Syd? *Syd!*"

It was Luke. That was Luke's voice. Relief made her knees give out, and she sat down hard, right there in the closet, knocking over fishing poles and lacrosse sticks and God knows what else.

The closet door was yanked open and there was Luke. The panic in his eyes would have been sweet if her relief hadn't morphed instantly into anger.

"What the hell did you think you were doing?" She nearly came out of the closet swinging that bat. "You damn near scared me to *death!*"

"I scared *you?*" He was just as mad as she was. "God, Syd, I came in here and you were gone! I thought—"

"You should have called me, told me you would be here early," she said accusingly.

"It's not *that* early," he countered. "It's nearly oh-one-thirty. What's early about that?"

It was. The clock on the VCR said 1:27.

"But..." Syd regrouped, thinking fast. Why had she been so frightened? She pointed toward the kitchen. "You came in through the back door. You always come in through the front—which was locked with a deadbolt, you genius! If you *had* been the San Felipe Rapist, I would have been trapped!"

She had him with that one. It stopped him cold and doused his anger. He looked at the lock on the door and then at her. She could see him absorbing the baseball bat that still dangled from her hand. She watched him notice the fact that she was still shaking, notice the tears that were threatening to spill from her eyes.

Damn it, she *wasn't* going to cry in front of him.

"My God," he said. "You don't have a key? Why the hell don't you have a key?"

Syd shook her head, unable to say anything, using all her energy to keep from crying.

Luke *wasn't* lying dead in the backyard. Thank God.

Frowning, he looked down at his belt, and pulled his cell phone free. It was shaking silently. He flipped it open, switched it on. "O'Donlon." He listened then said, "Yeah. We're both okay. She got..." He looked at her.

"Scared," Syd said, shakily lowering herself onto the couch. "I was scared. You can say it. I admit it."

"She didn't know it was me coming in," Luke said into his phone, "and she opted for the *hide* solution to the nightmare scenario." He looked at the baseball bat. "With maybe a little *fight* thrown in." He took a deep breath, running his other hand back through his hair, making it stand on end. "I came in, couldn't find her and—" He froze. He stood absolutely, completely still. "It's not?"

Syd's pulse was just starting to drop below one hundred, but something in his voice made it kick into higher gear again. "What's not?" she asked.

Luke turned to look at her. "Thomas says he heard your requests for a phone call, but that he couldn't get through. He said he called twice before he realized he couldn't hear the phone ringing over the microphones. Something's wrong with the phone."

Syd stared at him. "I got a phone call just a few minutes ago. Wes called, looking for you."

"Wes called *here?*"

"Yeah," Syd said. "Didn't you hear at least my side of the conversation?"

"I must've been already circling back," he said, "driving home—pretending I was coming from the base." He held out his hand to her. "Come here. I want you near me until we check this out."

Syd took his hand and he pulled her up from the couch as he spoke to Thomas once again. "Stay in position. Full alert. I want eyes open and brains working."

"This is probably nothing," he said to Syd, but she knew he didn't believe that.

The lights were still on in the kitchen. Everything looked completely normal. There were a few dirty dishes in the sink, a newspaper open to the sports page on the kitchen table.

As Syd watched, Luke picked up the telephone and put the receiver to his ear.

He looked at Syd as he hung it up, as he spoke once more to Thomas over his cell phone. "Phone's dead. Stay in position. I'm calling for backup."

A clean cut.
Probably with a knife, possibly with a scissors.

Lucky sat on his living-room sofa, trying to rub away his massive headache by massaging his forehead.

It wasn't working.

Somehow, someone had gotten close enough to the house tonight to cut the phone wire. Somehow, the son of a bitch had gotten past two experienced Navy SEALs and three bright, young SEAL candidates who had been looking for him.

He hadn't gone inside, but his message had been clear.

He could have.

He'd been right there, just on the other side of a wall from Sydney. If he'd wanted to, he could've gone in, used that knife to kill her as dead as the phone and been gone before Lucky had ever reached the back door.

The thought made him sick to his stomach.

As the FInCOM and police members of the task force filtered through his house, Lucky sat with Syd on the couch, his arm securely around her shoulder—he didn't give a damn who saw.

"I'm sorry," he told her for the fourteenth time. "I've been trying to figure out how he got past us."

"It's all right," she said.

"No, it's not." He shook his head. "We were distracted pretty much all night. It started around oh-dark-fifty when Bobby got a page from Lana Quinn. She sent him an urgent code, so he called her back. The rest of us were watching the house—it should have been no big deal. So Bob calls Lana, who tells him that Wes just came by her place, completely skunked. Wes told her he needed to talk, but then left without saying anything. She managed to get his keys away from him, but he walked to a nearby bar—a place called Dandelion's. She followed because she was worried, and sure enough, as soon as he got there, he tried to start a bar fight. She stepped in and he backed down, but he wouldn't leave with her. So she called Bobby."

Lucky sighed. "Bobby called Frisco, but he's got Mia

and Tasha to worry about, he can't just leave them home alone. Meanwhile, it's getting later and later. Lana's paging Bobby again, telling him she lost Wes in the crowd at Dandelion's, and now she's not sure *where* he's gone and—''

"Wait a minute," Syd said. "Lana *lost* Wes?"

"Well, no, not really," Lucky told her. "She thought she'd lost him for about twenty minutes, but he was only in the men's."

"He was in the men's room for twenty minutes?"

Lucky bristled. "No," he said. "I know what you're implying and *no*."

She held his gaze. "Dandelion's is only about a four-minute drive from here."

"Wes is not a suspect."

"I'm sorry, Luke, but he's still on *my* list."

"Lana took the keys to his bike."

"A clever move," she countered. "Particularly if he wanted to establish an alibi and convince everyone that he'd actually been in the men's room for all that time—instead of here at your house, at the exact time your phone wire was cut during a distraction that he knew about."

Lucky shook his head. "No," he said. "Syd, you've got to go with me on this one. It's *not* Wes. It can't be. You've got to trust me."

She gazed at him, looking into his eyes. She'd been scared tonight, badly. When she'd come out of that closet, that was the closest Lucky had ever seen her come to losing it. She was tough, she was strong, she was smart and she was as afraid of all this as he was. And that made her desire to catch this bastard that much crazier. Crazier and completely admirable.

She nodded. "Okay," she said. "If you're that certain…he's off my list. It's not Wes."

She wasn't humoring him, wasn't being patronizing. She was accepting—on faith—something that he believed in absolutely. She trusted him that much. It was a remarkably good feeling. *Remarkably* good.

Lucky kissed her. Right in front of the task force, in front of Chief Zale.

"Tomorrow," he said, "I'll talk to Wes. See if he wouldn't mind voluntarily giving us a DNA sample, just so we can run it by the lab and then officially take him off the suspect list."

"I don't need you to do that," she said.

"I know." He kissed her again, trying to make light of it despite the tight feeling that was filling his chest from the inside out. "Pissing off Wes Skelly while he's got a killer hangover isn't my idea of fun. But hey, I don't have anything else to do tomorrow."

"Tomorrow," Syd reminded him, "your sister's getting married."

Chapter 14

Luke O'Donlon cried at his little sister's wedding.

It wasn't a surprise to Syd. In fact, she would have been surprised if he *hadn't* cried.

He looked incredible in his dress uniform—nearly as good, in fact, as he looked naked.

Ellen, his sister, was as dramatically gorgeous as he was, except while he was golden, she was dark-haired and mocha-skinned. Her new husband, Gregory Price, however, was completely average looking, completely normal—right down to his slightly thinning hair and the glasses.

Syd stood at the edge of the restaurant dance floor, one of a very small number of relatives and intimate friends of the bride and groom, and watched as the newlyweds danced.

Greg made Syd feel slightly better about herself. If he could dare to *marry* Ellen, then Syd—also extremely average looking—could certainly have a fling with Luke.

"Have I told you how incredibly beautiful you look tonight?"

Syd turned around to give Luke an arched eyebrow. "That's slinging it a little thick, don't you think?"

She knew what she looked like. Her dress was black and basic, and yes, maybe it did hide her imperfections and accentuate the better parts of her figure, but it was a simple illusion. And yes, she *had* taken time with her hair and had even put on a little makeup this evening, but she was, at best, interestingly pretty. Passable. Acceptable. But not even remotely close to *incredibly* anything, particularly not beautiful.

Luke actually looked surprised. "You think I'm—" He caught himself, and laughed. "Uh-uh," he said. "Nope. No way. I'm not going to let you pick a fight with me over the fact that I think you look great."

He pulled her close and kissed her, surprising her by giving her a private kiss instead of a public one. It was one of those kisses that melted her bones, turned her to jelly, and left her dizzy, dazed and clinging to him. It was one of those kisses he gave her before he scooped her into his arms and carried her into his bedroom. It was one of those kisses he gave her when he wanted them to stop talking and start communicating in an entirely different manner. It was one of those kisses she could never, ever resist.

"I think you look incredibly beautiful tonight," he murmured into her ear. "Now what *you* do, is *you* say, thank you, Luke."

"Thank you, Luke," she managed.

"Was that so hard?"

He was smiling down at her, with his heavenly blue eyes and his gorgeous face and his sunstreaked hair. *He* was the one who was incredibly beautiful. It seemed impossible that the heated look in his eyes could be real, but it was. He'd somehow pulled her onto the dance floor, and as they moved slowly in time to the music, he was holding her close enough for her to know that that kiss had done the exact opposite of turning *him* to jelly.

He wanted her.

At least for now.

"You two are so perfect together." Gregory's mother, platinum-haired, rail-thin, with a smile as warm as her son's, winked as she danced past them. "We'll be dancing at *your* wedding next, won't we, Luke?"

Oh, God. How embarrassing. Syd kept her own smile pasted on as she quickly answered for Luke, saving him— and saving herself from having to listen to him stammer and choke on his hasty negative response.

"I'm afraid it's a little too soon for that kind of prediction, Mrs. Price," she called to the other woman. "Luke and I haven't really known each other for *that* long."

"Well, it's my son's wedding, and I'm predicting wonderful things for everyone," Mrs. Price enthused. "And my predictions usually do come true."

"In that case," Syd murmured to Luke as the older woman moved out of earshot, trying to turn this into a total joke, "maybe she could predict a lottery win for me. I could really use the cash. My car's in serious need of a complete overhaul."

As she'd hoped, Luke laughed.

Crisis averted, thank God. There was nothing that created tension quite like bringing up the subject of marriage with a man who, like Luke, was commitment-shy.

Syd didn't want him looking at her and feeling the walls closing in. She didn't want him to assume that just because she was female, she wouldn't be able to resist thinking about fairy-tale endings with wedding bells and happily-ever-afters. She didn't want him thinking that *she* was even *remotely* thinking about such an impossibility as marriage.

Marriage. Syd and Luke, *married?*

It was absurd.

It was insane.

It was…

Something she couldn't keep herself from thinking about. Especially not today.

There'd been a message this afternoon on her answering machine. *Think* magazine had called from New York. The series of pieces she'd written on women's safety, along with her proposal for an in-depth article on catching serial criminals, had given buoyancy to the resumé she'd sent them months ago. In fact, it had floated right to the top of their pile of editorial candidates' resumés. They wanted her to come for an interview with their publisher and managing editor, Eileen Hess. Ms. Hess was going to be in Phoenix for a few days at a conference. Perhaps it would be more convenient for Syd to meet with her there, rather than flying all the way to New York? It would be more affordable for Syd, too. They were a small magazine, and unfortunately they couldn't afford to pay Syd's airfare.

Syd had called back to let them know that she wouldn't be able to leave California until the San Felipe Rapist was apprehended. She didn't know how long that would be, and if that meant she'd be out of the running for the job, she hoped they'd consider her in the future.

She'd found out they were willing to wait. She could fly to New York next week or even next month. This job was virtually in her pocket, if she wanted it.

If she wanted it.

Of *course* she wanted it.

Didn't she?

Luke kissed her neck, and she knew what she *really* wanted.

She wanted Luke, ready and willing to spend the rest of his life with her.

Talk about pipe dreams.

Her problem was that she had too vivid an imagination. It was far too easy for her to take this make-believe relationship and pretend it was something real.

Syd closed her eyes as he kissed her again, lightly this time, on the lips, and she knew what the real problem was.

Her problem was simply that she loved him. And when she was with him—which was damn near all the time—the lines between make-believe and reality began to blur.

Yes, they were lovers, but no, she hadn't really moved in with him. That was just pretend. Yes, he'd told his friends that he loved her, but he'd never said those words to her, and even if he did, she wasn't sure she'd believe him, Lothario that he was.

Yes, she was here with him at his sister's wedding, and yes, they looked like a real couple. But in truth, they were merely co-workers who had become friends—friends who had a good time together in bed.

To think anything else would be a mistake.

But, as Syd swayed to the music, held close in Luke's arms, she knew the mistake had already been made. She was in love with him. There was nothing left to do now except endure the coming pain. And, like the removal of a Band-Aid, doing it fast and getting it over with always hurt far less in the long run.

After they caught the rapist, she'd go to New York. As fast as she possibly could.

The call came as Lucky and Syd were leaving the reception.

Ellen and Gregory had left for their honeymoon and, at nearly twenty-three-hundred hours, the party was winding down.

Lucky's pager and cell phone went off simultaneously.

His first thought was a bad one—that another woman had been attacked. His second thought was that it was good news. That Lucy McCoy had come out of her coma, or that they'd found Blue and he was on his way home.

The number on the pager was Frisco's—and so was the voice on the other end of the phone.

"Hey," Frisco said. "You're there. Good news. We caught him."

It was a possibility Lucky hadn't even considered, and he nearly dropped the phone. "Repeat that."

"Martin Taus," Frisco said. "Ex-regular Navy, enlisted, served here at Coronado during the spring and summer of 1996. Discharged in late '96 with lots of little dings against him—nothing big enough to warrant a dishonorable. He served time in Nevada in early '98 for indecent exposure. He's been picked up for sexual assault at least twice before, both times he got off on a technicality. He was brought in early this evening for questioning by the San Felipe PD. He just finished making a videotaped confession about twenty minutes ago."

Syd was watching him, concern in her eyes.

"They caught the rapist," Luke told her, hardly believing it himself.

"Are they sure?" She asked the question exactly as Luke asked Frisco.

"Apparently, he's been pretty specific in describing the attacks," Frisco said. "Chief Zale's getting ready to give a press conference—just in time for the eleven o'clock news. I'm heading over to the police station. Can you meet me there?"

"I'm on my way," Lucky said, and hung up.

Syd wasn't smiling. In fact, she looked extremely skeptical. "Do they actually have evidence, tying this guy to—"

"He confessed," he told her. "Apparently in detail."

"Can we talk to him?" she asked.

"Let's go find out."

Syd turned off the videotape and went back to her laptop computer, unable to listen for another second as the man named Martin Taus described the way he'd slammed Lucy McCoy into the wall. He knew the names of all the victims, knew the extent of their injuries. He was the right height, the right size, had the right hair—a short crew cut.

After Zale's press conference, Syd and Luke had waited for hours to see Taus, only to be told that the police were limiting the people in the interview room to the three FInCOM agents from the task force. When the police had tried to take a blood sample in order to match his DNA to that left behind during the attacks, Taus had thrown a nutty. He'd threatened a lawsuit if they so much as touched one hair on his head.

Normally, the police would get a warrant to search his home and take a hair sample from his hairbrush for the DNA test. But Taus was homeless. He lived under a bridge down by the water. He didn't even own a hairbrush.

Huang, Sudenberg and Novak were in there with him now, trying to talk him into consenting to the test. Once they succeeded, there would be a wait of a number of days before the results came in. But those results, along with Martin Taus's confession, would prove his guilt beyond a shadow of a doubt. With that confession and a guilty plea, they'd skip the trial and go straight to sentencing.

Martin Taus was going to go to jail for a long, long time.

Luke looked over Syd's shoulder at her laptop's screen. She was glad she'd made him stop at home to pick it up— at *his house,* she corrected herself—before coming to the police station last night. During all this waiting, she'd written a variety of different articles, from features to hard news, on various aspects of the case.

"Don't even *think* about reading over my shoulder," she warned him, her fingers flying over the keyboard, working on her story for *Think* magazine. She'd already sent the hard news story out electronically to the *San Felipe Journal,* and they'd called to tell her it was being picked up by *USA Today.*

"So you buy it, huh?" Luke asked. "You believe this is really our guy and, just like that, it's all over?"

"It *does* seem a little anticlimactic," she had to admit. "But real life isn't always as exciting as the movies. Personally, I prefer it *this* way." She looked up at him. "Are you finally ready to go?"

He sat down wearily next to her at the interview-room table. It had been a long night, and they were both still dressed in their formal clothes despite the fact that it was well after 8:00 a.m. "Yeah, I just wanted to see him," he said. "I just wanted to be in the same room with him for a minute. I knew if I stood there long enough, they'd eventually let me in."

"And?"

"And they did. He was..." Luke shook his head. "I don't think he's our guy."

"Luke, he *confessed.*"

"*I* could confess. That wouldn't make *me* the rapist."

"Did you even *watch* the videotape? It's chilling the way he—"

"Maybe I'm wrong," he countered. "I just...there was something that wasn't right. I was standing there, right next to him, but I couldn't put my finger on it."

"Maybe it's just lack of sleep."

"I know what lack of sleep feels like and no, it's not helping that I'm tired, but there's something else wrong," he told her. "All I'm saying is that I'm not just going to go along with Zale and stamp the case file 'solved' until the DNA tests come back with a match."

Syd looked at him with dismay. "Luke, that could be days."

He gave her a very tired version of his best smile. "Guess you'll just have to stay at my place for a few more days. Too bad, huh?"

She saved her file and shut down her computer, closing it up. "Actually," she said, choosing her words carefully, "I was just thinking how convenient it was that Martin Taus picked last night to get himself caught, because now

I can take advantage of a really excellent opportunity and drive out to Phoenix for a job interview.''

He sat back in his chair, his mouth dropping open. ''Since when have you been thinking about moving to Phoenix? To *Arizona*?''

''The interview's in Phoenix,'' she told him. ''The job's in New York. Remember? *Think* magazine. I told you I'd sent them my resumé for a position as an editor and staff writer.''

''New York?'' He swore. ''Syd, that's worse than Phoenix! You didn't say a thing about New York!''

''Well, where did you think a job like that would be?''

''Here,'' he said. ''I thought it would be here. San Diego, maybe. God, Syd, *New York*? Do you really want to live in New York?''

''Yeah,'' she said. ''I do.''

It wasn't really lying. Because she didn't really care where she lived. Her options had been split into only two possibilities. *With Luke* was her real first choice, but completely unrealistic. And everywhere else in the world fell under the heading *without Luke*. Everywhere else was exactly the same. New York, San Diego, Chicago. They would all *feel* exactly the same—lonely as hell, at least for a while.

''Wow,'' Luke said, rubbing his eyes. ''I'm stunned. I'm…'' He shook his head. ''Here I was thinking, I don't know, maybe that we had something here that was worth spending some time on.''

Syd couldn't keep from laughing. ''Luke. Get real. We both know exactly what we've got going. It's fun, it's great, but it's not serious. You told me yourself—you don't do serious.''

''Well…what if I've changed my mind?''

''What if you only *think* you've changed your mind?'' she countered gently. ''And what if I give up a great career move—something I've worked for and wanted for *years*—and your 'what if' turns out to be wrong?''

He cleared his throat. ''I was thinking, um, maybe you really could move in with me.''

Syd couldn't believe it. Luke wanted her to move in with him? Mr. I'm-never-serious? For a nanosecond, she let herself believe it was possible.

But then he winced, giving himself away. He didn't really want her to move in with him. He just wasn't used to being the one in a relationship who got dumped. It was a competitive thing. He was grabbing on to anything—no matter how stupid an idea it was in reality—in order to keep her around temporarily, in order to win.

But once he had her, he'd soon tire of her. And she'd move out. Maybe not right away, but eventually. And then she'd be in Coronado without Luke.

The job in New York wouldn't keep her warm at night, but neither would Luke after they'd split up.

''I think,'' Syd said slowly, ''that a decision of that magnitude deserves a massive amount of thought. On both our parts.''

''I've thought about it some,'' Luke said, ''and I know it's not…perfect, but—''

''Think again,'' Syd said, her heart aching. She couldn't believe she was the one who was turning him down, but what he was saying wasn't real, she told herself. It wasn't honest. ''Think about it while I'm in Phoenix.''

''New York,'' Lucky told Lucy McCoy as he sat beside her hospital bed. ''The job's in New York. Syd's having the interview right now, this morning in Phoenix, and of course she's going to get this job. I mean, who wouldn't hire her? She's brilliant, she's funny, she's a great writer, she's…she's perfect.''

Lucy was silent, her brain still securely locked shut by the coma.

Lucky lifted her hand to his lips and kissed it. "Come on, Luce," he said. "Wake up. I could really use some advice."

Nothing.

He sighed. "I feel like a complete ass—both for letting her drive to Phoenix by herself in that crappy car of hers, and for—" He laughed. "God, Lucy, you're not going to believe what I did. I asked her to move in with me for real. What a jerk. I couldn't believe the words were actually coming out of my mouth. I mean, I felt so cheap, like why am I only doing this halfway?" He lowered his voice. "I love her. I do. I never really understood this thing you've got going with Blue. Or Joe with Ronnie. I mean, I could *appreciate* it, sure, but I didn't *get* it. Until I met Syd. And now it all makes sense. My entire *life* makes sense—except for the fact that Syd is going to move to New York."

"So why don't you ask her to marry you?"

Lucky jumped, turning to see Veronica standing in the door. He swore. "Ron, are you taking lessons in stealth from the Captain? Jeez, way to give a guy a heart attack."

She came into the room, sat down on the other side of the bed, taking Lucy's other hand. "Hi, Lucy, I'm back." She looked up at Lucky and smiled. "Sorry for eavesdropping."

"Like hell you are."

"So why *don't* you ask Syd to marry you?"

He couldn't answer.

Veronica answered for him. "You're afraid."

Lucky gritted his teeth and answered honestly. "I'm scared she'll turn me down, *and* I'm scared that she won't."

"Well," Veronica said in her crisp British accent. "She'll do neither—and go to New York—unless you do something drastic."

There was a commotion out in the hall, and the door was pushed open. One of the younger nurses blocked the doorway with her body. "I'm sorry, sir, but it might be best if you wait for the doctor to—"

"I talked to the doctor on the phone on my way over here from the airport." The voice from the hallway was soft but pure business, honeyed by a thick south-of-the-Mason-Dixon-Line drawl. "It's *not* best if I wait for the doctor. It's best if I go into that room and see my wife."

Blue McCoy.

Lucky stood up to see Lieutenant Commander Blue Mc-Coy literally pick up the nurse and move her out of his way. And then he was in the room.

"Lucy." He didn't have eyes for anyone but the woman lying in the middle of that hospital bed.

Blue looked exhausted. He hadn't shaved in weeks, but his hair was wet as if he'd taken a short shower—no doubt for sanitary purposes—moments before he'd arrived. The look on his face was terrible as he gazed down at Lucy, as he took in her bruises and cuts and the stark white bandage around her head. He sat down on the edge of her bed and took her hand.

"I'm here, Yankee," he said, his voice breaking slightly. "I'm sorry it took me so long, but I'm here now." His eyes filled with tears at her complete lack of response. "Come on, Lucy, the doctor said you're going to be just fine—all you have to do is open your eyes."

Nothing.

"I know it's going to be hard. I know you must've gone through some kind of hell, and it's probably easier to stay asleep and just not have to face it, but I'm here, and I'll help you. Whatever you need," Blue told his wife. "It's going to be okay, I promise. Together we can make anything okay."

Blue's tears escaped, and Lucky took Veronica's arm and dragged her to the door.

Captain Catalanotto was in the hallway. Veronica launched herself at her husband. "Joe!"

Joe Cat was an enormous man, and he enfolded her easily in his arms and kissed her.

No, he inhaled her. What Joe gave to Veronica was beyond a kiss. Lucky turned away, feeling as if he'd already gotten a glimpse of something far too private.

But he couldn't help but overhear Joe's rough whisper. "Are you all right?"

"I am now," Veronica told him.

"Is Lucy...?"

"Still nothing," she told him. "No response."

"What does the doctor really say?" Joe asked. "Is there really a chance she'll just wake up?"

"I hope so," she told him.

Lucky had spoken to the doctor just a few hours earlier. He turned to tell Joe that but did a quick about-face. Big, bad Joe Cat was crying as he held on tightly to his wife.

"Everything's going to be okay," he heard Veronica tell Joe through her own tears. "Now that Blue's here, now that you're here...everything's going to be okay. I know it."

And Lucky knew then exactly what he wanted. He wanted what Lucy shared with Blue. He wanted what Joe and Veronica had found.

And for the first time in his life, he thought that maybe, just *maybe* he'd found it, too.

Because when Syd was around him, everything *was* okay.

He was definitely going to do it. He was going to ask Syd to marry him.

The door at the end of the corridor opened, and the rest of Alpha Squad came in. Harvard, Cowboy and Crash. And Mitch Shaw was back, too. Lucky walked down to greet them, shooting Mitch a quizzical look.

"By the time I found them," he explained, "they'd completed their mission and were on their way out of the mountains."

"How's Lucy?" Harvard asked. "We don't want to get too close—Blue and Joe were the only ones who had time to shower."

"Lucy's still in a coma," Lucky told them. "It's kind of now-or-never time, as far as coming out of it goes. Her doctors were hoping Blue's voice would help pull her back to our side." He took a step back from them. "Jeez, you guys are ripe." They smelled like a combination of un-washed dog and stale campfire smoke.

Stale smoke...

Lucky swore. And grabbed for his phone, punching in Syd's cell phone number. Please, God, don't let her be conserving her batteries....

She picked up after only one ring. "Hello?"

"Stale cigarette smoke," Lucky said. "*That's* what's wrong with this Martin Taus guy."

"I'm sorry," Syd said. "Who's calling? Could it pos-sibly be my insane friend Luke O'Donlon? The man who starts conversations in the middle instead of at the begin-ning?"

"Syd," he said. "Yes, you're funny. Thank you. Listen to me—Martin Taus isn't our guy. He's not a smoker. I stood right next to him, remember? I knew something was wrong, but I couldn't put my finger on it until two seconds ago. You said the man who nearly knocked you down the stairs smelled like Wes Skelly—like stale cigarette smoke, remember?"

There was a long silence. Then Syd laughed. "I could've been wrong. *You* could've been wrong."

"I could be," he agreed, "but I'm not. And you're not either. You need to be careful, Syd. You need to come right home." He corrected himself. "No, don't come home, come to the hospital. But don't get out of your car if the parking lot's deserted. Stay in your car, keep moving, call me on your cell phone and I'll come out to meet you, okay?

God, I can't believe you talked me into letting you drive to Phoenix!''

Another long pause. "Well," she said. "I'm sure you're dying to know—my interview went really, really well."

"To hell with your interview," Lucky said in complete exasperation. "You're driving me crazy. I need you back here, I need you *safe*. Get your butt home and, and…marry me, damn it."

He looked up and found Harvard, Cowboy, Mitch and Crash all staring at him.

On the other end of the phone, Syd was equally silent.

"Wow," Lucky said. "That didn't come out quite the way I'd hoped it would."

Cowboy started to laugh, but when Harvard elbowed him hard in the chest, he fell instantly silent.

Lucky closed his eyes and turned away. "Syd, will you please come back here so we can talk?"

"Talk." Her voice sounded weak. She cleared her throat. "Yeah, that sounds smart. You're in luck. I'm nearly half-way home."

Chapter 15

Fight, flee, hide, submit.

Hide was definitely not a working option in this scenario.

Please be there, please be there, please be there, Syd silently chanted as she dialed Lucky's number on her cell phone.

She held the steering wheel with one hand, her phone with the other as she drove. Her map was spread out on the seat beside her.

"O'Donlon."

"Luke, thank God!"

"I'm sorry, who's this?" Luke shouted. "I'm having a little trouble hearing—there's a lot of noise over here. Hang on, let me move into…" There was a pause, and then he was back, normal-voiced. "Sorry about that. Let's start over. O'Donlon."

"Luke, it's Syd. I have a little problem."

He didn't hear her. He spoke over her words as soon as he heard her voice. "Hey, excellent timing! I was just about to call you. I have some *great* news. Lucy's back! She opened her eyes about an hour after Blue arrived, and—get this! She looks at him and she goes, 'I'm bald. They had to shave my head.' Her first words after being in a coma for all that time. Typical woman—she nearly died and she's worrying about her hair. And it kills me that she knew. She must've been able to hear everything that was going on last week, because how else would she have known?''

"Luke."

"And Blue goes, 'I've always thought you'd look damn good in a crew cut, Yankee,' and it was all over. There were seven of us here—all SEALs, all crying like babies and—''

"*Luke.*"

"I'm sorry. I'm nervous. I'm talking because I'm nervous, because I'm scared to death that you called me back to tell me to go to hell.''

Syd waited for a few seconds to make sure he was finally done. "I called you," she said, glancing into her rearview mirror, "because I've got a little problem. I'm out here, in the middle of nowhere, and I'm...I'm pretty sure that I'm being followed.''

Lucky's heart stopped. "This is real, right?" he said. "Not just some make-believe scenario game you're playing?''

"It's real. I noticed the car behind me about fifteen miles ago." Over the telephone, Syd's voice sounded very small. "When I slow down, he slows down. When I speed up, he speeds up. And now that I'm thinking about it, I saw this car back at the gas station, last time I stopped.''

"Where are you?" he asked. His heart had started up again, but now it was lodged securely in his throat. He stuck his head out of the men's room, braving the noise out in the hospital cafeteria, waving until he caught Frisco's attention. He gestured for his swim buddy to follow him into the men's as Syd answered him.

"Route 78," she was telling him. "Just inside the California state line. I'm about forty miles south of Route 10, heading for Route 8. There's nothing out here, Luke. Not even another car, not for miles. As far as I can tell from the map, the next town isn't for another thirty miles. I tried calling the local police, but I couldn't get through. I'm not even sure what I'd say— Hi, I'm out here on the state road and there's a car behind me…? Maybe it's just a coincidence. Maybe…"

"Whatever you do," Lucky said, "don't stop. Don't pull over. Keep your car moving, Syd."

Frisco came into the men's room, curiosity on his face.

"I need the captain and the senior chief and a state map," Lucky told him. "I think Syd's being followed by the guy who put Lucy into this hospital."

Frisco had been at Chief Zale's press conference—the one in which the SFPD and FInCOM had announced that the San Felipe Rapist had been apprehended. But Frisco didn't ask any questions. He didn't waste any time. He nodded and went to get the other two men.

"Syd, I'm going to figure out a way to get to you," Luke told her. "Just keep heading south and west, okay? Stay on Route 78, okay?"

Syd took a deep breath. "Okay."

"Tell me about the car behind you." He sounded so calm, so solid.

She looked in the rearview mirror. "It's dark blue. Ugly. One of those big old sedans from the late seventies and…" She realized what she was saying. Dark-colored, old-model sedan. Ugly. That was how she'd described that unfamiliar car that had been parked on her street on the night Gina was attacked.

Behind her, the car started to speed up. The driver pulled into the oncoming lane.

"He's going to pass me," Syd told Luke, filled with a flash of relief.

The dark sedan was moving faster now, moving up alongside of her.

"God, this was just my imagination," she said. "I'm so sorry, I feel so stupid and—"

The sedan was keeping pace with her. She could see the driver through the window. He was big, broad, built like a football player. His hair was short and brownish blond, worn in a crew cut.

And he had a pair of feature-distorting panty hose over his face.

Syd screamed and hit the gas, dropping the phone as her car surged forward.

"Sit-rep," Lucky shouted into his cell phone. Damn, she probably didn't remember what sit-rep was. "Syd! What's happening, damn it?"

Joe Cat and Harvard pushed their way into the men's room, their faces grim. Harvard had a map, bless him.

Lucky's voice shook as he briefly outlined the situation, as he took the map from Harvard's hands and opened it. "She's heading south on 78." He swore as he found it on the map. "What the hell is she doing on route 78? Why not 95? Why didn't she cut over to Route 8 closer to Phoenix? Why—" He took a deep breath. "Okay. I want to intercept. Fast. What are my options?" He was praying that he wasn't already too late.

The phone line was still open, and he thought he heard the sound of Syd's car's noisy engine. Please, God...

Joe Cat looked at Harvard. "The Black Hawk that brought us here is probably still on the roof. It had more than enough fuel..."

Harvard kicked into action. "I'll round up the team."

"Come on, Syd," Lucky said into his phone as he started

for the roof. "Get back on the phone and tell me you're all right."

The car was starting to shudder and shake. It wasn't made to travel at seventy miles per hour for more than short bursts.

Syd had managed to pull out in front of the other car, but she needed both hands on the steering wheel to control the shaking. She could see her phone bumping around on the passenger's-side floor, next to her Club steering wheel lock. The phone wasn't *that* far away. If she could just take one hand off the wheel for a few seconds and...

She grabbed for it.

And missed.

Lucky took a quick head count as the Black Hawk helicopter rocketed east. Joe Cat, Harvard, Cowboy, Crash, Mitch. Also Thomas King, Rio Rosetti and Mike Lee—they'd been coming into the hospital, bringing flowers to Lucy when Harvard had grabbed them and dragged them to the roof. Nine men and...one *woman?* FInCOM agent PJ Becker, who hated to fly in anything smaller than a 737, was here, too. God bless her.

Her voice came through loud and clear over the radio headset Lucky had slipped on. "As Navy SEALs, you have no authority here," she told them. "So if anyone asks, this is a FInCOM operation, you got it? I'm the Officer in Charge, and you're—just think of yourselves as my posse. But that's just if anyone asks. This is your op, O'Donlon."

Lucky looked at the captain. "What weapons do we have on board, sir?"

"Considering that we pretty much came straight from a mission that called for full battle dress, we've got enough to outfit a small army."

"If this guy so much as touches Syd..." Lucky couldn't go on.

But Joe Cat knew what he was saying. And he nodded. "It finally happened to you, huh, O'Donlon? This woman got under your skin."

"She's irreplaceable," Lucky admitted.

Syd rode the clutch, trying to push a little extra power into her car's top speed. It was working, but for how long?

The temperature gauge was rising. It wasn't going to be long until she was out of time.

She had to get her phone off the floor. It had been at least ten minutes since she'd dropped it—Luke had to be going nuts. She had to talk to him. She had to tell him…what?

That she loved him, that she was sorry, that she wished it might've all turned out differently.

With a herculean effort, she reached for the phone and…

This time her hand connected with it. This time, her fingers scraped along the gritty floor mat. This time, she got it!

But the effort made her swerve, and she fought to control the car with only one hand.

Maybe it would be better if she died in a crash….

The thought was a wild one, and Syd rejected it instantly. That would be surrender of a permanent kind. And she'd never been fond of the surrender or submit solution to any "what if" scenario. If she were going to die, she would die fighting, damn it.

She tucked the phone under her chin and took a deep breath. The line was still open. She didn't have to redial, thank God.

"Luke?"

"Syd, this is Alan Francisco. Lucky's in a chopper, heading toward you, fast. He gave me the phone because he was afraid he'd lose your signal moving at that kind of speed. I'm in radio contact with him, though. Are you all right? I'm sure he's going crazy…."

Syd's heart sank. She wasn't going to get to talk to Luke. At least not directly. God, she'd wanted to hear his voice just one more time.

"It's him," she told Frisco. "The San Felipe Rapist. In the car behind me. He pulled alongside me—he's wearing panty hose over his face. He tried to run me off the road."

"Okay," Frisco said calmly. "Keep moving, Syd. Straddle the center line, don't let him get in front of you. Hang on—let me relay this information to Lucky."

"Alan," she said. "My temperature gauge is about to go into the red zone. My car's about to overheat."

Overheating. Syd's car was overheating.

"Can we make this thing go any faster?" Lucky asked Harvard.

"We're pushing it as it is," the senior chief told him. "But we're close."

"Close isn't good enough," Lucky growled. "Frisco. Tell Syd…" Everyone was listening. Everyone but the one person he wanted to talk to more than anything. "Tell Syd to hang on. Tell her to try to keep moving. Tell her if this bastard gets out of his car, if she's got any power left at all, tell her to run the son of a bitch over. But if her car overheats and the engine dies, tell her to stay inside. Lock the doors. Make him break the windows to get to her. Tell her she should cover her head with something, a jacket or something, so she doesn't get cut by the glass. Tell her…" He had to say it. To hell with the fact that everyone was listening in. "Tell Syd I love her."

"He said that?" Syd couldn't believe it. "He actually said those words?"

"He said, tell Syd I love her," Frisco repeated.

"Oh, God," Syd said, unsure whether to laugh or cry. "If he actually said that, he thinks I'm going to die, doesn't he?"

Steam started escaping from under the front hood of her car. This was it. "My radiator's going," she told Frisco. "It's funny, all those debates about whether to fight or submit. Who knew I'd actually have to make that choice?"

Luke wanted her to submit. He wanted her to stay in her car, wait for this behemoth to come in after her. But once he did, she wouldn't stand a chance.

But maybe, if she were outside the car, she could use her steering wheel lock as a very literal club. Maybe, if she opened the door and came out swinging...

"Tell Luke I'm sorry," Syd told Frisco. "But I choose *fight*."

Her radiator was sending out clouds of steam, and her car was starting to slow. This was it. The beginning of the end.

"Tell him...I love him, too."

Syd cut the connection and let the phone drop into her lap as the car behind hit her squarely. She had to hold on to the steering wheel with both hands to keep her car in the middle of the road. She had to keep him from moving alongside her and running her off onto the soft shoulder.

Except what would that do, really, but delay the inevitable?

Still, she couldn't quit. She couldn't just give up.

He rammed her again, pushing her up and over one last rise in the long, otherwise flat road stretching out in front of her, and...

And then Syd saw it.

A black speck, moving toward her, growing bigger by the second. It was some kind of jet plane or...no, it was a helicopter, moving faster than she'd ever seen a helicopter move in her entire life.

The sedan slammed into her again, this time pushing her off the road. She plowed into the soft dirt and braced herself for another impact. But the helicopter was on top of them then, swooping down like a giant, terrible, noisy hawk bent on revenge. It slowed only slightly as it turned, circling back, and Syd saw that the doors were open. There was a sharp noise—a gunshot—and the sedan swerved to a stop just in front of her. They'd shot out his front tire!

The helicopter was hovering, and at least a dozen men, armed to the teeth with enormous guns, swarmed down ropes.

Out her front window, Syd watched as the man who'd been terrorizing her was pulled from his car. He was big, but they were bigger, and even though he resisted, they had him down on his stomach on the pavement in a matter of seconds.

Her cell phone rang.

Syd picked it up. "Frisco?"

"No." The voice was Luke's. "I borrowed the captain's phone."

She looked up to find him walking toward her car, phone in one hand, gun in the other.

"How's that for timing?" he asked.

Syd dropped the phone and unlocked the door, and he pulled her up and out and into his arms.

Chapter 16

"His name is Owen Finn," Lucky reported to Frisco from his kitchen phone. "He was at the Academy, got into BUD/S, but didn't make it through the program. He rang out—it was during the summer of '96. Apparently he was a nutcase. One of those guys who had a million opportunities handed to him on a platter, but he just kept on screwing up. And whenever he did, it was never his fault."

"Yeah," Frisco said. "I know the type. 'I didn't mean to beat my wife until she ended up in the hospital. It wasn't my fault—she got me so mad.'"

"Yeah, right. Four months after he quit BUD/S," Lucky told his friend, "he was charged and convicted of theft. That got him a dishonorable discharge as well as time served. When he got out, as a civilian, he got caught in a burglary attempt, did time in Kentucky as well. I guess he sat there for a few years, stewing on the fact that—in his mind at least—his abysmal record of failure started when he rang out of BUD/S. As soon as he got out of jail, he headed back to Coronado, via a short stop in Texas where he robbed a liquor store. God forbid he should actually *work* to earn money.

"The police psychologist thinks he probably came back here with some kind of vague idea of revenge—an idea that didn't gel until he got here. This psychologist told me and Syd that he thinks Finn got mileage out of being mistaken for a SEAL in the local bars—he was built up from all those years of pumping iron in prison. He thinks Finn's first act of violence was a date rape—a woman who willingly left the bar with him. According to the shrink, Finn enjoyed the power and the fear, and realized how he could get his pound of flesh, so to speak. He started going down his list, hitting women who were connected to the people he wanted to hurt. Some of them were women he remembered from '96, some he did research to find. He was always careful only to go after the women who had definite patterns of time in which they were alone in their homes. Syd was an exception. And even then, he told the shrink he'd been planning to hit her in her motel room in Phoenix. She foiled his plan by heading back to California a day early. Thank God."

Lucky closed his eyes, unable to deal with the thought of what might've happened had she stayed in Arizona as she'd first intended.

"We're still waiting for Finn's DNA tests to come back, but this time I think we've got him," Lucky said. "He definitely smelled like cigarette smoke. As for Martin Taus, we're not sure yet how he was able to describe Lucy's attack so accurately. I think he must've met Finn in a bar."

"How's Syd doing?" Frisco asked.

Lucky laughed "She's writing," he said. "She locked herself in the guest room, and she's been writing from the minute we walked in the door. She's working on a short piece for *USA Today* about Finn—a kind of follow-up to those other articles she wrote.

"Did she, uh…" Frisco was trying to be tactful. "Did she give you an answer yet?"

"No." Lucky knew exactly what his friend was talking about. His marriage proposal. His incredibly stupid and all-too-public marriage proposal. It figured that Frisco would've heard about it. In fact, Mia was probably standing next to him, tugging on his sleeve, waiting for the word so that she could call Veronica with an update. And Veronica would talk to PJ, and PJ would tell Harvard, who would send out a memo to the rest of Alpha Squad.

The fact that Lucky had actually proposed marriage wasn't being taken lightly by his friends. In fact, it was serious business.

Serious business.

Serious…

"Hang on a sec, can you?" Lucky said into the phone. He set the receiver down on the kitchen table, then went down the hall, and knocked on the closed guest-room door.

"Yeah." Syd sounded impatient. She was writing.

Lucky opened the door and made it quick. "Do you have an estimate for when you'll be done?"

"Two hours," she said. "Go away. Please."

Lucky closed the door, went back into the kitchen and picked up the phone. "Frisco, man, I need your help."

Syd sent the article electronically, and shut down her laptop computer. She stood up, stretching out her back, knowing that she'd put it off as long as she possibly could.

Luke was out there in his living room, waiting so that they could talk.

To hell with your interview…. Get your butt home and marry me, damn it.

He couldn't have been serious. She *knew* he wasn't serious.

He'd been upset for a variety of reasons. He didn't like

the idea of losing her, of losing, period. This marriage proposal was just a knee-jerk attempt to make her stick around.

Tell Syd I love her.

Yeah, sure, he loved her. He'd probably said the same three words to the four billion women who'd come before Syd. She just couldn't take it seriously.

And she was going to have to tell him that. She couldn't—and wouldn't—take *him* seriously. She cared for him deeply, but she couldn't make such a big gamble. This was her life, after all. She was sorry, but she was going to take the job in New York.

She'd leave quickly. They wanted her to start as soon as possible. So she'd pack her things and go. One sharp pain, and it would be over. Like pulling off a Band-Aid, she reminded herself.

He probably wouldn't miss her for more than a week.

She, on the other hand, was going to miss him for the rest of her life.

She braced herself, squared her shoulders and opened the door.

Luke was in the living room, standing at the front window, looking out. He turned when he heard her, and she realized with a jolt of shock that he was wearing his dress uniform. His hair was combed neatly back from his face, every strand carefully in place. He wasn't wearing just his rows of ribbons on his chest, but rather the full medals. It was a wonder he could stand up with so much extra poundage weighing him down.

"Are you going somewhere?" she asked him.

"I think," he said, "that that should be my question for you." He looked so serious, standing there like that, all spit and polish, without a smile on his handsome face.

Syd sat down on the couch. "Yes," she said. "I'm going to New York. There was a message on my machine. They made me an offer. They want me."

"What about my offer?" Luke asked. "I want you, too."

She searched his eyes, but he still wasn't smiling. There was no sign that he was kidding, no sign that he acknowledged how completely out of character this was. "You seriously expect me to believe that you want to marry me?" She could barely say the words aloud.

"Yes. I need to apologize for the subpar delivery, but—"

"Luke. Marriage is forever. I take that *very* seriously. This isn't some game that we can play until you get bored."

"Do I look like I'm playing a game?" he countered.

She didn't get a chance to answer because the doorbell rang.

"Good," Luke said. "Just in time. Excuse me."

As Syd watched, he opened his door. Thomas King stood there, Rio Rosetti and Michael Lee right behind him. They, like Luke, were wearing their dress uniforms. Their arms were full of...*flowers?*

"Great," Luke said. "Come on in. Just put those down on the table, gentlemen. Perfect."

"Hey, Syd," Thomas said.

"If you don't mind waiting out on the back deck...?" Luke efficiently pushed them toward the kitchen door. "I've got a cooler out there with beer, wine and soda. Help yourselves."

Syd stared at Luke, stared at the flowers. They were gorgeous—all different kinds and colors. The bouquets completely covered the coffee table. "Luke, what is this for?"

"It's for you," he said. "And me."

The doorbell rang again.

This time it was Bobby Taylor and Wes Skelly. They both carried heavy boxes into the living room. Luke opened one and took out a bottle of champagne. He read the label. "Terrific," he said. "Thanks, guys."

"There're a couple bottles of non-alcoholic stuff, too,"

Wes told him. "For Frisco and Mia. We got it at the health food store."

"Hi, Syd," Bobby said. He pointed to the back of the house. "Deck?" he asked Luke, who nodded. He vanished, pulling Wes with him.

Flowers and champagne...? "Luke, what—"

Luke interrupted her. "Today you said that you love me. Were you serious?"

Oh, God. She was trying so hard to be realistic about this. "I thought I was going to die."

"So...you said something that wasn't really true?" he asked, sitting down next to her on the couch. "Something that you didn't really mean?"

Syd closed her eyes. She'd meant it, all right. She just probably wouldn't have *said* it if she'd known she was going to live.

"Do you love me?" he asked.

She couldn't lie to him. "Yes," she said. "But I don't—"

He kissed her. "The short answer's all I want."

Syd let herself look into his eyes. "It's just not that simple."

"It can be." He leaned forward to kiss her again, but the doorbell rang.

It was Harvard. What a surprise. He had PJ with him. And Crash and Nell Hawken. And Cowboy and Melody Jones. And Mitch and Becca Shaw. They were all dressed up, as if they were going to the opera or...

"Limos R Us," Cowboy announced with a grin. "Three of 'em. White, as ordered."

"Ready to roll, Lieutenant, sir," Harvard added. "Vegas, here we come."

Vegas? As in Las Vegas? Wedding capital of the world?

Syd stood up and looked out the window. Sure enough, three stretch limos, big enough to hold a small army, were idling at the curb. Her heart began to pound, triple time, in her chest. Was it possible Luke truly was serious…?

"Hi, Syd." PJ gave her a hug and a kiss. "You okay after this afternoon?"

Syd didn't have time to answer. PJ disappeared with the others, pushed into the kitchen and out the back door.

"So," Luke said when they were alone once again. "You love me. And I love you. I know this job in New York is good for your career, but you also told me that if you had a chance, if you could find a patron to support you for a year or two, you'd rather quit your day job and write a book." He spread his arms. "Well, here I—"

The doorbell rang.

"Excuse me."

This time it was Frisco and Mia. They came into the living room, followed by an elderly man in a dark suit who was carrying a large briefcase.

"This is George Majors," Frisco told Luke. "He owns that jewelry store over on Ventura."

Luke shook the old man's hand. "This is wonderful," he said. "I really appreciate your coming out here like this. Here, you can set up over here." He pushed aside some of the flowers on the table, pulled Syd down onto the couch.

Mr. Majors opened his briefcase, and inside was a display case of rings. Diamond rings and wedding rings. Syd couldn't breathe.

Luke got down on one knee beside her and took her hand. "Marry me, Syd." His eyes were so blue. She could drown in those eyes. She could lose herself forever.

Frisco cleared his throat and started inching toward the kitchen door. "Maybe we should—"

"Don't go anywhere. You guys are my best friends. If I can't grovel in front of you, who *can* I grovel in front of?" He pointed to the jeweler. "Him I don't really know, but I figure he's got to be a pretty cool guy to come all the way out here like this."

He looked back at Syd. "Marry me," he said. "Live here with me, write your book, have my babies, make my life complete."

Syd couldn't speak. He was serious. He was completely, totally serious. It was everything she had ever wanted. But she couldn't manage to utter even one short syllable to tell him yes.

And he took her silence for hesitation.

"Maybe I should put it like this," he said. "Here's the scenario, Syd. There's a guy who's never taken any romantic relationship seriously before in his life. But then he meets you, and his world turns upside-down. He loves you more than life itself, and he wants to marry you. Tonight. At the Igloo of Love Wedding Chapel in Vegas. Do you fight, flee, hide or surrender?"

Syd stared to laugh. "Igloo of Love?"

Luke was trying his damnedest to stay serious, but he couldn't keep a smile and then a laugh from escaping. "I knew you'd like that. With me, your life's going to be high class all the way, baby."

With Luke, her life was going to be laughter and sunshine all the way.

"I surrender," she whispered, and started to kiss him, but then she pulled back. She was wearing jeans and a T-shirt, and everyone else was dressed for…a *wedding*. "Tonight?" she said. "God, Luke, I don't have a dress!"

The doorbell rang.

It was Joe Cat and Veronica. Mia let them in.

"I have found," Veronica announced, "exactly what Luke asked me to find—the most *exquisite* wedding dress in all of Southern California."

"My God," Syd whispered to Luke. "You thought of everything."

"Damn right," he told her. "I wanted to make sure you knew I was serious. I figured if you saw that all my friends were taking me seriously, then you would, too."

He kissed her—and it was an extremely serious kiss.

"Marry me tonight," he said.

Syd laughed. "At the Igloo of Love? Definitely."

Smiling into his eyes, she knew her life would never be the same. She'd got Lucky. Permanently.

* * * * *

Look Who's Celebrating Our 20th Anniversary:

"Working with Silhouette has always been a privilege—I've known the nicest people, and I've been delighted by the way the books have grown and changed with time. I've had the opportunity to take chances…and I'm grateful for the books I've done with the company. Bravo! And onward, Silhouette, to the new millennium."

—*New York Times* bestselling author
Heather Graham Pozzessere

"Twenty years of laughter and love… It's not hard to imagine Silhouette Books celebrating twenty years of quality publishing, but it is hard to imagine a publishing world without it. Congratulations…"

—International bestselling author
Emilie Richards

If you enjoyed what you just read,
then we've got an offer you can't resist!

Take 2 bestselling
love stories FREE!
Plus get a FREE surprise gift!

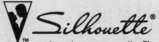

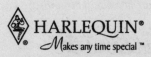

SILHOUETTE'S 20TH ANNIVERSARY CONTEST
OFFICIAL RULES
NO PURCHASE NECESSARY TO ENTER

1. To enter, follow directions published in the offer to which you are responding. Contest begins 1/1/00 and ends on 8/24/00 (the "Promotion Period"). Method of entry may vary. Mailed entries must be postmarked by 8/24/00, and received by 8/31/00.

2. During the Promotion Period, the Contest may be presented via the Internet. Entry via the Internet may be restricted to residents of certain geographic areas that are disclosed on the Web site. To enter via the Internet, if you are a resident of a geographic area in which Internet entry is permissible, follow the directions displayed on-line, including typing your essay of 100 words or fewer telling us "Where In The World Your Love Will Come Alive." On-line entries must be received by 11:59 p.m. Eastern Standard time on 8/24/00. Limit one e-mail entry per person, household and e-mail address per day, per presentation. If you are a resident of a geographic area in which entry via the Internet is permissible, you may, in lieu of submitting an entry on-line, enter by mail, by hand-printing your name, address, telephone number and contest number/name on an 8"x 11" plain piece of paper and telling us in 100 words or fewer "Where In The World Your Love Will Come Alive," and mailing via first-class mail to: Silhouette 20th Anniversary Contest, (in the U.S.) P.O. Box 9069, Buffalo, NY 14269-9069; (In Canada) P.O. Box 637, Fort Erie, Ontario, Canada L2A 5X3. Limit one 8"x 11" mailed entry per person, household and e-mail address per day. On-line and/or 8"x 11" mailed entries received from persons residing in geographic areas in which Internet entry is not permissible will be disqualified. No liability is assumed for lost, late, incomplete, inaccurate, nondelivered or misdirected mail, or misdirected e-mail, for technical, hardware or software failures of any kind, lost or unavailable network connection, or failed, incomplete, garbled or delayed computer transmission or any human error which may occur in the receipt or processing of the entries in the contest.

3. Essays will be judged by a panel of members of the Silhouette editorial and marketing staff based on the following criteria:

> Sincerity (believability, credibility)—50%
> Originality (freshness, creativity)—30%
> Aptness (appropriateness to contest ideas)—20%

Purchase or acceptance of a product offer does not improve your chances of winning. In the event of a tie, duplicate prizes will be awarded.

4. All entries become the property of Harlequin Enterprises Ltd., and will not be returned. Winner will be determined no later than 10/31/00 and will be notified by mail. Grand Prize winner will be required to sign and return Affidavit of Eligibility within 15 days of receipt of notification. Noncompliance within the time period may result in disqualification and an alternative winner may be selected. All municipal, provincial, federal, state and local laws and regulations apply. Contest open only to residents of the U.S. and Canada who are 18 years of age or older, and is void wherever prohibited by law. Internet entry is restricted solely to residents of those geographical areas in which Internet entry is permissible. Employees of Torstar Corp., their affiliates, agents and members of their immediate families are not eligible. Taxes on the prizes are the sole responsibility of winners. Entry and acceptance of any prize offered constitutes permission to use winner's name, photograph or other likeness for the purposes of advertising, trade and promotion on behalf of Torstar Corp. without further compensation to the winner, unless prohibited by law. Torstar Corp and D.L. Blair, Inc., their parents, affiliates and subsidiaries, are not responsible for errors in printing or electronic presentation of contest or entries. In the event of printing or other errors which may result in unintended prize values or duplication of prizes, all affected contest materials or entries shall be null and void. If for any reason the Internet portion of the contest is not capable of running as planned, including infection by computer virus, bugs, tampering, unauthorized intervention, fraud, technical failures, or any other causes beyond the control of Torstar Corp. which corrupt or affect the administration, secrecy, fairness, integrity or proper conduct of the contest, Torstar Corp. reserves the right, at its sole discretion, to disqualify any individual who tampers with the entry process and to cancel, terminate, modify or suspend the contest or the Internet portion thereof. In the event of a dispute regarding an on-line entry, the entry will be deemed submitted by the authorized holder of the e-mail account submitted at the time of entry. Authorized account holder is defined as the natural person who is assigned to an e-mail address by an Internet access provider, on-line service provider or other organization that is responsible for arranging e-mail address for the domain associated with the submitted e-mail address.

5. Prizes: Grand Prize—a $10,000 vacation to anywhere in the world. Travelers (at least one must be 18 years of age or older) or parent or guardian if one traveler is a minor, must sign and return a Release of Liability prior to departure. Travel must be completed by December 31, 2001, and is subject to space and accommodations availability. Two hundred (200) Second Prizes—a two-book limited edition autographed collector set from one of the Silhouette Anniversary authors: Nora Roberts, Diana Palmer, Linda Howard or Annette Broadrick (value $10.00 each set). All prizes are valued in U.S. dollars.

6. For a list of winners (available after 10/31/00), send a self-addressed, stamped envelope to: Harlequin Silhouette 20th Anniversary Winners, P.O. Box 4200, Blair, NE 68009-4200.

Contest sponsored by Torstar Corp., P.O. Box 9042, Buffalo, NY 14269-9042.

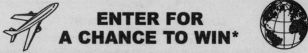

ENTER FOR
A CHANCE TO WIN*

Silhouette's 20th Anniversary Contest

Tell Us Where in the World
You Would Like *Your* Love To Come Alive...
And We'll Send the Lucky Winner There!

Silhouette wants to take you wherever
your happy ending can come true.

Here's how to enter: Tell us, in 100 words or less,
where you want to go to make your love come alive!

In addition to the grand prize, there will be 200
runner-up prizes, collector's-edition book sets
autographed by one of the Silhouette anniversary
authors: **Nora Roberts**, **Diana Palmer**,
Linda Howard or **Annette Broadrick**.

DON'T MISS YOUR CHANCE TO WIN!
ENTER NOW! No Purchase Necessary

Silhouette®
Where love comes alive™

Name:

Address:

City: State/Province:

Zip/Postal Code:

Mail to Harlequin Books: **In the U.S.**: P.O. Box 9069, Buffalo, NY
14269-9069; **In Canada**: P.O. Box 637, Fort Erie, Ontario, L4A 5X3

*No purchase necessary—for contest details send a self-addressed stamped envelope to:
Silhouette's 20th Anniversary Contest, P.O. Box 9069, Buffalo, NY, 14269-9069 (include
contest name on self-addressed envelope). Residents of Washington and Vermont may
omit postage. Open to Cdn. (excluding Quebec) and U.S. residents who are 18 or over.
Void where prohibited. Contest ends August 31, 2000.

PS20CON_R